Fast losing control of what she had hoped would be a magnificent climb down on Harriet and Caroline's part, Grandmama turned to face Jimbo. She'd never seen him so angry. There didn't seem to be quite so much pleasure in her challenge as there had been up to now. Obviously Sheila's popularity, though she couldn't think why, was much greater than she'd realised.

Holding her chin a little higher than normal Grandmama said quite clearly, 'All I was doing was giving a helping hand, assisting someone in dire need and what do I get in return? Insulted! Lady Bissett' – scathingly she repeated – 'Lady Bissett – I ask you! called me an old . . .' – there was hesitation here, should she tell? Yes, she must. She had to justify her actions, she really had – 'an old *baggage*! She only got what she deserved.'

Harriet smothered a grin.

Jimbo's face never slipped. 'Mother, I am ashamed. Whatever everyone will think of you I cannot imagine.'

'Well, I've resigned, so I'm not in charge any more. Perhaps now, everyone will be satisfied.'

'They won't forget though and neither will I.'

Educated at a co-educational Quaker boarding school, Rebecca Shaw went on to qualify as a teacher of deaf children. After her marriage, she spent the ensuing years enjoying bringing up her family. The departure of the last of her four children to university has given her the time and opportunity to write. Her latest novel in paperback in the Turnham Malpas series is *Intrigue in the Village*, and in hardback *Whispers in the Village,* also available from Orion.

By Rebecca Shaw

TALES FROM TURNHAM MALPAS
The New Rector
Talk of the Village
Village Matters
The Village Show
Village Secrets
Scandal in the Village
Village Gossip
Trouble in the Village
A Village Dilemma
Intrigue in the Village
Whispers in the Village

THE BARLEYBRIDGE SERIES
A Country Affair
Country Wives
Country Lovers
Country Passions

Scandal in the Village
TALES FROM TURNHAM MALPAS

Rebecca Shaw

An Orion paperback

First published in Great Britain in 1999
by Orion
This paperback edition published in 1999
by Orion Books Ltd,
Orion House, 5 Upper St Martin's Lane,
London WC2H 9EA

Reissued 2005

A CIP catalogue record for this book is
available from the British Library.

Printed and bound in Great Britain by
Clays Ltd, St Ives plc

The Orion Publishing Group's policy is to use papers that
are natural, renewable and recyclable products and
made from wood grown in sustainable forests. The logging
and manufacturing processes are expected to conform to
the environmental regulations of the country of origin.

www.orionbooks.co.uk

INHABITANTS OF TURNHAM MALPAS

Willie Biggs	Verger at St Thomas à Becket.
Sylvia Biggs	His wife and housekeeper at the rectory.
Sir Ronald Bissett	Retired trades union leader.
Lady Sheila Bissett	His wife.
James (Jimbo) Charter-Plackett	Owner of the Village Store.
Harriet Charter-Plackett	His wife.
Fergus, Finlay, Flick and Fran	Their children.
Katherine Charter-Plackett	Jimbo's mother.
Alan Crimble	Barman at the Royal Oak.
Linda Crimble	Runs the post office at the Village Store.
Bryn Fields	Licensee at the Royal Oak.
Georgie Fields	His wife.
H. Craddock Fitch	Owner of Turnham House.
Jimmy Glover	Taxi driver.
Mrs Jones	A village gossip.
Barry Jones	Her son and estate carpenter.
Pat Jones	His wife.
Dean and Michelle	Her children.
Revd Peter Harris MA (Oxon)	Rector of the parish.
Dr Caroline Harris	His wife.
Alex and Beth	Their children.
Jeremy Mayer	Manager at Turnham House.
Venetia Mayer	His wife.
Kate Pascoe	Village school head teacher.
Sir Ralph Templeton	Retired from the diplomatic service.
Lady Muriel Templeton	His wife.
Dicky Tutt	Scout leader.
Bel Tutt	School caretaker and assistant in the Village Store.
Don Wright	Maintenance engineer.
Vera Wright	Cleaner at the nursing home in Penny Fawcett.
Rhett Wright	Their grandson.

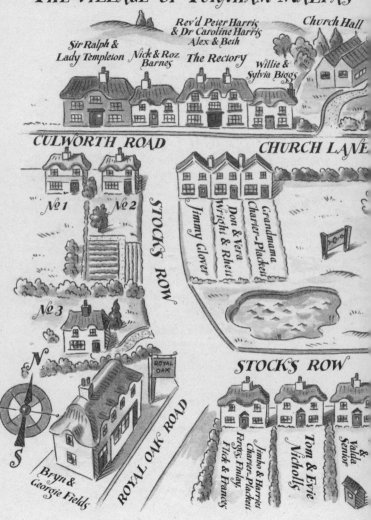

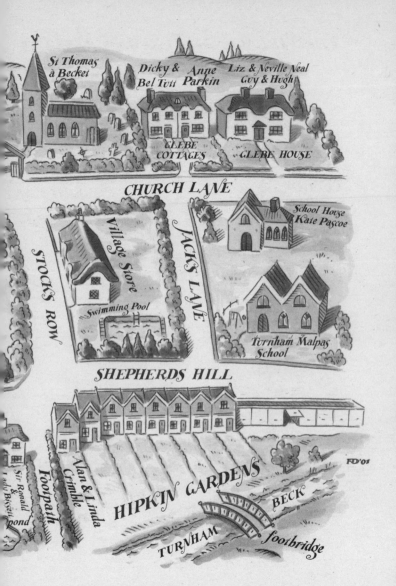

Chapter 1

'Talk of the devil! Here he comes!' Georgie finished pulling the pint, handed it over to her customer and waved to Dicky.

Bryn snorted his disapproval. 'Dicky Tutt! You mean you've lined him up to launch it? What does he know about show business?'

'He doesn't need to, he's a natural. A born comic.'

Dicky came bounding across to the bar and ordered his drink. 'Good evening one and all! My usual, please. And how's my Georgie tonight? Blossoming bright and beautiful as always.'

'Flatterer!' She drew him his pint and as he paid her she felt him give her fingers a slight squeeze. Georgie rewarded him with one of her stunning smiles. 'You're on top form tonight.'

'Of course. Heard the one about the dog with two tails?'

Dicky launched himself into his story with extra verve, knowing full well Bryn was on the qui vive as far as he was concerned. He'd honed to perfection the art of taunting Bryn and felt guilty but also elated by the knowledge. As

Dicky reached the climax of the story Bryn leant over the counter and waited for his chance to speak.

'Don't imagine for one moment that this is a dress rehearsal for a slot in this ridiculous showbiz scheme Georgie's come up with . . .'

Dicky pretended innocence. 'What ridiculous scheme?'

'This business of having entertainment on Fridays here in the bar. I've put my foot down about it. We're not. Right?'

'OK. OK. I'm either way. Doesn't bother me.'

'Well, don't come up with any more bright ideas for in here, ever again.'

'I didn't suggest it. It was Georgie's idea.'

Georgie intervened. 'It was, Bryn, honestly. It was me asked him. I think you're being daft. We could just try it once or twice and see what happens couldn't we?' She opened wide her lovely bright eyes and looked up at Bryn to plead her cause. 'Please, just once. Dicky would be a good one to start with. Dip our toes in the water, eh? How about it?'

Bryn twirled his Flying Officer Kite moustache and looked down into the pretty face of the woman he'd loved for twenty years. He wanted to please her, but something, he didn't know what, warned him to steer clear and he couldn't bring himself to agree. 'No. Sorry. It'd lower the tone.'

Dicky grinned up at Bryn. 'Eh! Come on, my jokes aren't mucky.'

'Not now they're not, but they might be once you get in your stride.'

'Oh no, they wouldn't be, I don't tell doubtful jokes. I've got all my Scouts to think of, got to keep their respect.'

'Anyway, it doesn't matter whether they're smutty or

not 'cos you're not performing in here, in this pub, whilst ever my name is over the door. I'm the licensee. Subject now closed.'

Jimmy Glover, for once drinking alone called across, 'Come on, Bryn, liven the place up. Bring more trade in, surely you can't object to that?'

'It's not bringing in more trade that I'm objecting to, it's what it might lead to that worries me.'

Georgie and Dicky exchanged a quick glance. She hastily served a whisky to a customer and as she pinged the till she said, 'There's nothing for you to worry about, it's just an experiment and Dicky's willing to give it a whirl and he's not expecting getting paid either. You know how everyone loves his jokes. Come on, Bryn, let's give it a try. Mmmmm?'

'Absolutely not.' Bryn began drying some glasses and turned his back to her.

She glanced at Dicky, pursed her mouth and shook her head. Dicky took the hint. He stood with his back to the bar and looked round. Jimmy was still alone and there were only three other punters in the bar besides him and Jimmy. There was no doubt about it, the pub could do with some new attraction to liven it up.

The outside door opened and in came Sir Ronald and Lady Bissett with their little Pomeranian.

Dicky called out to them, 'Evening Sheila! Evening Ron. This round's on me. What would you like?'

Sheila beamed her approval. She liked Dicky, he might be beneath her in the social scale but she liked him nevertheless. 'Gin and tonic, please Dicky. How are you?'

'I'm fine thanks. Ron, what's yours?'

'A pint of that special of Bryn's, please.'

Dicky ordered their drinks from Georgie and the three of them stood at the bar discussing the weather. Sheila's dog Pompom had to be kept on a tight lead because in his old age he had developed an alarming habit of sinking his teeth into the ankle of anyone who happened to displease him, and Dicky was a frequent target. Dicky moved away a few more inches when he heard a low rumble in Pompom's chest.

Sheila bent down to pat him. 'Now, Pompom, now, now, it's only Dicky. I think it's because he can't see as well as he did, he mistakes feet for cats.'

Dicky chuckled. 'Does he indeed. I'll keep my distance then if you don't mind!'

Ron, becoming increasingly hot in his ginger tweed Sheila insisted made him look like an English country gentleman, unwittingly brought up a subject of conversation close to Dicky's heart. 'I was thinking about you the other day, Dicky. Read an article in the paper about how successful clubs are nowadays, working men's clubs and suchlike. They're becoming the place to be discovered by a talent scout. They have entertainers, weekends – the big clubs get the big names of course, but they say the smaller clubs are a very good place to start. It named a few comics, and singers, who've got their feet on the ladder to success in the smaller clubs. I thought about you with your jokes. You'd go down wonderfully well I'm sure. I'm still laughing over that one you told us about the . . .'

Bryn poked a sharp finger into Ron's shoulder-blade. 'I don't know if this is all part of a plot, but don't encourage him if you please. I'm not having it and there's an end to it.'

Sir Ronald, surprised at receiving such a body blow, asked what made Bryn so annoyed, all he'd done was mention . . . ?

Sheila, feeling that a wholesale row was brewing and knowing she could never rely on Ron to be as tactful as

4

she always was, interrupted by saying, 'Let's hope this good weather holds for the Harvest Festival, all that effort we put in, it does so put people off from coming when the weather's bad.'

Dicky raised his glass to Sheila. 'I've nothing but admiration for you on that score, Sheila, every year I think the church can't look any better than it does this year and blow me next year it does. You've had some wonderful ideas in the past, and I've no doubt it'll be decorated even more brilliantly than last year.'

Sheila beamed with pleasure. 'Why, thank you. It's all team work really, my committee are very talented, believe me. You know, you really are the most charming man.' She tapped a lacquered fingernail on Dicky's sleeve. 'Most charming, your Bel did right to snap you up. In fact if you weren't spoken for I could . . .'

Ron like a terrier at a bone said, 'Bryn! Sorry! Didn't mean to give offence, though I don't know how I did, I was only . . .'

'Beg your pardon. It's just that Georgie here is wanting to start entertainment on Friday nights, and I won't have it. I thought you were encouraging her.'

Ron thumped the bar counter with delight. 'But there you are, there's his chance. Dicky here would be excellent. Just the man for the job! You'd do a turn wouldn't you?'

Deliberately Dicky pretended to be deaf to Ron's question. Pompom suspecting that Dicky's shoe was shuffling a little too near and the light tan of it was just the colour of that cat they called Chivers, lunged and snapped at Dicky's ankle. The lunge pulled Sheila's arm to its fullest extent and she overbalanced. Her glass, escaping her grasp, flew up before it fell down, and she tried to retrieve it as it passed her. Pompom took another snap at

Dicky's ankle as he tried to avoid the gin pouring down his jacket, Sheila made another try to catch the glass, Pompom took another snap and down Sheila went. Her foot slipped between the brass footrest and the front of the bar and they all heard the crack of bone as she landed, awkwardly trapped by the rail on which only a moment before her foot had been resting. Dicky just managed to save himself from falling on top of her and Pompom howled as Sheila's bottom almost flattened him.

Ron tried to lift her up. Georgie dashed round to the front of the bar shouting. 'Don't move her! I'm sure she's broken something.'

Sheila racked by searing pain and in shock, wept. Pompom hid under the nearest table. Dicky knelt down beside Sheila and put his arm round her. 'There there, keep quite still. Just a bit longer, yes I know it's uncomfortable crouched like that, but stay still just a bit longer till you know how you feel, then we'll move you.'

'Oh Dicky! It's so painful you've no idea. Whatever am I going to do?'

'Nothing for the minute. Then Bryn and your Ron, 'cos they're bigger than me can lift you onto a chair. It's your leg I'm afraid. It sounded like a break.'

'It is, I'm sure. That's all I need. The week before the Harvest . . .'

'Now. Now. Don't you fret about that. That's the least of your worries right now. Bryn, come and give a hand here will yer?'

Bryn came round and pushed his way between the customers. He peered anxiously at Sheila, took hold of her under her armpits and, very very gently, hoisted her up and propped her against the bar. She was ashen and sweating with the pain but felt slightly less ridiculous than when she'd been crumpled on the floor. She supported her bad leg. The pain she was suffering caused sweat to run off the end of her chin.

'God, Ron! I feel terrible . . .' Sheila's voice trailed off and she fainted. Bryn caught her with Ron's help.

Bryn shouted, 'Someone go get Dr Harris, and quick.'

Jimmy volunteered to go. He knocked loudly on the rectory door. When it opened Peter was standing there looking down at him.

'Rector! Sorry to trouble you this time o' night but could your good lady wife come. Sheila Bissett's had a bad fall and we think she's broken her leg and now she's fainted.'

'Oh goodness. Yes, of course.' He turned away from the door and using his most powerful voice called out, 'Caroline! there's an emergency. Can you come?'

Caroline dashed through from the kitchen. 'Shush! You'll wake the children! Well, Jimmy, hello, what's the matter?'

Jimmy was always impressed by Caroline. Her cheerful competence and generous smile never failed to lift his spirits, and her short dark curly hair and pale skin reminded him of . . .

'I'll explain as we go along. I'll return her to you quick as a flash, Rector.'

By the time Caroline reached the bar Sheila had regained consciousness and was seated on a chair.

'Oh Dr Harris! It's so kind of you to come. They shouldn't have troubled you!'

'Of course they should. Now let me look.' Very, very gently Caroline explored Sheila's leg causing her to wince several times. 'I'm sorry to hurt you. Unless I'm much mistaken it's more than a sprain, there is definitely a break there. It's hospital for you, Sheila, I'm afraid.'

Sheila put a hand on Caroline's shoulder. 'I rather

thought so. It's incredibly painful.' Two large tears fell down her plump cheeks. 'I'll have to be very brave, won't I?'

Caroline smiled and patted her arm. 'You will, but you are a brave person anyway, aren't you?' Caroline stood up. 'Sir Ronald, if we help her to your car could you . . . ? You'll get there quicker than waiting for an ambulance.'

'Yes, yes of course. I'll go right now and bring it round. I'll bring that old blanket for you, Sheila, keep you warm. Shock and that.'

Glaring meaningfully at him she said, 'You mean the car rug, don't you, Ron?'

Taking her meaning he said, 'Yes, of course, the car rug. The tartan one.'

'The Royal Stuart one,' Sheila called feebly after him as Ron hurried out. '. . . and my handbag . . .'

Pompom yelped from under the table. 'Oh, Ron's forgotten Pompom. I don't know what to do any more. It's all too much. Ohhh! the pain.'

'Don't worry, I'll take him home to the rectory with me. He can sleep in Mimi's old basket. Sir Ronald can collect him in the morning. No, change of plan, better still I'll bring him over to you and see how you are. Now you won't worry about him will you? I'll spoil him to death.'

Sheila's bottom lip trembled. 'It's at times like this that you learn who your friends are, isn't it? But I'll be in plaster for weeks and there's the Harvest, I can't let the Rector down.'

Looking down into Sheila's tear-streaked face Caroline forgot about all the times she had clashed with Sheila and felt nothing but pity for her. 'Don't you worry. You've made all the plans quite beautifully, and we'll carry them all out to the letter. Just think about yourself for now. There's the car. They'll give you painkillers and you'll be surprised how much better you'll feel when they've set it.'

Between them Ron and Bryn contrived to give Sheila a bosun's chair into the car whereupon she almost fainted again. Caroline bent down to speak to her. Tucking the car rug around her she said, 'Now, promise you won't worry about Pompom. I'll ring Casualty and tell them to expect you. God bless.'

Reluctantly Pompom allowed himself to be taken to the rectory, dragging his feet and protesting at every step.

'Now come along. Sheila's being brave and so must you be. I'm not putting up with any nonsense.' Hearing the firmness of her tone Pompom decided that he would have to give in and he followed her meekly back.

Caroline slipped her key in the door, briskly invited Pompom inside, locked it after her and called out, 'Peter! I've got Pompom, approach with caution please!'

He emerged from his study and made gentle clucking noises in an attempt to entice Pompom to restrain his vindictiveness.

'I'll keep him on his lead for a few minutes just in case.'

'Has Sheila broken her leg then?'

'Oh definitely. Ron's just taken her to hospital. It's quite a bad one I think. Poor thing.'

'You don't usually have sympathy for her.'

'Well, I have tonight. She's in awful pain. No, Pompom, behave yourself!'

Peter bent down and offered his hand, and Pompom sniffed it gently.

Triumphantly Caroline said, 'There you see, all he needs is firm handling. Now, young man, I'll get out the old cat bed and you can sleep in the kitchen, and no nonsense.'

By the time they'd settled the dog, reassured the cats, locked up and taken their cups of tea to bed it was half past eleven.

Peter was sitting up in bed reading when Caroline returned from the bathroom remarking 'I'm exhausted today.'

'Truth to tell you've not looked well for quite a while.' Peter closed his book and placed it on his bedside table. 'Do you think you're doing too much? Surgeries and such and Sylvia doing fewer hours?'

Caroline snapped at him, 'No, certainly not. I'm all right. Just too much to do at the moment.'

Peter apologised. 'I'm sorry, but you see what I mean, you don't usually snap at me.'

Contrite, Caroline said, 'You're right I don't. It's me who needs to apologise. Just had a bad week.' She climbed into bed and shuffled across into the safety of his arms. 'I do love you, but you really musn't mollycoddle me. I'm grown up now you know.' Putting her face close to his she ran the tip of her tongue around the edges of his lips. 'You're a beautiful man, do you know that? All six feet five, red–blond, blue–eyed, fresh complexioned bit of you. Every single bit.'

'Thanks, he said modestly.'

'Far more handsome than you've any right to be.'

'Thanks again he said, even more modestly.'

Caroline laughed. 'Well?'

'Well, what?'

'What are you going to say about me?'

'That you're beautiful in body, mind and spirit and suit me to the enth degree. I wouldn't swop you, not for anything.'

'That's not very romantic!'

'I didn't think you were in a romantic mood and you

haven't been for several weeks. I have begun to wonder why.'

Caroline turned away from him, drew the duvet up around her neck and said, 'I'm going to sleep now, so I'll say good night.'

'Good night, then, my darling girl.' He paused and then continued with, 'If you've gone off me I'd like to know.'

'Not really, just tired like I said.'

Thoughtfully, Peter leant over her and kissed her cheek. 'God bless you.'

'And you.'

Peter turned away from her and they lay back to back quite quietly for a while, so he never saw the tears which welled around her eyes and then slid silently onto her pillow. She brushed them angrily away but they wouldn't stop coming. Finally when there were no more tears left to cry she said, 'I love you, you know that don't you? For always and for ever no matter what. You love me, don't you? Really love me?'

'Absolutely. I tell you that every day of my life and mean it. Good night, my love.'

'Good night, darling. I'll go see Sheila straight after taking the children to school. I expect she'll be feeling very sorry for herself.'

'Indeed. Poor thing. It's no joke breaking a leg at her age.'

'You're right. It isn't.'

By some kind of intuitive telegraph most of the mothers at the school gate knew about Sheila's fall, and asked Caroline how she was.

'She was in an awful lot of pain last night, but I haven't heard anything this morning. I'm going right now to find out.'

'Give her our love. She might be an old bat, and bossy with it, but you can't help but feel sorry for her can you?'

Caroline laughed and agreed. 'She won't be a lot of use for the Harvest, so we'll all have to pull our weight on her behalf.'

'We all will, just give us the word.'

'Lovely, thanks.'

With Pompom in tow Caroline knocked on Sheila's door.

Ron opened it and invited her in, Pompom completely forgetting how Caroline had lavished loving care upon him in his hour of need, leapt about filled with excitement at his return and rushed to find Sheila.

She was sitting in an armchair still in her negligee and matching nightgown, with the broken leg, now in plaster, sticking straight out in front of her resting on a tapestry footstool. Pompom bounded about leaping up to reach Sheila's face to give it a welcoming lick.

'Down, Pompom, down, I say. Oh Ron, I can't bear him, take him away. Don't let him touch my le-e-g-g-g. Ohhhh!'

When Ron had safely shut Pompom in the kitchen Caroline asked how she had got on at the hospital.

'It was horrendous, they did their best though, we got home about one and I haven't had much sleep, however, I must say, I am feeling a little better this morning, thank you.'

'I thought you'd be in bed.'

'I can't stand lying in bed. So boring. No television, nothing to see. I thought I'd be more cheerful downstairs.'

'Of course you will. I told you last night you were brave and you are, you see.'

'I could soon cry. The slightest little thing.'

'Naturally.'

'I got the VIP treatment with you phoning up. Thank you ever so much.'

'Not at all. The least I could do. You're not to worry about a thing. Give me any messages and I'll attend to them and then Sir Ronald can spend his time looking after you.'

'That's most kind. We've been talking about the Harvest Festival decorations. I just don't know what to say. I don't see how I can help.' Tears began to fill Sheila's eyes. 'It's not fair it happening right now, of all the times to choose. One of my most crucial times of the year.'

'Say no more. I shall rally everyone and we'll all manage perfectly. You've got the file haven't you?'

'Oh yes, but I don't . . .'

'I know, you don't like other people to have it, that's quite understandable. On the Saturday you shall sit with it in your lap and give us our instructions and we'll do all the work. They'll all rally round, you'll see. I haven't got a surgery today so I shall get Willie to go into the church hall loft and get me the boxes of things out and tomorrow night at the committee meeting we'll have a good dust of everything and get fully sorted, repair anything that needs it . . .'

'I doubt I shall get there, Ron's speaking at a training session of trades union representatives in Birmingham tomorrow afternoon so . . .'

'You can't possibly manage on your own shall I . . . ?'

'No, please, you have enough on your plate and you've been too kind already, no, the children . . . well, I mean Louise and dear Gilbert, are coming and making my meal and settling me down for the evening. Ron will be back before bedtime, it's an early-evening meeting.'

'Are you sure? Because I can . . .'

'Absolutely. There were two corn dollies which needed

refurbishing and I never got them done and you remember we used . . .'

They heard the doorbell and listened to Ron answering it. Through the open lounge door the commanding tones of Grandmama Charter-Plackett could be heard enquiring if she could help.

Sheila visibly shrank into the chair. Caroline raised her eyebrows in despair.

Ron tried to put her off from coming into the house but she wouldn't hear of it. 'I must come in, I know how conscientious Sheila is, and I've come to relieve her of her worries. Is she in bed?' Without waiting for an answer she swept towards the staircase.

In a shaky voice Sheila cried, 'I'm in here, first on the right.'

Grandmama stood in the doorway, and surveyed the scene in the lounge. A proud autocratic woman in her seventies, dressed with her usual pin neat smartness and attention to detail, her hair rigidly set in waves and curls she nodded her head at each of them in greeting. 'Good morning, Caroline. Sheila. Now, how are things? I was so sorry to hear about your fall. I heard it was both legs and an arm. Obviously it's not.'

Sheila answered in a trembling voice. 'Oh no. Just this leg.'

'Is it agony, my dear? Of course it must be. Never had a broken limb myself, but I'm sure it must be excruciatingly painful. I've come to offer my services. She's not to worry about a thing, is she Caroline?' Before Caroline could answer Grandmama pushed on with her offer of help. 'Coffee! Yes, coffee. The kitchen, I'll do it.' She flapped her hands at Ronald. 'No, no, you've quite enough on with the dog and the house and the shopping. I'll do this for us all. You won't be staying, Caroline, will you? I expect you've a lot to do. Has the dog been out yet, Sir Ronald?'

He had only time to shake his head before Grandmama said, 'Well, in that case you take the dog while I'm here and then Sheila won't be left on her own. Sugar, Sheila?'

'Yes, please.'

Ronald scuttled out with Pompom thankful to have a reason to get out of her way. Caroline pulled a face at Sheila and then said loudly, 'I'll be off then.' Bending over Sheila's chair she whispered, 'Don't worry about tomorrow night, we'll attend to everything. You stay here and rest, OK?'

'Are you sure?'

'I am.' As she reached the door Caroline called out 'Bye-bye then. I'll call in tomorrow. I'm going, Mrs Charter-Plackett.'

'Very well, leave everything to me, my regards to the Rector!'

Chapter 2

Sheila's accident had been the main topic of conversation in the Store and Grandmama Charter-Plackett had determined as soon as she heard about it to step into the breach. If that common woman Sheila Bissett couldn't organise the Harvest Festival then she would. After all, it was only a bit of flower-arranging, any fool could do that. She'd taken her shopping home, put it away, remembered to check herself in the mirror in her tiny hall, wrapped the flowers Harriet had given her only two days ago in fresh paper and had sallied forth to Sheila's house.

On her way round the green she'd planned her strategy. The best approach would be sympathy to start with. Then she could move on to saying 'if', and 'but' and 'of course' and before she knew it she'd be in charge. Musn't appear too eager. The door chimes on Sheila's door had grated her nerves. Some people had no taste. Grandmama had followed Ron in, wincing at the decorations. Honestly, artificial flowers everywhere, whatever next. She bet her last shilling there'd be a lacy cover on the spare toilet roll in the downstairs lavatory. This wasn't going to prove much of a nut to crack, not for her anyway. She'd ease the way with a cup of coffee.

While the kettle boiled she found a vase and arranged the flowers with an imaginative flourish. Carrying them into the sitting-room she said to Sheila 'I've brought these, nothing like . . . fresh flowers is there?'

She held them close to Sheila and watched her sniff them. 'They smell gorgeous. Thank you so much. Most kind. Ron . . . Ronald isn't much good with flowers.'

'Well, there is a lot of skill in flower-arranging as you know. I'll put them here on this low table. The coffee won't be a minute now.' She twinkled her fingers at Sheila as she left for the kitchen. Mentally rubbing her hands she congratulated herself on the way things were going. Sheila was at her most vulnerable, she could tell that.

Grandmama carried in the coffee, placed it on the smallest of a nest of repro tables and when she'd settled herself back in her chair she chatted about this and that and gradually came round to how incapacitated Sheila would be for the next few weeks.

'They say I shall be in plaster for at least six weeks.'

'Oh dear. That will mean the end of October then at the earliest.'

'I'm afraid so. Such a nuisance. Ron . . . Ronald and I were hoping to go on Eurostar to Brussels in a fortnight, right after the Harvest Festival but we shall have to cancel. I couldn't manage that. At least with a bit of re-organisation I'll be able to manage the Harvest Festival arrangements though. It's so aggravating, it being one of the peaks of my flower year.'

'You don't mean you help with the Harvest Festival as well as all your other activities?'

'I'm the organiser!'

'Well! I'd no idea. But I should have realised, you being so involved with flowers at every turn. I wasn't here last year you see. Whatever will you do? How shall they manage without you?'

Sheila put down her cup and said 'Don't worry. I've got it all worked out. Louise, my married daughter you know . . .'

'No, I don't, I haven't had the pleasure.'

'You must have seen her about, she's married to the choir master Gilbert.'

'Oh, of course, that's your daughter. I hadn't realised.'

'Well, she put all the details on her computer for me last year, so she's printed it all out again and with one or two alterations I have everything at my fingertips. Ron can drive me round to the church and I shall supervise from the front pew.'

Grandmama shook her head in admiration. 'Well, I think that is most extraordinarily brave of you. That is a sacrifice above and beyond the call of duty.'

Sheila looked puzzled. 'Above and beyond . . . I don't understand.'

'It's people like you making those kind of sacrifices who are the back bone of village life.'

Sheila beamed her pleasure. 'Oh, I am, where flowers are concerned. I've organised the competition marquee for the last three Village Shows, this year's, last year's and the one before that which was the first and the hardest to do, and they've been a roaring success. Believe me, the Harvest Festival display will be nothing in comparison. No, nothing at all.'

Grandmama could see she was a harder nut to crack than had first appeared. 'A fall like you have had is a terrible shock to the system, you know. You do realise you're still in a state of shock.'

'Am I?'

'Oh yes, and it can be very dangerous to the nerves if you struggle on when really you should be resting. Breaking a bone is equally as serious as a major operation. And what would they be saying to you if you'd had a major operation? I can tell you. Rest, complete rest, no aggravation of any kind.' Grandmama nodded her head very wisely after delivering this salvo and Sheila began to be impressed. 'It's just the same as when you have the flu. Get up and about too soon and you're back in bed as soon as. These things take their toll.'

'I suppose they do. I have been feeling a little odd.'

Triumphantly Grandmama said, 'What did I tell you?'

'Perhaps I am trying to be too brave.'

'Exactly, but then you're that kind of person aren't you? You've the kind of grit we had to have in the War.'

'I don't remember much about the War, I was too young.'

A shade too hastily the reply came back, 'Oh well, of course, so was I, but my mother told me.'

There was a pause while Grandmama restructured her campaign. Sheila shifted uneasily in her chair, and her visitor gazed in admiration at the picture over the fireplace.

'What a wonderful picture. Who painted it?'

'I don't know who the artist was, it was a parting gift from the Union when Ron . . . ald retired. It's a very good likeness isn't it?'

'It is very good. They've captured his . . . *strength* haven't they? I admire strength in a man.' Frankly she thought it wooden and not one jot like the man himself but people like Sheila put such store by things like that. 'This list which . . . Louise was it? put together for you on her computer, do you think someone else should have a look at it too, you know, just in case you aren't able to cope as well as you would usually do? I'm not meaning to interfere but the show must go on as they say and it might be as well to have an understudy, mightn't it? What do you think? I'd be the last person to step in where I wasn't wanted, and of course your word is law, you've so much experience.'

Sheila, by now overwhelmed by Grandmama's arguments and not at all able to stand up for herself as she normally would have done, began to feel herself weakening. It would be good to have some help. Taking a look at the list wouldn't mean she was in charge would it?

'It's in the file in that drawer there at the bottom marked Harvest Festival.'

Grandmama was out of her chair and across the room almost before Sheila had finished speaking. She held up the file with a reverent air as though it was the prized acquisition of a major museum. 'Here we are. I'll wash up our cups, and then I'll leave you in peace to have a little sleep. Studying this file will be my first priority. Between us we'll get this sorted. Can't let the Rector down can we?'

As she left, Grandmama said, 'Now you're not to worry. I've met people like you before, working your fingers to the bone for everyone else with not a thought for yourself. Well, now someone is thinking about *you* for a change.' She patted Sheila's arm and continued, 'No, don't get up. There you go again, always thinking of other people. I'll let myself out. Have a good sleep.'

She spent the rest of the morning reading through Sheila's lists. There was no doubt about it, the woman was much better organised than she'd first imagined. Names, addresses, telephone numbers of her helpers. A plan of the church, with notes of who did what and where. A colour scheme carefully laid out with lists of fruits and vegetables and types of greenery necessary to achieve the right effect. One could be forgiven for thinking they were decorating Westminster Abbey for heaven's sake. Even a list of where and what they had stored in boxes for use from year to year. Plant holders, swathes, corn dollies, the list was endless.

She came to the conclusion this wasn't Sheila's plan. Behind this meticulous scheme there was a very different kind of brain from hers. Maybe it was that Louise. But the thought occurred to Grandmama that change was needed. It couldn't be the same as last year, not exactly the same. She'd have a word with the Rector. That was it. The Rector. She glanced at the clock. Twelve thirty. Time for lunch and then off to the rectory. No, she'd go now. Before lunch, try to catch him in.

'It's about the Harvest Festival. Is the Rector in, Sylvia?'

'The Rector's already got someone in his study right now, but I'll go give him a knock, if you'll wait here, Mrs Charter-Plackett.'

'Thank you.' Grandmama stood in the hall looking at the decorations. Much better taste here. Oh yes, the Rector and his wife were more her kind of people. She could hear Sylvia speaking to the Rector, then she came back into the hall.

'If it's about the Harvest Festival he says would you like to come through.'

Sitting in one of the easy chairs was Harriet with little Fran on her knee. Peter stood up to greet her.

'How nice, two Mrs Charter-Plackett's and a Miss Charter-Plackett all at the same time. What a pleasure. We're just discussing the Harvest Festival so you've come at the right moment.'

21

'Good afternoon, Rector.' Such a gorgeous man. Even a lady of her age found him . . . disturbing. 'Good afternoon, Harriet. Hello, Grandmama's favourite girl. What a coincidence.'

'Good afternoon, Mother-in-law. What brings you here?'

Grandmama tapped the file in her hand. 'I've got the master plan for the church here.'

Harriet registered shock. 'You have? How've you managed that? Sheila never lets it out of her sight.'

'My dear, she is desperate. This accident has completely thrown her, she's not at all well, she's just so grateful for my offer to step into the breach.'

'Sheila is? Is she? I'm amazed. Have you misunderstood?'

'Here is the evidence. I didn't steal it from her.'

Peter intervened. 'Does she not want to be in charge?'

'How can she? She can barely walk, and she's racked with pain. I've read through and made a few notes. The basic idea will be the same but I shall make a few minor changes, after all it will be boring if the same design is done year after year. I see you're down for the bread, Harriet. Usually a sheaf of corn design. Well, this time I think we'll have something more simple, I have in mind an extra large cottage loaf. More natural don't you think?'

'But I've always made a sheaf of corn.'

'My point exactly. Time for a change.'

Harriet, determined not to be steamrollered, said, 'I'd like to talk to Sheila about this. After all, she's the expert.'

Grandmama shook her head. 'Don't, when I left her she was going to have a sleep. She's not at all well. There's no need to worry her, believe me. This afternoon I shall telephone all the people who helped last year

22

and tell them of my changes of plan. She can't be at the meeting tomorrow night, so I've promised to chair it for her.'

'I see. Well, Mother-in-law,' Harriet lifted Fran off her knee and stood up ready to leave, 'I'm not at all happy about this. There's still two weeks to go, plenty of time for Sheila to have made at least a partial recovery and I for one am not prepared to go ahead without a word from her.'

Peter stood up too. 'I think we should leave the telephoning for a couple of days, that way we'll have a better idea of how Sheila is coping. I'm very grateful to you Mrs Charter-Plackett for stepping into the breach, but I would feel happier if I could be given the chance to speak to Sheila before anything definite is done. It is her baby as you might say.'

'Of course, Rector, anything you say, but you'll see it's me she wants to have deal with everything. There's absolutely no need for you to worry. Everything will go swimmingly, believe me. I shan't let you down. I might just make a few preliminary calls, break the ice so to speak.'

Harriet swept out hand in hand with Fran. 'Thanks, Peter, see you soon.' As she passed him she gave him a sceptical look of which her mother-in-law was blithely unaware saying, as Harriet left, 'I must give credit where it's due, she has made very careful lists about everything, there'll be no problems I can assure you.'

'In a village we have to step very delicately, I have known major incidents arise from quite insignificant beginnings. One can never afford to give offence of any kind, the repercussions can be so far reaching.'

Grandmama picked up her handbag, and smiled up at him. The combination of his red-blond hair and those blue all-seeing eyes was quite stunning. She reminded herself she was seventy-five. 'Of course I quite understand, there'll be no repercussions with this matter, believe me. If we're both on the same side . . .' Her smile was conspiratorial.

Peter's heart sank. The confrontations he'd had with Sheila in the past loomed uneasily in his mind. No one had told him when he was ordained that diplomacy would need to be high on his list of skills.

That afternoon several villagers received phone calls which pleased them not at all.

Chapter 3

The following morning Peter called in the Store for a few things he needed. Seeing Jimbo serving at the meat counter he called across, 'Good morning, Jimbo!'

'Morning, Peter! Nice day.'

'It is indeed. Lifts the spirits no end.'

There came a chorus of 'Good morning, Rector' and then the general hubbub recommenced. The Store was extremely busy for so early in the morning. There were three people waiting to pay at the till, a clutch of people taking advantage of the free coffee machine and gossiping by the ice-cream cabinet while they did so, and two people clustered around the post office grill listening intently to a story Linda was telling them from the other side.

He gladly embraced the sounds and smells of the Store, for not only was the weather uplifting this morning but coming in the Store was too. One was drawn in as though by a magnet to the warm welcoming atmosphere Jimbo had created: to the inviting displays, the bright lights, so clean, so smart, so enticing it was extremely difficult to leave without buying something. Jimbo might have been a merchant banker but he was a born shopkeeper too.

From the vivid colours of the greengrocery to the smart businesslike post office counter it was all so appealing and best of all his prices were competitive too, even though it was the only place to shop in the village.

Drifts of the conversations came to him as he studied the selection of toothbrushes.

'I'm telling you, I know. I saw. Dicky and Georgie have gone away together.'

'Noooo! They can't have.'

'They have. Her and Bryn had that row in the bar the other night and apparently, after Lady Bissett'd broken her leg and gone orf to 'ospital, it went from bad to worse. It's not right all that rowing in the bar.'

'Tisn't. I agree. But going off together! That's a bit much. Poor Bryn. I'd no idea that was the way the wind was blowing.'

'Neither 'ad I and I wouldn't have known if it hadn't been for the baby waking early and I was standing at the window rocking him and I saw Georgie come out of the pub and Dicky pull up in his car and she got in. She only had a small case so they can't be going for long. All tarted up she was and no mistake. I tell yer there's advantages in living at number three!'

'And 'im the Scout leader! Disgusting I calls it. Perhaps he was only giving her a lift to the station.'

'Got yer rose coloured spectacles on then this morning? So why wasn't he at Scouts last night then?'

The coffee drinkers were discussing other news.

'I see Lady Templeton's back.'

'Well, she won't say a thing, you know how kindly she always speaks of everybody.'

'Not always, she has been known to have her say.'

'She won't like old Mrs Charter-Plackett telling her what to do though will she?'

'No, she won't. And I'll tell you who else won't like her taking liberties.' The speaker nodded her head in the direction of the door marked *Private*. 'Mrs Jones. How Mr Charter-Plackett manages to keep the peace with 'er lording it over the mail-order office I'll never know. Still adds a bit of spice to life, doesn't it? Where would we be without someone to talk about?'

Peter, trying hard not to listen to these snippets of news, finally settled on a toothbrush and began contemplating the razor blades, hoping he'd remember which kind he used. He heard Mrs Jones call from Jimbo's mail-order office.

'Mr Charter-Plackett! Was that the Rector came in a minute ago?'

'The man himself. Do you want a word?'

Mrs Jones came through into the Store. 'I do. Bit private. Is it all right if the Rector comes into the back? Would you mind, sir?'

Peter had a very good idea what she wanted to see him about. 'I'm in a hurry, Mrs Jones.'

'Won't take long.'

She asked him to sit on her stool and propped herself against the racks where she stored Harriet's Country Cousin jams and marmalades.

'I've never had a lot of time for Sheila Bissett. She's a bossy interfering person who likes all her own way, *but* I had a phone call yesterday from the Duchess, sorry, Mrs Charter-Plackett.'

'Ahhh!'

'You know then.'

'I did ask her not to do anything until I'd had a word with Sheila.'

'Well, she told me that I was moved from being in charge of the window-sills to doing the small display we

27

always put in the choir vestry. I've done the window-sills for years. I have to admit that since Sheila took charge my window-sills have improved out of all recognition. I've liked what she's suggested and gone along with it. We've an understanding she and I. But I'm not being demoted to doing the choir vestry display. That's a kid's job.'

'I see. Did she give you a reason?'

'Something about the window-sills need to be coordinated with the rest of the church and it'll be better if the people doing the church itself do them. Meaning she's doing the church in place of Sheila, so she wants a bigger slice of the action. As you know, I don't like causing trouble,' mentally Peter raised his eyebrows at this remark, 'but I had to say something.'

'Leave it with me.'

'You'll have to move fast, she's rung I don't know how many people. They're all up in arms.'

'Oh dear.'

She nodded her head in the direction of the Store. 'You see it's a bit difficult for me working here and the Duchess being his mother, can't say too much can I?'

'I'm sure Jimbo knows his mother for what she is.'

'Maybe, but she is his mother after all. Got to press on, Rector. I'll wait to hear.'

'Right. I think she's only trying to help because of Sheila's accident.'

'No, Rector, she's taking charge. There's a difference.'

Peter paid for his shopping and went back to the rectory. He'd been in his study only a few minutes when Sylvia came in with his coffee.

'Thank you, Sylvia, here, look, I'll make a space.' He moved some papers further along his desk and she put down his cup.

'I expect they've all had a word have they, Rector?'

'About what?'

'About the Duchess going behind Sheila Bissett's back and reorganising all our arrangements?'

'Indeed they have. But I'm quite sure Sheila won't allow her to.'

'I think Sheila's too poorly to have any choice in the matter, she must be, she's let the Duchess have her precious file.'

'Well, Sylvia, I think we can just wait and see. I'm sure she means well.'

'She also went up to the Big House yesterday afternoon and sweet-talked them into letting her borrow lots of potted plants from the glasshouses so it's going to look more like a garden centre than anything. Also she's going to buy palms and rubber plants and charge them to the church. It's going to look ridiculous.'

'Charge them to the church?'

'Yes.'

'I did warn her to tread carefully.'

'Well, if that's the Duchess treading carefully, heaven alone knows what'll happen if she puts the boot in. And Lady Templeton has been compulsorily retired, too.'

Peter smiled at her. 'Leave it with me. Thanks for the coffee.'

After Sylvia had left Peter sipped his coffee while he thought up a way to soften Grandmama's overbearing scheming. He'd ask Caroline. Her commonsense approach to life most often produced an answer for him to questions of this kind. After all, she was on the committee and might resolve the problem for him. Grandmama was well meaning but so domineering. He glanced at the study clock. Eleven. Three hours before she got home. Somehow problems never seemed so bad when she was home.

But he had this niggling worry about Caroline. Nothing

specific, but he knew things weren't right for her. They never had secrets, well only that one which he'd handled so badly he'd nearly lost Caroline, and the guilt had made him want to die. But not now. No secrets now, except . . . He picked up the photograph he kept on his desk. It was of her and the twins taken about two years ago. Alex so like himself and Beth dear little Beth . . . He shut his mind off from thinking about whom she was like, with her blonde hair and rosy rounded cheeks. With the best will in the world you couldn't say she resembled Caroline.

The phone rang.

'Turnham Malpas Rectory, Peter Harris speaking.'

'Peter, it's Harriet Charter–Plackett. Is Caroline there?'

'She's taking surgery this morning, she won't be back until about two-ish.'

'Ah! I need to speak to her about tonight, the Harvest Committee. Ask her to ring as soon as she gets in? It's urgent.'

'Sure. Are you cancelling it with Sheila not being there?'

There was a pause and then Harriet answered, 'Not exactly. But it's urgent.'

'Understood.'

Caroline returned Harriet's call from the telephone in the study and Peter couldn't understand the intrigue which was afoot. After she'd put down the handset he asked her what was going on.

Caroline tapped the side of her nose with her forefinger and said, 'It's a secret, the fewer people know the better.'

'Darling!'

'It's better you don't know. Has Sylvia left my lunch out?'

'She has. What's Harriet up to?'

'Will you have a drink with me, tea, juice, coffee?'

'No, thanks. Will Jimbo like this secret plan?'

In truth Jimbo didn't. At that very moment, just like Peter he was questioning *his* wife about her phone calls and Harriet was answering him with undisguised glee.

'We've all rung each other up and decided to boycott the meeting.'

'Why?'

'Because your mother thinks she is taking us over and we're not putting up with it.'

He'd looked at her in astonishment. 'You mean mother's going to be there at the meeting and no one else?'

'Exactly. Sheila told Caroline yesterday there was no way she would be able to cope with getting to the meeting so that's what we've decided, we're not going either. I wish I was a fly on the wall and could see your mother's face when she realises no one's turning up.'

'How could you do that to her, Harriet?'

'Very easily.'

'She's your mother-in-law.'

'You don't need to remind me. I know!'

'I think that is the unkindest thing I have ever known you do.'

'I beg your pardon.'

'You heard.'

'Whose side are you on?'

'Yours, of course. But . . .'

'You are siding with your mother, ergo you are *not* on my side.'

'But there are limits, and in this case . . .'

'Sorry, Jimbo, but none of us is going to the meeting and that's that. You'd do well to remember the promise you made to me before she came. You promised me you'd back me against your mother in any dispute.'

'I always do.'

Harriet pointed her finger at him. 'You're not. You pledged yourself to be on my side. I didn't want her to come to live here, we've never got on and we never will. She's an interfering, bossy, inconsiderate, overbearing, insensitive woman with no finer feelings *at all*. But, she's your mother and I agreed I wouldn't object to her coming to live near her only family in her . . . well, I was going to say in her declining years but I take that back because they're not declining, not one bit. But I warn you, you are skating on very, very thin ice here . . .'

Jimbo was shocked at the threat in Harriet's voice and decided to deflect his anger from her onto other members of the committee. 'I'm appalled at Caroline and Liz not going, the others perhaps but not them. Caroline especially.'

'You can be as appalled as you like because it won't make one jot of difference, we are not going to the meeting. Someone has to take a stand.'

'For a person who has in the past complained about Sheila Bissett's tactlessness and bossiness you amaze me.'

'Do I indeed? Well, being annoyed with her is something quite different from standing by and allowing the niche she has carved for herself to be dismantled piece by piece by your battleaxe of a mother.'

Harriet stood arms akimbo glaring at him.

'Does Sheila know about this?'

'No. We daren't tell her because she can't keep a secret as we all know to our cost.'

'Is Peter privy to it?'

'We've all taken a vow of silence, so I'm pretty certain Caroline won't have told him.'

'If he knew he'd be livid. He'll blame me. I've a good mind to ring him.'

'Don't even think of it. Because if you do . . .'

'Yes?'

'If you do . . . your life won't be worth living and I mean that. I have *never* been more serious in my life.'

On that Harriet left the sitting-room and went into the kitchen, crashing about in there as though she was demolishing it cupboard by cupboard. Jimbo knew that things were bad when she was like that. He did think of quietly going round to his mother's house and telling her what was afoot, but changed his mind when he recollected how much he loved his home to be a haven, not just for him, but for his children too. There was no doubt about it, this time for the sake of peace it was his mother who would have to be sacrificed.

Grandmama Charter-Plackett, fully expecting that Sheila would not come, as she was still in pain despite the tablets from the hospital, was looking forward with pleasure to chairing the Harvest committee meeting. It was her first opportunity to prove her mettle since she'd moved into the village. This was something she could really get her teeth into.

It was being held in the small committee room in the church hall. She was there first and turned up the thermostat on the radiator. That Willie Biggs was very parsimonious with the heating. The church could well afford to keep the hall warm, after all she understood Mr Fitch had paid for it to be installed so they only had the running costs to contend with. She glanced at her watch, only five minutes to go, they were all running late. Still it was a weekday evening and everyone had things to do before they came out. How did Caroline manage to keep her job with all the other things she was involved in to say nothing of those two little shockers. She'd never known two such adorable but inventively naughty children in all her life. Thank God she hadn't had twins. Two at a time! Heavens above!

There came a shuffling at the door and a voice calling out. She went to see who it was. The last person she'd expected to see, nor indeed wanted to see, was Sheila, but there she was.

'Hold the door for me, Mrs Charter-Plackett, please. Thank you.'

Between them they got her through the door and onto a chair. Sheila, panting with exhaustion slumped onto the chair and heaved a sigh of relief. 'I'd no idea how far it was from our house to the church hall. I'm sure they must have moved it further away since I was last here!'

Her mind working overtime trying to adjust to this unwelcome surprise, Grandmama took Sheila's crutches and propped them against the wall. 'You really are extremely brave, Sheila. Considering the pain you're in. I . . . We never expected you here tonight. You shouldn't have come. No, you shouldn't.'

'Well, I have. Didn't want to let everyone down. Ron's not due back till late tonight, he's been delayed, and so when Gilbert and Louise left for home I thought, sitting here all by myself and that meeting going on, it's no good I've got to go. I thought I'll manage somehow. So here I am! But it's nearly killed me. Where's everyone else?'

'I don't know, they're all busy people, don't worry they'll be here shortly.' Grandmama was in a serious dilemma. Her idea of being in charge, which she admitted she was perfectly capable of being, was in serious jeopardy now Sheila had arrived.

'Oh, good! I see you've brought the file. I'll have it

34

back. Thank you.' She held out her hand. Grandmama didn't have an answer to this, and short of saying 'absolutely not' which in the circumstances she couldn't justify, she had to hand it over. She made a last-ditch effort. 'Are you sure? Are you really well enough to cope?'

Immediately Sheila was struck by a lightning flash of understanding. 'Am I sure? Of course I'm sure. I sincerely hope you weren't expecting to take over? Were you?'

'Of course not! Simply trying to help a . . . friend in distress. Of course I wasn't.'

Sheila opened the file and the first thing she saw was a list in Grandmama's handwriting.

'What's this list?' Sheila took out her reading glasses, placed them on her nose and studied the list. She didn't speak, but she did flick through her computer lists. Here, there and everywhere were red ink notes and crossings out. She was in such a temper that the file, almost as though it had a life of its own flew into the air and fell on the floor at Grandmama's feet, who automatically bent down to pick it up.

Sheila shouted. 'Don't dare! Don't you dare pick it up! Not taking over! That was an absolute lie! You've changed everything.'

'No I haven't, just made a few notes here and there.'

'A few notes! You've massacred my plans. All your pretending to be helpful, you've ruined it. Have you told everyone you're in charge? Have you?'

'Not really, no.' She wasn't accustomed to opposition like this, but she'd no intention of allowing this situation to become her Waterloo. She'd have to regain the lost ground and quickly.

Despite her extreme discomfort or maybe because of it

Sheila almost screamed, 'Not really! I don't believe that. I'm in charge! Do you hear. I will not be usu . . . usur . . . I will not have you taking over. This is my pigeon.'

'Well, really! I was only trying to help. I'm sure you would have made changes, you can't have it the same every year and . . .'

'It isn't the same every year! We develop it. Your trouble is you think you know better than everyone else. Well, you don't. You can't just come to this village and ride roughshod over everybody.'

'Let's face it, Sheila, they're not exactly at the leading edge all these people are they? They need a push here and a nudge there to bring them into the twentieth century never mind the twenty-first. Between us, you and I could make a real difference. You with your knowledge, me with my style. We'd be a stunning combination.'

Grandmama could be very persuasive when she chose and Sheila went silent. Having organised the big Village Show Competition marquee so successfully three times now, she'd grown in confidence and in the realisation that she had a real part to play in village life. There was no longer a need to stand her ground against stiff opposition as she had in the past. She'd arrived. Now the Duchess was undermining her all over again.

'No good being a stunning combination if we've no committee, is it?'

Grandmama looked round the room. 'You're quite right. Where is everybody?'

Sheila looked at her watch. 'We did say seven thirty. Or I did. Did you change it?'

'No, of course not.'

'There's no "of course" about it. You'd change anything you wanted if you'd a mind to it. It won't do. I'm not putting up with it. Pass me the file. Please.'

Grandmama picked it up and handed it to her. 'There you are.'

Now the papers had been reshuffled by the fall, the top most one was the one where Grandmama had reallocated the tasks. 'What's this? Lady Templeton always does the organ flowers. You can't reorganise her. She's aristocracy.'

'Oh come, come. She was only a solicitor's secretary, you really can't call her aristocracy.'

'Muriel *is* Lady Templeton whatever you might say and I'm not moving her without her consent.' Sheila glared at Grandmama. 'Has she said she doesn't want to do it?'

'Well, I haven't had a chance to speak to her, she's only just back from holiday.'

'Right that's it. I'm taking this file home and I'm getting Louise to print it all out once more and I'm starting from scratch, again. You're having nothing to do with it.' She took another look at the list. 'And, look, what it says here. Palms and things in front of the lectern. The Rector's wife always does the lectern arrangement from time immemorial. Dr Harris will be most offended. You're a stupid interfering old . . . old . . . old . . . *baggage*. Pass me my crutches.'

Grandmama's mouth twisted into something like a smile. She sat quite still. Sheila persisted. 'Please.'

'You'll have to wait for the rest of the committee. I'm not having some trumped up trades union leader's wife speaking to me as you have done, knighted or not. No one speaks to Katherine Charter-Plackett like that. No one. So you can sit there until tomorrow morning as far as I'm concerned. I'm going home now.'

Sheila suddenly realised the impossible position she was in. She couldn't get off the chair without help, and she couldn't reach her crutches from where she sat. She couldn't reach a phone to call for help either; the Duchess had her absolutely in her power. Then another thought intruded. Where was the committee? Her devoted committee who'd never let her down, ever. Had they abandoned her? They certainly hadn't come. Was everything she'd worked for in ruins? She glanced surreptitiously at her watch. Twenty minutes to eight. They weren't going to come now. They always had a nice coffee before they started and Caroline or Harriet brought cake and it was all friendly and gossipy and thoroughly pleasant.

'You wouldn't dare walk away and leave a sick helpless woman.'

'I would. You've spoken to me as I've never been spoken to in my life. You're a common little woman.'

That remark struck home. Sheila had known for years that she lacked good taste. But ever since Ron had put his foot down that time when it was the Flower Festival in the church and she'd gone out with him and bought that green suit which everyone had liked and she'd stopped peroxiding her hair, she really had tried. But she knew that every now and again that lack of taste manifested itself in some ridiculous buy she made and then regretted. It was a continuous battle that, keeping the common side of her under wraps, and now this terrible woman had unearthed it all over again.

'How dare you say that! Who do you think you are?'

Grandmama stood up. This distasteful conversation really must be brought to a close. 'Well, I know who I am, do you know who you are? I'm going home.'

'Righteo, Duchess. You go. It'll be all round the village tomorrow, what you've done to me. It'll be a really juicy piece of gossip for them all. Do you no end of good. I don't think. We've now no committee, all because of you, so the Harvest Festival will be in ruins and I can't face telling the Rector. I don't know what he'll say.'

'Duchess? Who calls me Duchess?'

The tone of her voice gave Sheila the idea she might, just might, be able to get back at her and really slap her down. Her lip, unaccustomed to curling, did so as she said, 'Everybody does, didn't you know?'

But the shot misfired. Grandmama drew herself up, picked up her crocodile handbag, bought in Harrods years ago but still as good as new, and said, 'Well, at least people do have respect for me then. I'd no idea.' She smiled and left.

Chapter 4

'So, there she was waiting. 'Er leg too painful to stand on and she was too unbalanced with the weight of the plaster to hop. She'd been there an hour when I found her.'

Vera laughed till the tears were rolling down her cheeks. Willie knew it was funny but he didn't think it was that funny. He'd had to get his Sylvia to bring her car round and give Sheila a lift, because she'd been too distraught and exhausted to tackle the walk home. For once in his life he'd felt sorry for Sheila, really sorry.

Eventually Vera had calmed herself enough to speak again. 'But what I don't understand is where were the rest of the committee?'

'They'd agreed not to turn up, believing Sheila would never get there anyway, and that would leave the Duchess high and dry with no committee to boss around and it would serve her right.'

Vera picked up her glass to finish the last few drops of her shandy when a thought struck her like a thunder bolt. 'But Harriet Charter-Plackett's on the committee. Do you mean she dared do that to her own mother-in-law?'

'Yes, apparently she did, and her and Jimbo had a terrible row about it. He said she should go out of loyalty to 'is mother and she said she shouldn't out of loyalty to Sheila and the rest of the committee. Right bust-up I understand. Bel Tutt said they still weren't speaking this morning, so when Harriet went in to 'elp in the Store while little Fran was at playgroup, they passed messages to each other through her and Linda.'

'That must have been a laugh. Still it's not nice when yer in-laws come between yer. Jimbo and Harriet are really keen on each other, aren't they? I'm glad you mentioned Bel Tutt though.' She nodded her head in the direction of the bar counter. 'Is it true do you think about Georgie and Dicky?'

'Look, two people happen to go away for a couple of days at the same time. It doesn't mean they've gone together does it?'

'No, but Bel's 'is wife, why hasn't she gone? There's no reason is there?'

From where he sat Willie had a good view of the saloon door. He was about to answer Vera when he turned and, looking straight into her eye, he said, 'Don't look now, she's just come in. She's at the bar ordering a drink. Alan's serving 'er.'

'Bel?'

'Yes. She's coming over. Don't say a word.'

'Right.'

'Hello, Bel. Coming to join us?'

Bel estimated whether or not she could squeeze in next to Willie on the settle but decided the gap was too narrow and lowered herself onto the chair next to Vera, who, bursting to know the real truth of Dicky and Georgie's holiday situation, blurted out, 'Lonely on yer own with Dicky away?'

Bel studied Vera's face. 'You could say that.' She took a long draught of her shandy, put the glass down on the table and looked about her.

Not to be put off with such bland meaningless statements Vera asked, 'Gone somewhere nice has he?'

'You could say that.'

Willie became embarrassed, sometimes Vera could be just too inquisitive. 'I hear there's been trouble at the Store today.'

Bel's face lit up. 'You could say that. Linda and me, we've been at our wits' end. Was I glad when it got to half past eleven and I could nip off to the school. Mind you Mr Charter-P wasn't much better in the afternoon. He has got a point though, she should have supported his mother.'

Vera was enraged. 'Support the Duchess? I don't see why she should. She's an interfering old bag . . .'

'Vera!' Willie hissed between his teeth.

'Old basket then.'

Bel smiled for the first time. Bel's smiles were worth waiting for. They illuminated the whole of her large round face. Her smiles touched not only her lips which curved up at the corners most attractively but her cheeks lifted, her eyebrows and even her forehead rose up and a light burst forth from her eyes. Her smooth pink and white skin glowed with her delight.

'She's a right case is that mother of his. She comes in to the Store sometimes with a determined look on her face and you can see Mr Charter-P brace himself for a fight. She makes suggestions about him changing things round and if it was hers she'd do this and that. Quite often though you know she's right but he wouldn't admit it to her. When she's gone he'll prowl about for a bit and then change things about just like she's said, then he shrugs his shoulders and winks at me. Some of her ideas are good, but some well . . .'

Vera's thirst for knowledge still not having been assuaged she pressed on with her enquiries. 'The midnight hike. Our Rhett's all organised. You'll be taking it all on your own, with Dicky away?'

Bel looked at her. 'He's back tomorrow. Wouldn't miss a hike, not Dicky.'

'Oh I see I thought . . .'

'What?'

'Oh nothing.'

Willie mused. 'Curious name Bel, how did it come about?'

'Isobel actually, but I couldn't say it so I said Bel and it stuck.'

To encourage Bel to further revelations Vera commented 'There was that Belle Watling in *Gone with the Wind*. Our Brenda's favourite book, that's why she called our Rhett, Rhett. Poor kid. He doesn't half get teased.'

'He should change it. He could change it to Robert or Roland or Richard.'

'That's what your Dicky is isn't it, Richard.'

'You could say that.'

'Funny how Dicky is short for Richard, they don't seem to belong do they? Not like Les for Leslie?'

'You could say that.'

'Perhaps he couldn't say it either, just like you.'

'I suppose.'

Bel sipped her drink. Willie wondered what to say next and Vera remembered she had to get to bed in good time as she was on early turn.

'I'll say good night then. Nine thirty for the hike, Bel?'

Bel nodded. 'Outside the church hall. They can eat the

food in their fingers, but tell him to bring a cup of some kind.'

'Will do. Night, Willie.' Vera wended her way out, speaking to a few people before she left. Bel watched her leave.

'Quiet for you is it without Dicky?'

'It is. Good company is Dicky. Georgie not in?'

'No. They had a row did her and Bryn and she's hopped off on holiday. Over your Dicky.'

'Over Dicky?'

'Didn't you know? She'd asked him to do a turn. A comic turn like. You know what Dicky's like with his jokes. She's wanting to start up having entertainment here in the bar and Bryn won't have it and she had Dicky lined up for the first turn.'

'I see.'

'Didn't he tell yer? Could have been the start of a showbiz career! Yer never know.'

Bel finished her drink, heaved her bulky body out of her chair, took her glass to the counter and left without another word.

Next morning in the Store Bel was very quiet. Jimbo noticed and put it down to missing Dicky. He'd quite enough on his plate though without worrying about other people's marital problems. He'd been in hell for over twenty-four hours now and hell didn't suit him. The children had become seriously fractious because of the atmosphere at home and little Fran had cried at having to go to playgroup. He hated her to cry. Couldn't bear it in fact, but what was worse was Harriet having shut him out.

Caroline came in. 'Morning, Jimbo. Morning, Linda.'

'Good morning, Dr Harris. How's things?'

'OK thanks. How's that little Lewis of yours?'

44

'He's doing fine. Alan's that delighted with him. He's such a sunny little boy. Your two OK at school?'

'Oh yes fine. Before I know it they'll be in Kate's class and ready for leaving! Just got these two letters to post. They're both going to India.'

'Put them on the scales then, please!'

'There we are.'

'Eighty pence each.'

'Thanks. Harriet about?'

Linda nodded. 'In the back in the kitchens. Treat with care!'

Caroline raised her eyebrows and Linda pointed to Jimbo and pulled a face.

To Linda's disappointment her next customer was the Duchess. She'd promised herself that she would treat her with the barest civility for what she'd done to Sheila Bissett. Leaving her all alone in that state, it simply wasn't right.

'Good morning, Linda. I have a registered parcel to post. How are you, my dear, today? Baby being good?'

'Yes, thank you. That'll be four pounds twenty-two.'

'Four pounds twenty-two? Are you sure?'

'Registering is very expensive.' Rather maliciously Linda added, 'If you can't afford it, proof of postage is cheaper.'

'There's no need to be insolent, my girl. Jimbo! Come here.' He came across. 'The cost of posting this parcel is outrageous. Can't you make it cheaper for me. I am family.'

'Not on the post office counter, Mother. Sorry.'

'Very well, though I don't see why not. Register it, please, it is rather important. Don't mistake me, I can afford it, it's just that it seems so disgracefully expensive for such a very small parcel.'

45

'It does weigh quite heavily though.'

Grandmama put her change in her purse and as she snapped it shut she asked, 'Is my daughter–in–law in?'

'Er . . . yes.'

'In the back?'

'Er . . . I think so.'

'Well, is she or isn't she?'

'Well, yes, she is . . . I think.'

Grandmama found Harriet propped against one of the huge freezers, talking to Caroline.

'Harriet! I've been waiting.'

'What for?'

'For an apology.'

'For what?'

'Your behaviour at the meeting.'

'I wasn't there.'

'I know, that's what I meant.'

Caroline began to excuse herself, but Harriet stopped her. 'No you stay, please. You can be a witness.'

'I don't think I . . .' Caroline tried to make her exit as gracefully as she could, but Harriet held her arm.

Grandmama directed her glance at Caroline. 'You owe me an apology too, Dr Harris.'

'Me? You will not get an apology from me!'

'You both do. You both thought that Bissett woman wouldn't be there and you deliberately refused to come to the meeting, obviously intending to make a fool of me.'

Jimbo's voice interrupted the confrontation. 'I'm very busy but I've broken off to remonstrate with you about last night. I was very upset about them boycotting the meeting but no longer upset when I heard what you'd done to Sheila. It was quite dreadful. I did hear correctly, did I?'

Fast losing control of what she had hoped would be a

46

magnificent climb down on Harriet and Caroline's part, Grandmama turned to face Jimbo. She'd never seen him so angry. There didn't seem to be quite so much pleasure in her challenge as there had been up to now. Obviously Sheila's popularity, though she couldn't think why, was much greater than she'd realised.

Holding her chin a little higher than normal Grandmama said quite clearly, 'You did. All I was doing was giving a helping hand, assisting someone in dire need and what do I get in return? Insulted! Lady Bissett' – scathingly she repeated – 'Lady Bissett – I ask you! – called me an old . . .' – there was hesitation here, should she tell? Yes, she must. She had to justify her actions, she really had – 'an old *baggage*! She only got what she deserved.'

Harriet smothered a grin.

Jimbo's face never slipped. 'Mother, I am ashamed. Whatever everyone will think of you I cannot imagine.'

'Well, I've resigned, so I'm not in charge any more. Perhaps now, everyone will be satisfied.'

'They won't forget though and neither will I.'

His mother rounded on him. 'Jimbo! It was your wife who insulted me the most. She should have supported me and come to the meeting no matter what the others said. My own son's wife! My daughter-in-law!'

Jimbo, furious, came out in defence of Harriet. 'My dear wife is quite capable of making her own moral judgements, she doesn't need me to vet her actions. The way things turned out, it's my opinion she did the right thing.'

'How could you? I came to live here looking forward to your support.'

'And you'll have it, so long as you behave yourself. Now please, Mother, leave before any more damage is done.' Jimbo stood aside from the doorway and waited for her to leave. Grandmama opened her mouth to protest, changed her mind, gathered the remnants of her dignity together and prepared to leave.

She strode from the freezer room intending to find a way out other than going through the Store, but due to her fury she was too confused to find one. Rather than ask for help she marched between the customers who had gathered to eavesdrop on what was being said, and then on past the till. Someone slyly sang the *Dambuster's March* in time to her masterful stride. As she shut the door a cackle of hysterical laughter rose to a crescendo. But the laughter was hastily cut short when Jimbo came through from the back. He glared round at everyone, and they quailed at the anger in his face. Then, his sense of humour being restored by remembering that Harriet had said quietly as his mother left, 'Thank you, Jimbo, darling', he raised his boater and bowed to them all.

Chapter 5

Caroline had gone straight back to the rectory after leaving the Store. She closed the door behind her and stood with her back to it, leaning on it. That woman would be the death of her. Hell's bells. She'd felt quite guilty enough not going to the meeting, because it did seem a nasty trick to play, but to be told she should apologise! That really was too much. They'd finally tamed Sheila into being more reasonable and now she'd been replaced in the aggravation stakes by Katherine Charter-Plackett. These things are sent to try us she thought. But I should never have answered her back like I did. As the wife of the rector, as the Duchess said, she shouldn't have. But of late her own worries seemed to override her innate good manners. The rectory was quiet. Peter was out, Sylvia was in Culworth at the dentist's and the children at school till half past three. Nearly five years old. Where had all the years gone? She'd have a quiet coffee all by herself and read the morning paper. Hopefully the telephone wouldn't ring.

The kitchen was warm. She adored this kitchen. She loved its bright walls, the pine table, the big Aga. She remembered what it had been like when they'd first moved in. Thirty years of a bachelor rector in residence had taken its toll. Peter had declared they'd never get the Aga into shape at all, old Mr Furbank must never have used it preferring the nasty little table-top gas cooker which they'd had removed, but some careful cleaning and a genius of a man who understood cookers had seen to that. Now it was her pride and joy. Though it was Sylvia who used it more than she. Thank heavens for Sylvia.

The coffee was jolly hot. She found the newspaper and carried it and her coffee into the sitting-room. Bliss! One peaceful morning all to herself. Though she loved general practice it was so draining, one always saw people when they were at their lowest ebb. Lowest ebb. The thought which had been pushing about in the back of her mind returned. She, a doctor, who'd said so many times as gently as she could 'it would have been so much more sensible to have come to me as soon as you realised, wouldn't it' and here she was doing just that. Ignoring it. It was telling Peter which was going to be so difficult. That was what she dreaded. She could face it, but Peter wouldn't be able to. She knew, even without his frequent affirmation of it, that without her he would be totally desolate. Love like his made hurting him horrifyingly easy.

Caroline picked up the newspaper and tried to concentrate, but every piece of news she read was full of doom and gloom. Was there nothing happening that was joyous? Apparently not. She laid the newspaper down again and tried to face up to her problem. Having been born with a badly deformed womb and now being more than sure that there was something insidious growing on her ovaries it seemed as though there would be nothing left in her to make her feel a woman. The phone rang.

'Darling! Peter here! Look, I've got held up here in Culworth. Seeing as you're having the day off why don't you come in and have lunch with me? We don't often get the chance do we?'

'Sylvia isn't back yet for a while.'

'Never mind. She won't be long, leave her a note and put the answer machine on till she gets back.'

'Shall I?'

'Yes, please!'

Caroline didn't feel like being happy. She simply wanted to hide and to be left alone. But the pleasure in Peter's voice! She really couldn't deny him. A café in Culworth wasn't exactly the right place for telling one's loved one about operations, so she could justifiably put off telling him.

'You're right! I'll come! One o'clock at Abbey Close?'

'Lovely!'

When she saw him coming, striding eagerly out of the Abbey Close towards her she wept inside. There was never going to be a right time to tell him. The smile of greeting on her face was genuine though. The very sight of him lifted her spirits. His vigour, his thick red-blond hair, the lovely glowing smile on his face which the sight of her had inspired. How could she break his heart?

'Darling!' Peter took hold of her elbows drew her close to him and kissed her full on the mouth. She kissed him back with a desperate fervour.

'Peter! I don't think rectors are supposed to kiss like that in public!'

'Why not? I'm not a saint! And I am married to you! Where shall we go?' He tucked her hand into the crook of his arm and smiled down at her.

'Not the George. Not at lunch time. They always take so long to serve.'

'Well, then. How about the Belfry Restaurant? Right here.'

'OK. The Belfry it is.'

The waitress suggested a table in the window, which someone had just vacated.

'Well, as I'm playing hookey I might as well be seen by everybody from the abbey.'

'No point in doing things by halves is there?' Caroline gave him her coat and he hung it up for her beside his cloak. She'd bought him the silver clasp for it when they'd first got married. He needed a new cloak now. She'd buy him one as a surprise, measure this one with her dressmaking tape. The cloak would have to be specially made because of his height.

'Miles away? I asked what you would like?'

'Sorry, darling.' Caroline looked at the menu and all she could see was lasagne. 'I'll have lasagne.'

'Are you sure? My treat?'

'Absolutely. Thanks. Just coffee. I won't have wine with driving straight back.'

'No, of course not. I think I'll have the steak and all the trimmings.'

'Good, you need something to fill that frame of yours!'

'You laugh, but for days now the laughter hasn't reached your eyes.'

Caroline pulled back from people watching and stared at him. She'd forgotten how perceptive he was. 'I've had an altercation with the Duchess this morning. She claimed I was without honour. And Harriet too! I'm afraid I gave her a mouthful and stormed out.'

'Oh dear! That's not my Caroline at all. Quite out of

character. But that's today. What happened to all the other days when you haven't . . .'

The waitress came for the order and when she'd gone Caroline gave him a blow by blow account of the happenings in the Store kitchen. 'So to conclude Harriet and Jimbo have been restored to each other, so all's well with their world.'

'Might be all well with theirs but not with yours. Are you overtired? Look, you don't have to go to the practice. I'm sure there's plenty of eager young things only too willing to take your place. Have a rest for a while. You've been working, albeit part time, for a good while now and I would appreciate you being at home. Is that the problem do you think, that you're overtired?'

A short portly figure marched by the window. Caroline waved. 'Oh, look there's the Dean going past. Turn round and wave!'

'Hope he doesn't come in. Oh! he hasn't.'

'Nice man, the Dean. I like him.'

'Wet!'

'Peter!'

'Stop changing the subject.'

'I didn't make him walk by.'

'I wouldn't put it past you.'

He sat twisting his ring round and round and round. Caroline read the signs. He was worried about her but he didn't know why, his suggestion of being overtired was simply a stab in the dark to get the real truth from her. Well, she wasn't going to tell him, not today. Not till she knew for certain.

'I'm just tired I expect. It's quite hectic working and then having two four-year-olds when I get home and at the weekend. You're always so busy then you see.'

'Yes.' Peter looked across the restaurant. She obviously

wasn't going to tell him. But he knew there was a problem. But what? Maybe she didn't know what it was either, just a general feeling of unsettledness. He was selfish. He'd brought her here, buried her in the country-side and it was all getting too much. Perhaps he should get out . . . for her sake. 'I've been thinking about a change.'

Caroline didn't answer until the waitress had finished serving them. 'Thank you. Parmesan? Yes. Thank you.' She brought her attention back to him. 'A change?'

'Yes, we've been here over five years, perhaps it's time . . .'

'Do you seriously fancy a move?'

'Do you?'

Caroline hadn't begun her lasagne. She'd picked up her fork intending to start but there was a strange tone in Peter's voice she was wary of. She put down the fork and sat back. He was scrutinising her face, watching for the slightest sign, anything at all that might give him a clue.

She answered him very quietly. 'The only reason we would move, my darling, is because *you* want to. That was the agreement we had. Your mission in life has a higher priority than mine. I can get a job anywhere I want to. That's our rule. OK?'

'But perhaps rules need changing?'

Very firmly Caroline answered 'Not this one.'

'So this sadness isn't . . .'

'Isn't anything. I've come out to enjoy your company. Isn't it great that Alex and Beth have settled so well at school. I was dreading Beth being difficult, when you remember how bad things were when she started playgroup. She loves her school dinners, I suggested packed lunches but she's refused them.'

Peter decided to cheer himself up for Caroline's sake. 'Yes, it is. It's a great relief.' Then another thought occurred to him. 'It's not the children starting school is it? Made you feel like a spare part?'

'A little teeny bit. But I can't keep them at home for ever can I? I grew up and so must they. Alex gets more like you every day.'

'He does, doesn't he?'

'Beth gets more like Suzy.' There came a silence when Caroline said that. She knew he found it hard when she mentioned the children's mother but there was no point in pretending Suzy had never existed. They only had to look at Beth to know she did.

'Yes, that's true.' Peter pushed his unfinished meal away from him, placed his knife and fork side by side, and sat back to look at her. 'So is that it? Is it this barren thing come back to haunt you?'

So near the truth. Maybe now was the moment, but there was a flurry of new arrivals and a man's cultured voice saying delightedly, 'Peter! Caroline! How lovely to see you. Not often you get away together for lunch! This is our first time here, we usually go to the George but they had a conference there today and it was far too busy for comfort. Muriel, my dear, look who's here.' Peter stood up as Muriel joined Ralph.

'How lovely! It must be good if the Rector and his wife are lunching here! What a nice surprise.'

Caroline, seeing a way out of her problem, began pulling out the chair beside her. 'Look, do join us.'

Muriel glanced at Peter, recognised a desperate kind of sadness, and shook her head. 'Certainly not! You both look to be enjoying being by yourselves for a change. We shan't intrude. Come, Ralph! Bye-bye! see you soon! Enjoy your lunch.'

Caroline caught the sound of Ralph protesting but Muriel was being quite firm with him.

Peter said, 'Well, that ruse didn't work did it? By the look on your face they were heaven-sent.'

'I did not come out to lunch to be psychoanalysed. You're my husband not my therapist. Finish your lunch! Eat up your greens! I'm sure your nanny must have said that to you many times!'

'She did! She was a tartar! Once I . . .' Caroline let him ramble on about his nanny, back on safe ground she thought thankfully. He took the hint and they chatted about everything under the sun including Dicky Tutt and Georgie Fields.

'Caroline, do you really think they've gone away together?'

'I shouldn't imagine so. You know what the village is like for inventing things on the slightest pretext! I saw Georgie crossing over to the Store when I was locking the door, whether Dicky is back as well I don't know. Everyone else thinks they have. Bryn apparently is like a bear with a sore head and Bel has gone silent and that's not Bel. She's as good as Jimbo for livening us all up!'

'He's the Scout leader you see. One has to be so careful even in this day and age.'

'But poor Bel! Poor Bryn!'

'It can't be very funny in a small community like Turnham Malpas, where we all know each other's business before we know it ourselves.'

'Apparently Jimmy nods his head very wisely but keeps his lips clamped and won't tell anyone what he knows.'

'Does he indeed? Honestly, it's always the same. I wonder what he knows? Help! I'm getting as bad as everyone else. One little hiccough and they have you dead and buried!'

Caroline didn't laugh. Neither did Peter when he looked at her face.

In bed that night Caroline watched Peter getting undressed. 'I don't think you've put an ounce of weight on since we married.'

He went to stand in front of the mirror. 'I don't think I have. In fact I know I haven't. Weighed myself a few weeks ago and I'm exactly what I was then.'

'Well, you do work hard at keeping fit. I admire your strength of character in going running in all weathers.'

'Habit. Jimbo doesn't come every morning like he used to, only about three times a week, says he doesn't have the time any more. I've warned him all the weight he's lost will slowly go back on again. But he claims he's so busy now with all his enterprises, he's on his feet all the time so he reckons he doesn't need it quite so much. Won't be long.'

He went to the bathroom. Caroline curled up on her side preparing to go to sleep. She'd tell him when . . . no she'd tell him tonight. No, she'd wait until she got a date. That was it.

Peter got into bed and drew her towards him and they lay, him with an arm under her neck and his other arm across her waist. He nuzzled his face into her hair and said 'Love you.'

'Love you too.' Caroline put an arm across his chest and hugged him.

'I'm sorry you're upset, would making love be any comfort to you?'

She released herself from his arms. She couldn't face that. 'No, I don't think so.'

Peter lay silent for a while, frighteningly puzzled by her refusal. 'That must be the first time ever you have refused.'

Trying to put a lighter note in his voice he joked, 'Are you turning into one of those women who get convenient headaches? Ten years of marriage and you've had enough!' He turned to watch her face, but it gave nothing away.

'That was a cheap joke. Of course not!'

He hadn't switched the light off on his side and he reached over and moved the lamp slightly so that the light fell on Caroline's face. Peter saw the beginning of tears. One escaped and trickled down her cheek. He wiped it away with his thumb.

'My darling girl, whatever the matter is, there's nothing which cannot be said between the two of us. We don't have secrets, you and I. We are truthful with each other.' He moved to take hold of her again. 'You and I.'

She shrugged herself away from him. 'Not always, Peter, not always.'

Twice he opened his mouth to speak, and twice he silenced himself. Then he said, 'I was terrified of hurting you.'

'But I would have preferred to know.'

'Then if you would have preferred me to have confessed and cause you dreadful pain when it might not have been necessary, though in the end of course it was, why can you not be truthful to *me* now, if that's what *you* would have preferred then?'

'All I can promise at this moment is that I will tell you when I can.'

'That's the best you can do?'

'At this moment. Yes.'

He couldn't bear the closed up, shut off Caroline who lay curled tightly on the other side of the bed. 'I need to hold you close. Nothing more. Is that OK?'

She was across the bed and in his arms weeping almost before he'd said 'OK?'

'Darling! darling! There! There!' He held her close, soothing her as he did the children when they had nightmares. 'Gently! I've got hold of you. There's nothing can harm you. I won't let it!' When the tears subsided he found a tissue and wiped her face for her. 'Listen! There is nothing in this world we can't face together. Now, is there?'

'No.'

'Well, then. I won't ask you again. You tell me what's troubling you when you're good and ready. Good night, and God bless you.' He pushed her hair away from her face and gently kissed her forehead, the kiss was a token of his love for her; it lacked desire, it lacked lust, it lacked a lover's touch, it was quite simply his salute to her as the person to whom he was giving his total, all adoring, all encompassing support.

And she loved him for it.

Chapter 6

The morning of the Harvest Festival dawned bright and sunny. There was a sharp autumn nip in the air but, as everyone declared when they opened their curtains first thing, 'Grand day for the Harvest. Sky's real clear.'

At a quarter to ten the ever burgeoning ranks of Scouts and Cubs, Guides and Brownies streamed up the church path carrying their harvest gifts. The church was already almost full and although Willie with Sylvia's help had filled in every available space with extra chairs from the Sunday School they were beginning to run out of seats. Eventually they had standing room only behind the font, and Willie thought one more person and we shall have to build an extension.

But what a feast met their eyes. Being a special day the church silver, for which they all had great affection after their fight to save it, gleamed on the altar and the great candlestick stood behind with its huge creamy white candle lit. Its flickering light shone on the festoons of flowers and greenery overflowing from the sill of the great altar window. Huge vases of flowers and foliage stood around on the floor. In front of the lectern was a vast arrangement of orange and yellow flowers with delicate grey-white eucalyptus leaves cascading from it. Caroline had spent a long time on Saturday morning getting it just right, and even someone who knew nothing of flowers would see it was special.

Each window-sill down the sides of the church was decorated with fruit and berries and greenery. Small trails of ivy trickled over the edges dropping down the stone walls beneath. Mrs Jones couldn't keep her eyes off them. She hated the thought of dismantling it all on Monday morning. Best do it tonight she thought, get it over with, though she'd be in the way of the people making up the parcels to go out to the children's home and the old people. Still she'd be quick. The stone pillars had swathes of yellow and white cactus chrysanthemums securely anchored to them, the trailing greenery softening the sandy coloured stone, apparently held there by magic.

Sheila, from her privileged position in the front pew where she sat to allow her to prop her broken leg on a kneeler, if she just craned her neck a little could admire most of the church excepting the arrangement in front of the organ seat. She was overwhelmingly well satisfied with how things had turned out. In fact, despite all her problems of not being mobile, of nearly losing control to the Duchess, of pain and anxiety at the restraints her broken leg put upon her, she was intensely proud.

All their planning had worked out beautifully, far far better than she could ever have hoped in the circumstances. They'd had such a jolly meeting at her house after that dreadful night when she'd thought her committee had abandoned her. Louise had printed out all the schedules for her again and they'd got together and cancelled all the Duchess's changes and restored the friendly atmosphere as though nothing had happened at

61

all. Mrs Jones had her window-sills back and Lady
Templeton her organ arrangement, Harriet had made a
sheaf of corn as everyone loved her to do, and under
persuasion from Dr Harris they'd agreed to allow the
Duchess to arrange the flowers along the screen to the
memorial chapel as a gesture towards good relations.
Altogether the whole thing had become a major triumph
for her, for the committee had demonstrated their loyalty
to her beyond anything she'd any right to expect.

Grandmama Charter-Plackett arrived late. She had
thought about not coming at all. That would show them!
How she disapproved. But then it occurred to her that
they wouldn't care anyway. Probably wouldn't even
notice she wasn't there. So she'd planned to arrive at the
last minute.

At the organ Mrs Peel, quite by coincidence, was
playing a particularly triumphant piece when Grandmama
entered. Without realising it she marched down the aisle
in time to it, looking from side to side for a seat, but there
were no seats to be had. She'd hoped to be able to squeeze
into the Templeton pew right down there at the front but
it was filled by Muriel and Ralph and that gaggle of four
Prior girls, some poor relations of Ralph, she understood,
though it seemed surprising that he should have poor
relations with his background.

There was one small space in the rectory pew. Caroline
caught her eye and shuffled the twins further up and
Grandmama could just get in next to those two awful
sisters, Valda and Thelma Senior. Why they should have a
prominent seat at the front of the church just because
they'd decided to attend every single service that ever was
held after being scared out of their wits with that witchcraft business last year before she'd arrived, she really
couldn't think. She just hoped they'd both remembered to

wash properly before they came, they really were in very close proximity.

Caroline smiled a greeting when Grandmama got up from her knees. She was in church so she'd better be magnanimous so she smiled Caroline a greeting in return. She had to admit the church looked wonderful. Her own arrangement along the foot of the screen carved in memory of the fallen looked excellent. That was a prime site if ever there was one. Those blood-red blooms Mr Fitch had let her have mixed with the dark dark shiny green of the foliage and the red berries certainly were very fitting. Very appropriate. In fact everywhere looked very tasteful. Though the palms and rubber plants would have added that extra . . . no perhaps they wouldn't after all. She reluctantly had to agree that Sheila Bissett knew her stuff.

The Rector came in. He was a lovely young man. Pity Caroline was looking so thin. She was sure she'd aged ten years since that altercation in the Store kitchen. Though the twins must be very wearing. Alex was singing gobbledegook, out of tune, at the top of his voice and didn't know when to stop for the end of a verse, and Beth was trying to tie her shoe laces and Alex's together. Really! Caroline didn't even seem to notice. She had eyes for no one but the Rector. And no wonder. That snow-white surplice he was wearing, dripping with antique lace made him look . . . well just too utterly . . . Grandmama pulled her mind back to the service.

If it was the last day of September today then her hospital check-up must be on Wednesday. Ten thirty if she remembered rightly. Oh good! lunch at Jimbo's today. How nice. She could just see Fergus and Finlay in their Scout uniforms and down the other side just out of sight she knew Flick must be standing with the Guides. Fran she couldn't see, Jimbo and Harriet must have been very late, because she hadn't spotted them when she came in.

There was that Dicky Tutt! What cheek he had. Standing there bold as brass, the self-righteous little man. They all said he'd been away with Georgie, disgraceful. Hymn book in hand, singing his head off as though butter wouldn't melt in his mouth. Holding himself up as an example to all those boys. She'd tell Jimbo to remove her grandsons from such a disgusting influence. If she glanced just behind her to her left she could see Georgie Fields, at the end of the pew. Good thing, she was only tiny she wouldn't see a thing if she wasn't on the end. Such a pretty woman. No longer in the first flush of youth but very attractive still. Georgie was watching Dicky! She was. How dare she. People had no shame nowadays. What could she see in him? He was a runt of a man really. Not quite small enough to be a jockey but not far off. That Dicky Tutt was kneeling in prayer. She peeped at him from between her fingers. Crossing himself too! A wonder he wasn't struck by lightning. She'd have a word with the Rector. The kind of thing he was getting up to gave the Anglican Church a bad name, to say nothing of the Scout movement.

When prayers were finished and Dicky stood up to sing he looked across at Georgie. Oh! My goodness! Dicky had twinkled his fingers at her and winked! Georgie was blushing. At least she'd shame enough to blush anyway. Bryn, standing next to Georgie, tall and well able to see Dicky, went a dull red. Grandmama thought, he knows. He knows! There must be something in it then. He's fuming. Georgie in her confusion dropped her hymn book. Not a few heads turned to see. Bryn bent down to pick it up for her. From the corner of her eye Grandmama saw him, *positively* saw him make up his mind. Before she knew where she was Georgie's elbow had been gripped by Bryn and he was manhandling her down the aisle. Perhaps manhandling was too strong a word but she was speeding down the aisle, her feet scarcely touching the stones.

Willie, standing by the door, hastily opened it and let them out. The singing trailed to a standstill, leaving Mrs Peel playing to herself and then she stopped playing thinking she must have played one too many verses. Only Peter's voice carried on without a falter, though Grandmama knew he knew because she saw him watching. Mrs Peel caught up with him and the congregation rallied and attempted to continue singing.

Peter carried on as though nothing had happened, and gradually the congregation pulled itself together. Though Grandmama guessed that quite a few of them would beat a rapid retreat to the Royal Oak at the end of the service.

Just when everything had settled down and she was enjoying the children doing their little play and the parents were beaming with satisfaction at their unbelievably talented children, Caroline fainted. Not dramatically or noisily, she simply slid off her seat and fell into the side aisle. Because the church was so crowded no one noticed at first what had happened. Grandmama was the only one alert enough to take action. She squeezed past Thelma and Valda who were dumbstruck, and past the two children who were beginning to cry and didn't know what to do, and knelt down beside Caroline. She took off her fur jacket and propped Caroline's head on it. Sylvia miraculously appeared from behind her and said, 'I'll get a drink of water. You stay with her.' Grandmama fumbled in her handbag and found her smelling salts. Old-fashioned they might be but she was taking the only possible course of action.

Sylvia went into the choir vestry and by now there was a lot of attention being directed at their part of the church. The children carried on with their play and Peter sitting on a chair with his back to the congregation watching them didn't notice what had happened.

The smelling salts brought Caroline round in a moment. Grandmama whispered, 'No, don't get up, not yet. Lie quite still.'

Sylvia came back carrying an old cup. 'It's all I could find. Here we are, Dr Harris, have a sip. That's it. There we are. Sit up a bit. Lovely.'

Grandmama whispered, 'We'd better get her out into the air. You get the twins.'

Caroline struggled to pull herself together, fearful of disturbing Peter's service. 'I'm so sorry. It's the heat. I'll get up now.'

Grandmama who was supporting her agreed. 'We'll go outside where it's cooler. Come along.'

The congregation was clapping the children and it wasn't until Peter turned to address it that he saw Grandmama helping Caroline out, with Sylvia following behind with the children. Willie, after a consultation with Sylvia, crept down the aisle to whisper to Peter. He nodded his head and then continued to announce the next hymn.

As Mrs Peel launched herself into the first line Peter went down the aisle and into the porch. Supported by Grandmama, Caroline was standing just outside breathing deeply and beginning to revive.

'Peter! It was the heat in there and the smell of the flowers. Please darling, you go back in, I'll be all right . . .'

He took her hand and squeezed it. 'Darling! I'm so sorry you're not well. The fresh air's making you feel better is it? Thank you Mrs Charter-Plackett for helping. I'd no idea.'

'You get back inside. We can manage. I'll take her back to the rectory as soon as she feels able.' She let go of Caroline and wafted her hands at Peter. 'Go along now. Everything's under control.'

'Will you be all right if I go?'

'Of course. I'm much better now.' So he went but didn't know how he would get through the rest of the service. But it was like she said, the church was hot and the smell of the flowers too. Then he remembered their conversation in bed the other night. 'I will tell you when I can.'

The children were clinging to Caroline's skirt not knowing how else to show their concern. Sylvia said, 'Come along, children, you lead the way. We'll get the kettle on and you can give Mummy a lovely cup of tea. She'll like that won't she?' They scurried away each holding one of Sylvia's hands looking back all the time as they walked down the path. Caroline could hear Beth saying 'Is my Mummy *very* poorly, Sylvie?' Oh God, she was. She watched them walking away. She had to be strong, for their sakes. She had to fight.

Grandmama helped her home as soon as she felt able to walk. She didn't come in; left her at the door for Sylvia to take care of, and went back to the service.

Only by a supreme effort of will, apparent to everyone there, did Peter manage to see the service through to the end. As he stood shaking hands with everyone and accepting their concerns for Caroline the truth dawned on him. How selfish could a man be? Occupied with his own work, striving to be a good pastor to his flock, being a father and a husband, the one thing he should have noticed he hadn't. Caroline had been losing weight. In fact she looked quite ghastly. She'd been uncharacteristically short-tempered with him and irritable with the children and not the slightest bit interested in him as a man. Be blunt here, he thought, she hadn't wanted sex, and that had always been one of the mainstays of their marriage.

He was standing at the door nearly twenty minutes, longing to leave, but so many people to see. So many reassuring him that Caroline would be all right, no wonder she fainted. So hot. Lovely service. Thank you, Rector. Lovely as usual. Never better. Sheila came hobbling out on her crutches with Ron in attendance.

'Sheila! Many many thanks . . . The church looks wonderful, truly wonderful! Never better.'

Overcome by his gratitude she muttered her thanks.

'Will you thank your committee personally from me? I'm so grateful for all you do.'

'Of course I will, they are a brilliant team, they've really rallied round this year. And thank you, I'm glad you liked everything. It's time you went home to Dr Harris. See how she is.'

'I will shortly. Mind how you go.'

Finally he excused himself and left.

Sylvia had settled the children down with some toys and Caroline was sitting at the kitchen table sipping tea. The colour had come back into her cheeks and she greeted him with something like her usual enthusiasm.

'So sorry, Peter, for causing a sensation in the service. I really do apologise. I know how important it is to you.' She turned up her face for him to kiss. Peter bent down and kissed her cheek.

'Please don't apologise. I'm only too sorry I couldn't leave to bring you home myself. Sylvia, Willie has nearly finished. You go home and get him lunch. I can cope.'

Sylvia standing out of the line of Caroline's vision pointed her finger at Caroline and said, 'Are you sure?'

'Absolutely.'

Sylvia nodded her head in the direction of the hall. 'I'll leave then.'

He followed her out of the kitchen, closing the door behind him.

Sylvia didn't speak until they'd reached the front door. 'She hasn't confided in me, but you must get her to confide in you. I don't like the look of things, Rector. Not at all.'

'I've tried, but she won't. We've agreed she'll tell me when she's good and ready.'

'Then you'd better try your utmost. This business of you not trespassing on each other's ground is quite out of place now. That girl in there is either ill or there's something worrying her quite dreadfully. I'll be here first thing tomorrow.' With her hand on the front door latch Sylvia turned back and said, 'Remember, I shall want some answers tomorrow morning or else. I think a lot about Dr Harris, you know. It needs sorting.'

Peter stripped off his cassock and hung it in the hall cupboard, braced his shoulders and returned to the kitchen with the firm intention of finding out.

'Don't seem right coming straight in 'ere from church, but I'm dying to know what's going on.' Vera, accompanied most unusually by Don, settled herself down with Jimmy at his favourite table.

Don raised his glass of orange juice and said, 'Here's to you both.'

'And to you,' Jimmy answered. 'Nice to have some male company. Don't expect Willie will be in today he doesn't on Sundays and not with Dr Harris being taken bad.'

'One time if yer fainted like that it meant one thing.'

'What?'

'Yer were in the club.'

'That's not likely is it. We knows they can't have children.'

Vera's theory having been dismissed she felt quite deflated and sighed. 'Yep! I expect we do. And we know it's not him at fault. He's proved that.'

'Well, then.' Jimmy glanced about him. 'Eh! Georgie's just come in. Got changed out o' that sparkly suit she wears on her rare excursions into church and she's smiling like there's no tomorrow. The cheek of it.'

'Bold as brass that Dicky waving and winkin' in church. Be different if they were kids and single.'

'Well, yer know when Cupid's arrow falls . . .'

'Cupid's arrow! They should 'ave caught it and sent it flying back. At their age, they ought to have more sense.'

Jimmy laughed. 'This wife of yours is very indignant, could she be just a bit jealous, Don? Did you see 'em?'

'No.'

Bryn was busy serving with a grim smile on his face. Even his Flying Officer Kite moustache appeared to be bristling with annoyance. Georgie was pulling pints too, but well down the other end of the bar.

Jimmy called out, 'Feeling better Georgie? It was hot in there wasn't it?'

Bryn scowled. Georgie said, 'It was very hot. I wonder no one else had to leave.'

Someone said, 'They did. Rector's wife left just after you. Went clean out on the floor. Terrible white she was.'

'Oh! So I wasn't the only one then. There we are, one pound eighty please.'

As the customer pocketed his change he said, 'Thought you looked flushed Georgie.'

'I said it was hot.'

70

Jimmy slyly remarked, 'Your Bryn sized up the situation in quick sticks, 'ad you out in a flash.'

Bryn glared at Jimmy and for a second Jimmy thought he would be coming across and thumping him but the moment passed and Jimmy took a hasty gulp of his ale.

Vera was scandalised. 'Honestly Jimmy! You'll be getting a black eye, you will.'

'Not me, but he might.' He nodded his head in the direction of the saloon door.

Vera and Don twisted round to look. Bel and Dicky had just come in. It was so rare for them both to come in together that everyone would have stared in any case but today, this lunchtime, they not only stared they were appalled. Dicky really was sticking his neck out coming in. Bryn could have a very short fuse on occasion, and as he was something like twice as big as Dicky things could get lively. Roast beef and Yorkshire pudding could wait, something more appetising was on the menu.

To everyone's intense disappointment Bryn's attention was taken by a problem in the dining-room so he had to leave Georgie and Alan behind the bar.

Vera shouted across. 'Good turn-out for the Scouts this morning, Dicky! They're a credit to yer!'

Dicky, who'd changed out of his Scout uniform and was looking quite the dandy in a rather startling bright red polo-necked sweater and black and white checked trousers, shouted 'Thanks Vera! They're a good set of boys, all of 'em! See you've dragged that husband of yours in. What are you getting up to nowadays, Don?'

Don lifted his glass in acknowledgement. He was known as a man of few words was Don but this time he excelled himself. 'More to the point, Dicky, everyone's asking what *you're* getting up to nowadays?'

An audible gasp went round the bar. Vera choked on

her drink and had to search for a hanky to dab her chin. As for Jimmy, well there was no other word to use but to say he guffawed. The customers round the table by the fireplace burst into side splitting laughter, but Bel went bright red and looked at the floor and Georgie shook her head in warning which Dicky chose to ignore. 'Oh, this and that yer know,' he said. He raised his glass to Georgie and grinned. 'This and that. Eh! Georgie, have you heard the one about the husband who went home early from work one night and found his wife in bed with . . .'

Bel hit him very hard on the side of his head with the flat of her hand. If his head wasn't ringing with the blow everyone else's was. Then she hit him again on the other side with the other hand. He began backing off but she followed him right round the bar, giving him another good slap with every step she took.

'I'll teach you to show me up in public!' When she was opposite Georgie she stopped slapping and faced her over the bar. 'But for this counter between us I'd be slapping you too!' Bel grabbed hold of Dicky by the neck of his sweater and frogmarched him out. As the saloon door shut on them they could hear Dicky shouting 'Bel! Bel! I haven't finished me drink! Have a heart!'

The customers nearest the windows rushed to watch them go by.

'She still hasn't let go!'

'He's twisting and turning!'

'She's hit him again!'

'He's got away!'

'He's coming back!'

'No, he isn't.'

'Yes, he is!'

'He is! He is! Oh, my God!'

Bryn walked back into the bar from the dining-room at

this moment and they all quickly sat down, but their excitement was trembling in the air. Bryn looked round for answers but there weren't any. Everyone was avoiding meeting his eye. He looked at Georgie but she found an urgent necessity for rooting about under the bar for a clean cloth to polish some glasses.

The door burst open and back in came Dicky. He was red faced and breathing fast but never one not to face up to a challenge, he'd come back in to finish his drink. He marched to the bar conscious that all eyes were on him, and as he loved the drama of it all he decided to play his audience to the utmost.

Picking up his drink he stood facing everyone and drank a toast to them all. First to one group and then to another. There were a few sniggers, then downright laughter and then loud applause. But he hadn't realised that Bryn was there watching his every move.

Dicky put his empty glass down on the bar, did a few tap-dancing steps and then bowed. As he straightened up Bryn caught hold of his arm.

'Out, you little runt! Out! You're banned!!' Dicky was dragged across the floor for the second time in as many minutes. Bryn flung him out, not caring what happened to Dicky as he staggered down the two steps out onto the road, and when Bryn came back in he slammed the door shut with a loud bang.

'Alan! Where's Alan?'

'Here.' Alan lurching in from the cellar with a crate of bottled beer in his hands asked 'What's up?'

'Can you manage for ten minutes?'

'Yes, of course.' Bewildered he looked round for a clue as to what was going on. But there wasn't a single person looking in his direction, they were all watching Bryn who was glaring at Georgie. She was eyeing the distance between her and the door marked *Private*. Bryn went towards her, a menacing look on his face.

She started to retreat. With a beautifully filed and lacquered finger she prodded the air between her and Bryn. 'You lay one finger on me and I'm out the door and never coming back!'

'Never have done and don't intend to start now. In the office this minute.'

He opened the door into the back and stood aside for her to go through first. Before he shut the door on them they heard Bryn say, 'And now, madam, I want to know what's going on.'

Don finished the last of his orange juice and with a deadpan face, said to Vera, 'Having brought things to a head, I think it's time we went home and you made me my dinner.'

Chapter 7

Grandmama had thought of asking Harriet to take her to the hospital for her check-up but in the event Harriet was too busy so she'd booked Jimmy to take her in. The bus was so smelly and the times so inconvenient that it was easier to go in with him. This was the first check-up she'd had since moving to Turnham Malpas. They said they'd transferred all her notes so it should just be a formality. She hated having to go, in fact this time she might suggest she never went again. After all, there'd been no recurrence in five years now, there was no more requirement for wasting their time.

She asked Jimmy to drop her off at the main entrance, she wasn't having him know she was going to the cancer treatment department, or else it would be all round the village in no time as she'd found to her cost with the Harvest débâcle. The main entrance was obviously part of the original hospital but over the years it had quadrupled in size, and she couldn't find her way. She asked a nurse, she was brown but seemed to know what she was talking about, and set off to follow the directions.

The arrows on the direction signs appeared to point not

only straightforward and left and right but, rather significantly, heavenwards too and Grandmama became confused. She pushed through some swing doors and found herself in the antenatal clinic. Really! She waited to find a nurse to ask where to go, but there was only a receptionist sitting at a desk on the far side, so she tripped across between the children and the toys and the mothers in various stages of pregnancy, so many in fact she wondered if they hadn't got television in Culworth yet, and went to ask. The receptionist was on the telephone so Grandmama had to wait. One of the doors marked with a newly painted sign saying *David R. Lloyd-Jones, Consultant* opened and out came Caroline Harris! Of all people! What a coincidence! A very distinguished looking man came out with her and they shook hands and she heard him say 'Good luck' and Caroline said 'Thanks for everything', checked her watch and hurried away.

Well, well. So she was right. It was a baby after all. Looking thin and preoccupied must be bad morning sickness, it took some people like that. Well, fancy! After all these years. A baby.

Grandmama realised the receptionist was addressing her. 'Excuse me! I said "Can I help you?"'

'I think I must be in the wrong department.'

'I would think so too.'

Grandmama's intense eyes gave the receptionist a bleak look and then asked directions. Having had them explained to her twice because she was so excited with what she'd just seen she couldn't take them in, she departed in haste, she was going to be late if she didn't hurry.

Peter couldn't concentrate, he was waiting for Caroline to ring, for today was the day she got the result of her scan. He'd offered to take her in to Culworth and wait with her but she wouldn't hear of it. Now he wished he'd insisted.

'I've a surgery straight afterwards, there isn't any point. I'll ring at lunchtime to let you know. It would mean going in two cars anyway. It's better this way.'

'Look, how about going private?'

'Certainly not. I'm a doctor, I can't take advantage of a privileged system when the majority of my patients can't. That wouldn't do.'

'Of course not, I see that.'

He went to the garage and got her car out for her and brought it round to the front of the rectory.

'Oh thanks, darling.'

'Least I can do. Caroline, I . . .'

She'd cut in to prevent him from saying something encouraging which might penetrate the wall she'd built round herself. 'When I've had my appointment I'm going to see David Lloyd-Jones, I don't need to refresh your memory about him do I?' She'd smiled wickedly at him.

'Of course not! Has he taken up his appointment already then?'

'Started on Monday. Want to congratulate him.'

'So long as that's all!'

'Peter! After all these years! You're not still jealous!'

'Not really. No.' He'd looked away.

'You are! Well, well. Must go or I'll be late.'

He'd kept the conversation as she wanted it. Ordinary. Unemotional. Brisk. If that was how she coped then he'd have to go along with it. 'Bye then! Don't forget to ring!' He'd longed to kiss her, hold her, hug her, longed to suffer it for her, anything but this.

He'd watched her drive away and then stepped into the house thinking about the Sunday when he'd walked back into the kitchen after Sylvia had gone and he'd found Beth sitting on Caroline's knee being cuddled. Her thumb was in her mouth and Caroline was rocking her. 'I do love you, Mummy. Are you better now?'

'Much better, darling. Much better.' Alex had got up from the floor and gone to stand beside her. He'd leaned against her legs, put an arm round her waist and said, 'You're a doctor, can you make yourself better?'

'Sometimes, but sometimes even doctors need help.'

Beth lifted her head from Caroline's shoulder and asked, 'Are you going to need help now?'

'Perhaps.'

Alex said, 'When I'm grown up I'm going to be a doctor.'

Beth wrinkled her nose. 'I'm not. It's nasty being a doctor. You have to stick needles into people like they did when we had our booster to go to school. That was horrid. It hurt.'

'My needles wouldn't hurt. I wouldn't let them. I could make you better couldn't I, Mummy?'

'Of course you could.'

Beth gave him a push. 'You couldn't, you're too little.'

'I'm not!'

'You are!'

'I'm not am I, Mummy? I'm bigger than Beth aren't I?'

Before Caroline could answer Beth sprang off her knee and shouted 'You're not, you're not, we were both born together, so you can't be.'

'I am, look!' They stood back to back and Peter had to confirm that Alex was indeed taller than Beth.

Beth moaned, 'It's not fair.'

'Men are always taller than their mummies. Look at Daddy.'

'They're not! Mr Tutt isn't. He's little and Mrs Tutt is big.' She stretched her arms as wide as they would go.

Caroline had to laugh. 'Go away you two. I want to set the table for lunch. It's been in the oven for ages and I can smell it's more than ready.'

After lunch the two children had gone to play on their bicycles in the back garden leaving Caroline and Peter to finish their coffee.

'Lovely service, Peter, and didn't the church look wonderful? Best ever I think. I was really chuffed with my arrangement. The eucalyptus leaves against the dark wood looked great, they almost lit it up.'

He didn't answer.

Caroline said, 'Hellooo! Anyone at home?'

'Oh yes.'

'Well?'

Not looking at her while he answered Peter said, 'How much longer are you going to leave me in the dark?'

Caroline looked out of the window and watched the children racing each other down the path. Beth's sturdy little legs were pedalling as fast as she could make them, yet Alex's long ones, pedalling far more leisurely, were pulling him ahead of her.

'Well? You haven't answered me. I treasure you, I cherish you above and beyond anyone else on this earth, and yet I am not to know.'

She poured him more coffee, passed him the sugar.

'My darling girl, *it is crucifying me.*'

'*And me.*'

Peter waited. The kitchen clock struck the quarter hour.

Caroline gave a huge sigh and said quietly, almost inaudibly and very very slowly, 'There's no kind way of saying this, no way of letting you down gently, so I might as well say it straight out. I've had a scan because they

79

think . . . they think I might have a growth on my ovaries. I get the results on Wednesday.'

From outside came the excited laughter of their two children. Inside, the kitchen boiler burst into life and the clock ticked away the seconds. Long startling frightening seconds during which Peter almost suffocated with shock. For Caroline's sake he took a deep deep shuddering breath and then another. And then a third, before he had his voice under control. 'My darling! Why ever haven't you told me before? How long have you known?'

'A while.' She reached across the table and stroked his hand.

'What can I say which doesn't sound empty and trite? I am deeply sorry. You've been carrying this burden all alone. How can I possibly have failed you so much that you felt you couldn't share it with me? I am so, so, sorry that I've let you down.' He placed his free hand on top of hers. 'I shan't treat you like a fool and say are you sure, might there be some mistake, I know you too well for that.'

'There is no mistake, darling. And you haven't let me down. It's my fault, I couldn't bear to tell you. I didn't want to break your heart.'

'My heart! What's *my* heart got to do with it? It's you who has it to face.'

'You have it to face, too. Let's be frank. If it's worse than they think then . . . it may mean you coping on your own.'

'Dear God! Dear God!' Peter sat with his elbows resting on his knees and his head in his hands. He sat up again. The shock of what she'd said had drained all the colour from his face, it was deathly white. Just as slowly as she had spoken when she'd broken her news he said, 'Let's look on the bright side. We musn't assume the worst. It could

80

be a matter of a simple operation and hey presto! it's all over and done with. Obviously you'd have to take care and perhaps only work a few hours, not try to do too much, but there's no reason why things couldn't be back to normal in no time at all. Is there?'

'None at all.' Caroline smiled bravely, and he recognised the bravery and held out his arms to her. She got up and went to sit on his knee. 'This is why you fainted is it? I can scarcely manage to ask this but, are you in a lot of pain?'

'Sometimes. But maybe it's all in the mind, fright you know. That's why I get snappy.'

'Snappy? I hadn't noticed! Wednesday. Three days. Will you go to the surgery just the same?'

'Yes, it's easier that way. Keep busy, you know. No time to dwell.'

Peter sat patting her arm, stroking her knee, rubbing his cheek against her hair. 'I've been so blind. I've been absolutely unforgivably blind.'

'I told you not to ask didn't I?'

'I shan't do as you say ever, ever, again. Never. If I want to question something I shall. This not trespassing is ridiculous.'

'No, it's not. It's agreeing that we are two intelligent human beings with rights to our own thoughts and decisions. What could you have done if you'd known? Nothing. No one can.'

'I could have been more considerate.'

'You are already far more considerate than is good for me. I haven't told anyone at all. No one knows and I don't want them to.'

'We shall have to tell Sylvia.'

'Why?'

'Because she told me as she left just now that I . . . that she wanted some answers on Monday or else.'

'I wonder what "or else" will be?'

'Caroline, you must tell her, or I will. It's only fair. We may need to rely on her.'

She held Peter's face between her two hands and studied him closely. With her fingers she traced his eyebrows, and then with her thumbs gently closed his eyelids and kissed them sweetly. 'You are my beloved. All the David Lloyd-Jones in the world can't hold a candle to you. And why I don't know. I wasn't really a church person at all you know, so it wasn't your dog collar that did it, but that morning when you walked into my surgery with your bad throat and your streaming nose and red watery eyes and that dreadful cough and your face all flushed . . .'

'Heavens above! I can't have looked very appealing!'

'You didn't. But you twanged my heart strings and they've never stopped twanging since.'

Peter grinned at her. 'I've often wondered what that curious noise was when I got close.'

'Oh that noise! That's my hormones clamouring!'

Peter began laughing but it changed to tears. She kissed his tears away. 'Stop or I'll be crying too.'

'You're being so brave. I've discovered I'm not brave at all.'

'You will be, just you wait and see.' She got off his knee. 'Let's clear up. The children are very quiet, just look out and see what they're doing.'

He blew his nose, ran his fingers through his hair, and then went to look out of the window. 'You're not going to like this.' He raced out of the back door leaving it wide open. Caroline hurried to see. Alex was balanced on top of the wall and was preparing to leap down into the back lane. Beth was coming back in through the gate hobbling, both her knees badly grazed and holding her hand as though it hurt. Great fat tears were beginning to roll down her lovely rounded cheeks. 'Oh heavens!'

They'd had them both to sort out as, before Peter could reach the wall, Alex had jumped. The drop was something like five feet and the surface of the ground uneven, so he'd hurt himself too.

After they'd settled them both in front of the television well bandaged and drinking hot sweet tea, which Alex declared doctors always said you needed for shock, Caroline had sighed and said 'Never a dull moment!'

So here he was waiting for the telephone to ring. He'd tried concentrating on some study he wanted to do in preparation for the following Sunday but he might as well have been reading the *Radio Times* for what good it did him. Peter's thoughts were interrupted by the phone ringing.

It was Caroline. It was only eleven o'clock. 'I'm coming home.'

'Oh, right!'

'Won't be long.'

'No, right. Drive carefully. Take care.'

Then she told him as soon as she got in. The growth was larger than they'd anticipated and they had to operate a.s.a.p. He hugged her tightly to him. 'Sort of in the next few weeks, when there's a bed, kind of thing?'

'No, this Friday. Gave me a day to get organised.'

'That must mean . . .' He stopped and changed tack. 'There's no organising to do.'

'There is. We have to tell the children, for one thing. I've two meetings next week, I shall send my apologies, say I've had a clash of appointments or something, anything, anything at all, but I don't want people to know.'

Very gently Peter said, 'We can't disguise the fact that

you're going in to hospital. They'll have to be told something.'

Caroline slumped down into Peter's chair, laid her head on his desk and wept. She was inconsolable. Her sobbing tore at Peter's heart. In all their lives together he'd never seen her so deeply, so torturously distressed, and there seemed to be nothing he could do to reassure her, to give her comfort. He stood beside her helplessly hugging her shoulders. Gradually the sobbing slowed and she turned to him, put her arms around his waist, and pressed her head against his body.

'Oh Peter! I do need you. Please help me!'

Chapter 8

Grandmama had been invited to take coffee with Muriel on the morning after her hospital appointment. Despite herself she couldn't but be flattered at the opportunity. Muriel might be a retired solicitor's secretary but she was still called Lady Templeton and had that lovely man Ralph for a husband. Grandmama paid meticulous attention to her toilet and emerged at eleven o'clock feeling on top of the world. As she turned the key in the lock and stood back to admire her cottage with something akin to love in her heart, some children from the school came past, walking in a neat crocodile. With them was that nice girl Kate.

'Good morning, children! Good morning, Miss Pascoe!'

'Good morning, Mrs Charter-Plackett. Isn't it lovely today?'

'It certainly is. Out for a walk?'

'We're going for a visit to Nightingale Farm.'

'How lovely! You've chosen the right day! Bye-bye, children.'

'Bye-bye, Mrs Charter-Plackett.' She distinctly heard at

least two of them say 'Bye-bye, Duchess' but she didn't fix them with her most disdainful eye, they were only being complimentary.

Muriel answered the door when she rang. Muriel in smart checked trousers and a lovely rose silk blouse. Give her her due she could dress well, but considering the money they had she should look smart.

'Good day to you Muriel!'

'And to you Katherine. Do come in. Lovely day.'

'It is indeed.'

Ralph came from his study. 'Good morning, Katherine.'

'Dear Ralph! And how are you?'

'Well, thank you, yes, very well. I'm leaving you two ladies to your coffee, I've a business meeting. See you after lunch, my dear.' Ralph kissed Muriel on the lips, when Grandmama thought a kiss on her cheek would have sufficed. She hated it when sex came into a relationship between two people at their age. It amounted to obscenity.

Muriel patted his cheek. 'Take care, Ralph. No fast driving!'

'As if I would!' He laughed and Grandmama saw the young man he used to be and for a second was quite envious of Muriel, but she'd invited her into the sitting-room and the moment passed.

'The kettle's just boiled, I'll make the coffee.'

Grandmama placed herself in the chair, which from its size she guessed was Ralph's. Really this room did have charm. There were a lot of uncoordinated things in it which Ralph must have collected during his years abroad but somehow he and Muriel had made it all gel and the room was welcoming and attractive and it had warmth. The colours of the furnishings were pleasant to the eye too. Lovely mellow creams and soft browns, and a hint of peach which spiced the overall impression.

'Here we are!' Muriel placed her tray on a small table in front of the fire. Grandmama was very gratified to see that the family silver had been brought out in her honour. Coat of arms no less!

Muriel poured the coffee into a china cup so thin Grandmama thought she could see right through it. There was a matching plate and she put on it two of the homemade biscuits Muriel offered her.

'This is delightful. So civilised!'

'We are!' Muriel laughed.

'I didn't mean *you* weren't, but some of them around here are definitely not civilised.'

'It doesn't do to think that you know. They're all kind well-meaning people. Salt of the earth.'

'Well! After what happened on Sunday in the public house, I do wonder!'

'It all adds to life's rich tapestry.'

'I know something to add even more to life's rich tapestry as you call it. Oh yes. I had occasion to visit the hospital yesterday . . .' Muriel's instant concern for her made Grandmama have to reassure her. 'Only for a check-up, I shan't have to go again.' Muriel relaxed and Grandmama continued her story. 'I got lost, it has such a bewildering layout and I had to ask at reception in the antenatal clinic which way to go. Well, I was waiting while the receptionist finished a long-winded conversation about a changed appointment or something and who should I see! Guess!'

'I don't know. A patient you mean?'

'Yes, exactly that.'

'I don't know anyone expecting a baby in the village.'

'Well, there is someone. She fainted on Sunday.'

Muriel was nonplussed. 'Fainted on Sunday! Someone else fainted too then?'

'Only one, my dear Muriel, only one.'

'You can't mean Caroline.'

'The very one. Coming out of the consultant's room. He said "Good luck" and she said "Thanks for everything". I guessed when she fainted that that might be it, but I got confirmation didn't I? Otherwise what would she be doing in the antenatal clinic? She doesn't work at the hospital does she?'

'Not any more. No. But I understood . . .'

'So did we all, but there are things that can be done nowadays aren't there and she has been looking decidedly peaky of late. Morning sickness of course, but you won't know about that.'

'Well, no, I don't. I'm amazed though. Truly amazed, oh she will be pleased. So very pleased.' Muriel clapped her hands with delight. 'How absolutely lovely.' She sipped her coffee, took a bite of her biscuit and then said, 'But we'd better not say anything, you never know.'

'Why ever not?'

'Because . . . well, I don't know why but it would be indelicate and thoughtless to spread the news, just in case . . .'

'Indelicate in this day and age? When they're doing it, well *almost* doing it I hope, in full view on the television, I don't think we need to be coy about it!'

'Doing it? Doing what? Who is?'

'Really, Muriel, I sometimes wonder if you are in the real world at all. However to use your own words I will refrain from being indelicate and we'll close the subject.'

Muriel sat silently contemplating her guest, thinking about Caroline and Peter. They couldn't be. On the other hand Katherine did have a point, and she was very astute,

88

it must have been Caroline she saw. A lovely glow filled her, she felt so warmed by the news. But she wouldn't say a word to anyone, well only to Ralph.

'If I might be so bold, Katherine, I think it would be best for them to tell us the news themselves. Perhaps it's early days and they're not quite sure, sometimes there are mishaps.'

'But everyone will be so pleased for them. I know, I am. Those twins might be Caroline's pride and joy but every time she looks at them she can't fail to remember how she came by them.'

Muriel was indignant. 'Well, really!'

'Who wouldn't want children to that gorgeous man. I think he's the most attractive man I've met in years. Were I but thirty years younger, well between you and me, forty years younger, I could set my cap at him.'

Muriel began to boil. 'I think you need to choose your words more carefully. "Set your cap" indeed. I've never heard such a thing.'

'Grow up, my dear. You can't mean to tell me you haven't noticed how attractive he is, the sheer delight of it is *he* isn't aware he is! I bet there's many a female heart fluttered madly when he's looked at them with those deep blue eyes of his. I should think he has to fight them off in droves! It must be a constant worry to Caroline, especially when he's strayed once and with such dire consequences!'

Muriel positively steamed. She got to her feet and proclaimed, 'I had looked forward very much to this morning but I'm rapidly beginning to regret inviting you. I don't know how you can have such thoughts running through your head.' She heaved in a great breath and continued fiercely, 'It's preposterous! Indeed outrageous!'

Grandmama's cup rattled in the saucer, she was so

incensed. She placed it on the little side-table by her chair and stood up. Her cheeks were wobbling with fury. 'That's the last time I shall tell you any news Muriel Templeton! Preposterous indeed! Outrageous! I'm only speaking the truth, as you well know. What's wrong with the truth?'

'Sometimes it's best left unsaid.'

'Is it indeed. When I'm proved right about the baby I hope you will eat your words and apologise to me! I think it best if I leave now. Thank you for the coffee and good morning to you.' Grandmama left Muriel's sitting-room in a rage. She had to struggle to get the front door opened, and when she did she couldn't face the thought of going home and being in a rage all by herself, but didn't know where to go.

Then she decided, and stormed off in the direction of the Royal Oak having a real need of something to fortify herself after that little confrontation. She pushed open the saloon door and marched in. It was the first time she'd been in there and she was agreeably surprised by the furnishings and the general pleasurable air of the place. Quite upmarket she thought. Georgie was behind the bar.

'A whisky, please. Make it a double.'

'Why, how nice to see you, Mrs Charter-Plackett.' Georgie served her and said, 'On the house, seeing as it's your first visit.'

'Why thank you.' She downed it in one go.

'My word, you look as though you needed that.'

'I did. There are times when Muriel Templeton's Goody-Two-Shoes attitude is distinctly trying. I'll have another.'

'Very well.'

She downed the second one and then proffered a ten-pound note. 'Take for two, I need another, but I'll drink that slowly with water. I don't like standing at the bar, would you care to sit down and join me, you're not busy.'

'For a while yes, I will.'

'Take for another drink for yourself then.'

'Thanks.'

Grandmama went to sit by the log fire in the huge inglenook fireplace. At least it's a genuine one she thought, not made with modern bricks trying to look ancient by being blackened with synthetic soot.

Georgie chose a stool and sat down beside her. 'A fire's comforting isn't it?'

'It is. I like my cottage for having an open fire. You can dream dreams.'

'Ah! Yes.' Georgie sat, drink untouched, staring into the fire.

'You look as though you have dreams to dream.'

Georgie sighed. 'Ah, well!'

'I heard about Dicky.'

'You did?'

'Listen to me, my dear, if you will. I know I don't know you very well, but perhaps I can offer some advice, you should *never* pass up a chance of happiness. Life doesn't present us with many bouquets and when it does, one should hold out one's hands and grasp it.'

'Think so?'

'I'm sure so. There's nothing worse than living with regret. Nothing. Believe me. I know.' She sipped her whisky and decided to change the subject. 'I know you won't have heard this, because I think I'm the only one to know, except for Muriel Templeton that is, but I believe we shall be hearing the patter of tiny feet at the rectory before long.'

Georgie's face changed from dejection to delight. 'Really! I'd no idea. Well, that's wonderful! Really wonderful. Dr Harris will be thrilled. Is it she who told you?'

'No, but quite by chance I met her in the antenatal clinic at the hospital. And after fainting on Sunday . . .'

'I didn't know that.'

'Well, you went out before it happened. That Dicky is certainly a card isn't he? Bold as brass.'

Georgie blushed. 'I do wonder what he'll do next.'

'Bryn angry?'

'Oh yes. He is. Poor Bryn. We've been married twenty years and each year that goes by I . . .'

'I know. Even the smallest habit annoys.'

Georgie looked at Grandmama, grateful for her insight. 'That's just it. All the magic's gone. Every single little bit. I sometimes think if he asks me once more to do a job for him, you know, order this, order that, wash this, wipe that, ring him, ring them, I'll murder him. He thinks because it's for the business I should find it fun. Well, I don't, not any more. The only conversations we have are about work.'

'Tell him.'

'I have but he can't understand what I'm talking about.'

'More fool him, try once more and then go in search of your own happiness.'

'Hop it you mean?'

'Yes, go. Is that what Dicky wants?'

'He's never said, not yet. He can't really, we've not reached that stage. And then there's Bel.'

'Of course. Poor Bel. It can't be fun for her.'

'It's not fun for any of us.' She got up to go, a customer had come in, and she left Grandmama sitting by the fire. Georgie's cheerful 'Hi there! What can I get for you?' sounded false, but the customer didn't appear to notice.

Grandmama finished her whisky and thought next stop

the Store. There were a few things she needed and she was dying for Harriet to hear about the baby.

'Hello, Linda! Harriet in?'

'Just gone to collect Fran. Mr Charter–Plackett's in his office though.'

'Thank you, dear.' She marched into the back, nodded in passing to Mrs Jones, and headed for Jimbo.

'Hello, Mother. Here take a pew. Won't be a minute.' Without getting up he pulled a stool out for her from beside his filing cabinet and continued tapping away on his computer. Grandmama waited. She never thought of Jimbo as an organised person but here in his office he most certainly was. Everything filed away, labelled, standing straight, even his desk was uncluttered. He stopped typing and swung his chair round to face her.

'And what can I do for my dear mother today?'

'I'm forgiven then?'

'For what?'

'Making all that stir about the Harvest. I'd no idea it would cause so much trouble. They do get on their high horses don't they?'

'Well, you're a newcomer, it'll take you about fifty years to be accepted for what you are.'

'Too damn late for me then.'

'Almost too damn late for me!'

'Oh, I don't know, I think you're doing all right. Everyone always speaks well of you.'

'Till I offend their sensibilities and then it'll be curtains for Jimbo Charter-Plackett and Company.'

'Nonsense! It was really Harriet I intended to see. I've got wonderful news.'

Jimbo's love of gossip made him prick up his ears at the prospect. 'What? Tell me.'

'I do believe Caroline Harris is expecting a baby.'

Jimbo met this gem with total silence.

Rattled by his silence Grandmama demanded, 'Well? Aren't you pleased for them?'

'I don't know all the details of why she can't have children, obviously Caroline hasn't confided something so sensitive to either Harriet or me, but I think you're wrong. What makes you think she is?'

Grandmama told him. He shook his head. 'Look, she has all sorts of medical connections, both her parents are doctors, she knows all kinds of medics, it could just have been a visit to a family friend. Take my advice and say no more.'

'Don't be ridiculous. They'll want everyone to be pleased.'

'Not if it's not true they won't.' Jimbo stood up. 'Time I was relieving my help.'

'The trouble with everyone in this village is that they're all too good to be true. That Muriel Templeton is a pain, she was quite . . .'

'Have you told her?'

'Yes.'

'Well, at least she won't spread it around. Now do as I say and not another word.'

He got engrossed behind the till so it wasn't until he heard a customer relaying the news to a neighbour whom she'd bumped into while choosing a card for her dad, that he looked up and saw his mother outside on the seat with a tight knot of villagers around her and he realised too late she'd done exactly the opposite of his advice.

The village hummed with the news that night and those who hadn't been told in person heard it over the telephone. Delight broke out like a rash.

Not wanting to worry them for longer than there was any

need, they'd broken the news to the children about Caroline going into hospital that afternoon, when Sylvia brought them home from school.

Beth had understood immediately. 'You are very poorly then, Mummy?'

'Yes, I am. They're going to take away what it is that's making me have tummy ache.'

Alex looking relieved said, 'Oh, if it's only tummy ache take some of our tummy ache medicine, we don't mind sharing do we, Beth?'

Beth looked scornful. 'You are silly.' She walked away, took out the doll she liked the best and sat down and began to rock it, her thumb in her mouth.

Alex burst into tears and rushed to Peter for comfort. 'I don't want my Mummy to go into hospital. Tell her she's not to.'

'If you had tummy ache and needed to go to hospital I wouldn't stop you from going there to get better would I? So we mustn't stop Mummy. We want Mummy to get better don't we?'

'Yes, but there'll be no one to tuck me up at night and give me a kiss.'

'Well, you'll have to make do with me and your Sylvie, just for a while and you'll be able to talk to Mummy on the telephone too, won't he Mummy?'

'Of course. Every night.'

'Will it be weeks and weeks and weeks and weeks?'

Caroline answered 'No, of course not. Just a little while.' She looked to see how Beth was coping and saw the reason for her silence. She was rocking rapidly backwards and forwards and great rivers of tears were running down her cheeks. 'Beth, come to Mummy.' She shook her head. 'Please, darling, Mummy wants a cuddle.'

Beth dropped her doll and raced into Caroline's arms.

95

With her chubby little arms wrapped tightly round Caroline's neck she cried, 'Oh, Mummy, I do love you.'

'I love you too, so very, very, much.' Then she too burst into tears. Alex struggled down out of Peter's arms and went to hug his mother.

Peter, his eyes brimming with tears said, 'This won't do. We've all got to cheer up. Mummy won't be away long and we've all to be glad she's going to get better. Now, come on, let's dry our tears. Each one of us. Poor Mummy is going to be sad if we all cry, and that's not fair. Come on you two, cheer up! We must all be brave.'

There came a knock at the sitting-room door. It was Sylvia. She'd been crying too. 'I'll be here eight at o'clock tomorrow as usual, Dr Harris, good night. Rector, there's just a message I have to give to you, could you come?'

She led the way into his study. 'Close the door, sir.'

'Couldn't it wait?'

'No. It couldn't I'm afraid. I don't know how to tell you this, but forewarned is forearmed, I'm glad it was me went to collect the children, and do you know why?' Peter shook his head. 'Because the news is all round the village that . . . I don't want to say this at this moment but there's no way I can get out of it, you've got to know . . . there's a rumour started that Dr Harris is . . . pregnant.'

'What?!'

'Shhh! It's true, there is. How or why it started I do not know, but there we are. And I said I didn't know what they were talking about and I was very upset, as if things aren't bad enough as it is.' Sylvia sat down on the nearest chair and sobbed.

Peter clenched his fists. The crushing weight of it all was unbearable. Just when they were needing support. That this should happen now. He stood silently for a minute and then said, 'Thank you, Sylvia, for letting me know. Nothing could be further from the truth, could it?'

Sylvia made a brave attempt to collect herself. 'Indeed not. I want you to know I shall do absolutely everything I possibly can to make things go smoothly. I shall do as many hours as need be and I shan't expect paying for it, in fact I shall be insulted if you offer it. If, though I don't suppose it will be necessary, you need to stay very late, like all night late at the hospital, Willie, that is if you don't mind him being here but I wouldn't want to be on my own with the children just in case, and I, we'll sleep in that room I used to use when I first came. I've already put sheets on the bed. So there's no need to worry.' She wiped her nose and said, 'I think the world of her you know. I can't hardly bear it.'

'Neither can I. But she's being so brave.'

'I wouldn't expect anything else. She's strong but that doesn't mean she isn't afraid. Shall we tell the truth then?'

'We can't avoid it. Just enough of the truth, not too much. She doesn't want a big fuss. Thank you, Sylvia.'

'Remember anything at all, any time. I shall come in every day, Saturdays and Sundays too. So don't worry about that. We shall probably have her home in no time at all, and then we can look after her ourselves and get her better, eh? I'll be off now. I'm sorry I had to tell you that, but I had to hadn't I? Couldn't have you being greeted with congratulations not having been forewarned.'

'That's right. Thanks.' Peter nodded not able to trust himself to say any more.

'I'll be off then. We'll be thinking about you both. Good night.'

Damn them! Damn them! How on earth had they got hold of such a heartbreaking idea. It wouldn't have been amusing at the best of times, but now! Thank God, he'd

97

been worried about getting back in time and had asked Sylvia to pick up the children. If Caroline had gone! It didn't bear thinking about. If he'd gone he'd probably have hit whoever'd said it.

He heard Caroline calling, 'Peter? Is everything all right?'

Opening the study door, he checked there were no tears on his face, and called out brightly, 'Everything's fine. Just coming.'

Chapter 9

It didn't take much imagination to guess who it was who'd climbed up the church tower and out onto the parapet to fasten the banner up there to the square bit of the tower below the spire. *Happy Birthday Georgie* it read, in bright pink letters on a white background. The letters ran in a line one below the other right to the bottom where it had been secured to the drain pipes either side of the tower door.

The stockman who'd rented one of Ralph's houses in Hipkin Gardens was the first to see it when he left for milking at Nightingale Farm at half past four. The next was Malcolm from the dairy coming specially early to do his round because his girlfriend was due any minute and he wanted to get back as soon as he could. There wasn't much Malcolm didn't know about the village and he chuckled to himself, wondering what their response would be when they woke to find that. They couldn't miss it. Definitely they couldn't!

The people in the queue waiting for the first bus into Culworth reeled with laughter.

'Oh God! It must be Dicky!'

'He's a right one.'

'And not half!'

'But poor Bryn.'

'Poor Bel.'

'Whatever next.'

'Wish my husband would think up something like that for my birthday, I'm lucky if I get a card when he gets home from work. Thinks he's done wonders "Well, yer've got it on the day 'aven't yer?" he goes. Huh!'

'I'd wring his neck if it was my wife!'

'Give over! You couldn't knock the skin off a rice pudding, you couldn't!'

Willie, unable to sleep because Sylvia had been tossing and turning all night worrying about Dr Harris, went out earlier than usual to set about his duties of putting the heating on and getting the children's hymn books out ready for the school Friday morning service, except Kate Pascoe would have to conduct it seeing as the Rector would be taking Dr Harris into Culworth as soon as they'd seen the twins off to school. He went through the lych gate and took his regular long distance view of the church before he headed up the path. He couldn't believe his eyes when he spotted the banner. Not that it took much spotting it was so big, you couldn't avoid it. Blowing there, brazenly in the breeze! Just wait till he got his hands on that Dicky Tutt. Always supposing it was him. But it must be. Certainly wouldn't be Bryn. Nice chap but not very imaginative.

'The fool. The absolute fool. That Dicky needs his brains examining.'

Willie unlocked the church and went to switch on the heating. Rector didn't like the church to be cold. My, what changes he'd wrought since he came. Wasn't like the same place. Everything alive, bouncing with energy.

Congregation bigger than it had ever been in his lifetime, and all of 'em people who *wanted* to be there, not coming just because it was the thing to do.

Halfway down the aisle Willie stopped in his tracks. This morning of all mornings he'd have to have a quick word with his Maker. He wasn't what could be called a praying person, due respect and all that, but not prayerful. But this morning he went to kneel in the little memorial chapel, where he knew Peter prayed every morning of his life except today, and said a prayer for Caroline. 'I may not be much cop Lord, at praying but, by Jove, I'm praying today. I 'aven't got words like the Rector has, no book learning yer see apart from the village school, but if yer can listen to a prayer from an ordinary man then this is it. Whatever you do don't call on Dr Harris to be one of your angels this week. Nor for that matter any day in the immediate future. The Rector needs her something bad and them children which, as you know Lord, she took under her wing under very difficult circumstances, they don't half need her too. Matter of fact, we all do, she's such a good young woman and we all love her. So if it pleases you Lord, leave her with us. Amen. By the way, I shall be back tomorrow, expecting to thank you for bringing her through the operation. Amen.'

He got up from his knees and for extra measure crossed himself, then set off to get the big step ladder to see if he could reach the banner and drag it down.

When he got outside with the ladder he found Dicky standing on the church path with his camera, laughing fit to burst.

'Hey! Willie doesn't it look good. Won't she be pleased?'

'Pleased! See here, it won't do. Simply won't do. When the Rector sees it he'll be livid.'

'Livid? Whatever for?'

'The church isn't here to display your love messages, Dicky Tutt. It's disgusting!'

'Disgusting! What's disgusting about being in love?'

'You're both married or has that escaped your notice? You ought to know better.'

'You're a spoilsport you are. Move your ladder and buzz off and do whatever you're going to do and then you won't be the wiser. I want to take a photo.'

'I'll do no such thing. Hop it, go on, hop it.'

'Come on, Willie, you know what it's like when you're in love. Give us a chance. I want her to have a memento. Go on, just one teeny weeny photo. No one will know.'

'It'll be you having the memento if you don't move, and your memento'll be a black eye. Now get off home to Bel. You ought to be ashamed.'

A thought suddenly occurred to Dicky. 'What are you doing with that ladder? You're not thinking of taking Georgie's banner down?'

'I am.'

'You're not.'

'We've the school coming for morning prayers in an hour. I'm not having the evidence of your . . . your illegal amours 'anging 'ere for them to see.'

'But that means Georgie won't see it, she never gets up before nine with working late.'

'Hard cheese.'

'Just one photo, that's all I ask.'

'No. I'm not moving from this path.'

'Right then, I'll have you on the photo, and it'll look as if you helped me to put it up.'

Willie already angry almost exploded and he shouted, 'Don't you dare. Take your damned camera away.'

Dicky laughed, went much further down the path

turned round and took several photographs. He guessed that Willie would be hardly recognisable because he had to stand so far away to get the whole of the banner in, but so long as Willie was left in doubt that was all that mattered.

'I'm having them developed this morning at a shop near work, I'll let you have a couple of prints!'

'Don't bother!' Willie propped the ladder against the church wall and set off down the path to see Dicky off church property. Dicky dashed away, still laughing, leaving Willie angrier than he could remember ever having been. He knew the Rector wouldn't see the banner before he left, it was out of sight from the rectory, but he didn't want him coming back from the hospital and finding it there.

But no matter how he tried he couldn't budge it. Now what could he do? There was no way he could climb up the tower steps. He hadn't done that for years, not since he was a boy when he'd been taken so ill climbing them on the annual saint's day. He'd managed to get to the top and then all but collapsed when he'd gone out and looked over the edge and seen how high up he was. So ill he was paralysed and they'd had to carry him down. Acrophobia they'd said it was and he'd never climbed the tower since. He'd have another go and then . . . but it wouldn't come down. Drat that Dicky. Drat him. He'd have to get Jimmy. He'd do it, he'd go knock him up right now. But Jimmy must have left early, because there was no reply.

Peter came home from the hospital, parked his car outside the rectory and went straight to Church to say his morning prayers. He saw the banner as soon as he went through the lych-gate. He guessed immediately that it must be Dicky's doing. Why on earth hadn't Willie got it down?

'I tried, sir, I did, but I couldn't budge it.'

'Not even from the top? What on earth has he fastened it with then?'

Willie looked uncomfortable. 'Well, not from the top, no.'

'Why ever not? I would have preferred the children not to see it.'

'So would I, sir.'

'Then why ever not?'

Willie shuffled his feet and then had to confess. 'You see, Rector, I never go up there.'

'Never go up there?'

'I've got acrophobia?'

'What's that?'

'Fear of heights.'

'Are you telling me that you've been the verger all these years, how many is it now?'

'Fifteen.'

'And you've never been up there?'

'I am.'

'Who does then? Who sweeps and things?'

'Jimmy. He does it for me.'

Despite his anxiety Peter had to laugh. 'Well, well.'

Willie had to ask. 'How's the Doctor, is she all right? When you left her, you know?'

Peter said, looking anywhere but at Willie, 'Being brave, not wanting to worry me. They said to ring about four, but I think I'll go rather than ring.'

'That'll be best. Yes. Now about this banner. I've knocked at Jimmy's door but he's not in.'

'I'll do it. Have you the key? How did Dicky get in?'

Willie scowled his annoyance. 'I don't know, but when he gets back from work I'll ask him. Taken a photo of it he has. I could strangle him.'

'I'm not too pleased with him myself.'

'You'd better take scissors or, I know, I've got my Stanley knife in my tool box in the boiler house, I'll get that.'

Peter began the long climb up the stone spiral staircase. It was narrow, and the steps too small for his large feet, it had been built for men much shorter than himself. Once he caught his knee on the rough stone walls, twice he caught an elbow. As he climbed he thought about the bells being rehung and them ringing out across the fields. That would be wonderful. He imagined the sounds of the bells calling people to worship again like they had done for hundreds of years. Thank you Mr Fitch. In fact thank you Mr Fitch for the central heating, for the newly repaired organ and now thank you Mr Fitch for the bells. Decent chap but he seemed to have been born without a heart, though he had been visibly moved by Sadie's death. Death. For now he wouldn't think about it. Not today. He climbed the rest of the stairs, pushed open the trap door and climbed out.

He'd been up before on All Saint's Day each year but then it was always so busy that there wasn't time to contemplate the view. He unfastened the Stanley knife, secured the blade in place and went to cut the ropes holding the banner. Dicky had certainly done a good job. He leaned over to shout to Willie, and saw Georgie standing on the path talking to him. Even from such a height he could see she was agitated, and when she saw him looking down at her, her face flushed red.

'OK, Willie! Here goes!' Peter sliced through the ropes and the banner fell fluttering to the ground. He watched Willie begin cutting through the bottom ropes and then turned his attention to the view. From this side he could see the village. As he walked round the parapet he could see the Big House, then Bickerby Rocks, the fast moving traffic on the bypass and, he thought he could just catch a glimpse of the great spires of Culworth Abbey something like eight miles away. Between Turnham Malpas and Culworth were rolling fields, some still stubble, some already ploughed for next year. Next year. Would there be a next year for him? If Caroline . . . But then there'd be the children. He'd have to keep going for their sakes. Prayer. He'd go say prayers.

By the time he got to the bottom of the tower Georgie had gone and Willie was still struggling to fold up the banner. 'Too blowy, sir, can't keep control of it.'

Between them they managed to roll it up and store it in the boiler house.

'Tell Dicky I want to see him. Not today, I've other things on my mind but I'll see him tomorrow some time. Georgie, what did she think?'

'Half embarrassed, half delighted. He'd rung her from work and told her to come out to have a look. He's a fool is Dicky.'

'More than a fool. Just going to say prayers. Here's the tower key.'

As Peter was leaving the church after his prayers he met the Duchess coming in with an armful of flowers.

'Good morning, Mrs Charter-Plackett! Lovely flowers.'

'I'm taking a turn at doing the altar flowers with Sheila Bissett being laid up! I would normally have done them Saturday morning but I'm going out with Harriet and the children so I thought I'd do them today. Aren't they lovely? Mr Fitch gave me them. Such a kind man.'

'Very generous.'

'He is. I can't let this chance go by, seeing as we're on our own. Will you allow me to say how pleased I am?'

'How pleased you are?'

'Yes, about the, well I know it's a secret, but about the baby. I saw Caroline in the hospital in the antenatal clinic. I suspected as much when she fainted in church, but when I saw her there I knew. You must be thrilled and I expect she is too.' She was so delighted with herself she didn't notice the change in Peter's expression.

'It's you then who spread this rumour?'

The Duchess was about to exonerate herself from being a rumour-monger when something in his tone of voice pulled her up short.

'Rumour?'

'Yes. In truth she's having an operation today. I took her to the hospital this morning. For cancer. Ovarian cancer.'

The Duchess was left standing completely devoid of speech. She watched Peter walk down the path, and disappear from sight as he passed Willie's cottage. The blood hammered in her head and she couldn't see properly. Whatever had she done? That poor man. He wouldn't have said that just to upset her would he? Not something as serious as . . . cancer? She knew all about the fear that word instilled in one's soul. She'd known all about that, oh yes. But a young woman Caroline's age and with children to bring up. It didn't bear thinking about and here she'd been telling everyone . . . She'd never live it down. Fifty years Jimbo had said. It might as well be one hundred and fifty. Well, she hadn't meant to be malicious. Not at all. She was only going on the facts. Facts? People fainted for all sorts of reasons, as had Caroline. Obviously she *had* been seeing a friend in the antenatal department. It took her well over an hour to arrange the flowers. She'd so looked forward to doing it and now she couldn't make them look good for love nor money. Flowers! She never wanted to see another flower as long as she lived. Lived. What if Caroline . . . She'd better have a quick word of prayer before she left. In fact she'd better be on her knees all day. Contrite heart. That was what she'd better have. A contrite heart.

Unable to wait any longer and wanting to be out of the house before the children came home from school and begged to go with him, Peter left the rectory at half past two. He drove steadily because he knew his mind was elsewhere. Past the dreaded crossroads where he'd had that strange encounter with the tractor, and on into Culworth. It was always difficult to find a space in the hospital car park at any time of day, but he could take advantage of the fact he was an official hospital padre and he parked in the space specially reserved for them.

Being familiar with the hospital layout he was in the ward in no time at all. The nurses greeted him and assured him things were going fine, she was recovering nicely and yes of course he could see her.

She was laid flat on her back, fastened to a drip and what seemed to him a multiplicity of tubes and wires.

'Caroline! Darling! It's Peter.'

Her eyelids fluttered and then opened, she looked vaguely at him and a smile started on her mouth but she slid back into sleep before it had happened. He found a chair, put it beside the bed, sat down and took hold of her hand.

Helpless. Totally vulnerable, his Caroline was right now. Always so organised and energetic. So loving and kind and considerate. He didn't deserve her. This business of having to put others before his own, it was asking too much of anyone. A nurse came in to do routine checks.

'Good afternoon, Reverend. You're not to worry, you

know, she's doing fine.' She patted Caroline's cheek and said, 'Dr Harris! Hello!' Caroline stirred and opened her eyes. 'All right?' There was no answer, Caroline was sleeping again.

'Everything seems OK. She won't be talking for a while yet. Why don't you go for a cup of tea or something? Another hour and she'll be coming round properly.'

'I do have another patient to see. I might do that and then come back.'

'Good idea.'

But he wasn't prepared for what he saw when he came back. He couldn't see her for the hospital staff filling the room.

'Stand away!' They all stepped back from whatever they were doing and he had a clear view of Caroline's body jerking with the electric shock. The monitor was displaying a straight line, no heartbeat at all. A nurse was counting and rhythmically pressing her hands on Caroline's chest and they were giving her oxygen and everything fell into a sort of chaotic madness and all Peter could do was call out 'Caroline? Caroline?'

Someone snapped 'Get him out!'

'Come along, sir, leave her to us.' He felt hands steering him towards the door. He didn't want to go out. His place was beside *her*. Peter turned to go back in. 'Better leave her to us. We're doing all we can.' He felt hands pushing him away again. The sounds of instructions, of haste, of a kind of controlled desperate energy came through the door. She couldn't be left alone not right now. He went back in. They were too busy to notice him. The line on the monitor was straight.

'Caroline! Caroline!' He called in his loudest voice. The sound ricocheted back off the walls, deafening in its intensity in that small room. There was a blip on the screen, and another and another, then the line went straight again and then restarted irregularly, and suddenly the blips were regular and the razor sharp alertness in the room reduced and with it the intensity of the last few minutes. There was an audible sigh of relief.

'Right. Thanks everyone, she's back.' The line on the screen had a reassuring steadiness about its blips. The doctor stood beside the bed, cautious, alert, checking the controls, watching her breathing, observing her colour.

The staff began putting away the equipment disappearing to other duties leaving Peter with Caroline and the doctor. He became aware of Peter standing the other side of the bed ashen and trembling and saying 'I'm not leaving. I'm staying here. No one is making me leave. Do you understand? I won't be turned out. I'm staying with her.'

'Of course. All night if you wish. My word, she gave us a few anxious moments there. Can't do to lose a good doctor can we?'

Peter's voice was shaky. 'Nor a good wife, come to that.'

'No, indeed. Definitely not. I'm so sorry. A doctor will be in and out and a nurse will be in very frequently to check her but should you have any anxiety just ring. We'll need to find out what caused that little hiccough, if we can.'

'Little hiccough! She died!'

The blips continued steadily.

'Her heart stopped momentarily.'

'Well then, she died. Don't try to pacify me with euphemisms, I'm not for pacifying. In any case it was longer than a moment.'

'I'm sorry, very sorry.'

The blips kept going on, beating away.

'What caused it?'

'Bad reaction to the anaesthetic possibly. We'll have to find out. Most unexpected. Anyway, things have settled down now. If you need anything you've only to ask. She should be making good progress from now on.'

Less ashen than he was and with the trembling under control Peter thanked him. He pulled forward his chair, which had been pushed out of the way in the emergency, and sat down again beside her. Her hand he took in his own and bent his head to kiss it. He felt a very slight squeeze of her fingers and he thought he saw a tiny almost imperceptible smile on her lips.

Then his reaction began. Sweat rolled down his face as though he'd been running a marathon in a scorching midday sun. His knees went to jelly and his hands were shaking so violently he had to release Caroline's for fear of upsetting her. A nurse came in to check the monitor, but didn't speak. Peter couldn't have answered her if she had; his throat had closed up and his teeth were clamped tightly together. The nurse noted his ashen complexion and the sweat running down his face.

'Everything's going to be fine, Mr Harris. Look.' She pointed to the blips. 'No need to worry. Not now.'

He nodded.

'I'll go put the kettle on, make you a cup of tea.'

The tea was in his shaking hands almost as she spoke. Time, somehow, had done a head over heels. He tried to get the cup to his mouth. But he shook so much it was spilling everywhere. The nurse took it from him and held it to his mouth herself. He was icy cold. The tea was burning hot.

'Go on, drink some more, it'll do you good.'

Slowly the shaking stopped and he took charge of the

cup himself, with one eye on the screen he finished the tea right to the bottom of the cup where he could see grains of sugar undissolved.

The nurse held out her hand to take his cup. 'Another one?'

'Yes, please. I'm so thirsty.'

'You've had a bit of a shock, that's why.'

'You could say that.'

'Well, more than a *bit* of a shock. Won't be a minute.'

Briefly he went to the telephone to speak to Sylvia and explain he wouldn't be coming home just yet, possibly not until the early hours and he would be glad if she and Willie could stay and could he speak to the children and yes, Caroline was doing fine and thank you for everything. He reassured the children, yes, Mummy is doing very well. Yes, he was staying with her for a while and be good for Sylvia. Yes, he'd be home in the morning. Night, night, Beth. Night, night, Alex. Yes, he'd give Mummy a great big kiss. Night, night, sleep tight. God bless you both.

Chapter 10

If he could, Jimbo avoided working in the Store on Saturdays but this Saturday it was unavoidable. Added to which Harriet was upset about Caroline, his mother was distraught at what she'd done and generally he sensed a black cloud over his life he could well have done without.

Life must go on though, he'd lined the morning papers up neatly on their shelf by the till, he'd tackled the meat counter, the vegetables were looking their sprightly best, the stationery racks were filled to bursting and it was October and Christmas would be upon him before he knew where he was. Last night had been a good night. If there was one thing he liked it was a good party and that twenty-first last night had been such good fun. He remembered he must ring Pat Jones and tell her how pleased he was with her efforts. People were a continuous surprise to Jimbo, who'd have thought Pat had such potential. Well, that was one thing he could give himself a pat on the back for, finding her potential and putting it to work to his advantage, and hers come to think of it.

The bell jingled and in came Peter. To Jimbo's eyes he looked terrible. Gaunt, exhausted, shredded with anxiety.

'Good morning, Peter. Well, what's the news?'

'When I left about three this morning she was beginning to shape up nicely. I've rung just now and she's continuing to improve, so I'm taking the children to see her this afternoon.'

'Thank God for that!'

'I have. Just got some shopping to do, I want to take something in for her, and Sylvia wants a few things too. I'll just take a look round.'

'Feel free. I'd be grateful if you'd take her some flowers from Harriet and me. With our love.'

'Thank you, thank you very much, she'll like that.' Peter took a wire basket and began to do his shopping. He'd just picked up the milk and a box of eggs when the doorbell rang, and in came Dicky. He saw Peter's red-blond hair over the top of the shelves and began to beat a quick retreat, but Peter straightening up saw him as he was making his escape. 'Dicky! I need a word!'

Reluctantly Dicky turned back and shut the door.

'Now look, Peter, it was a harmless . . .'

'See here, your personal life is your affair, but when it intrudes on the church then it becomes mine. What were you thinking of?'

Dicky looked down at his shoes, put his hands in his pockets and then looking up at Peter said, 'To be honest I don't know. I can't help myself. It's out of my control.'

'Is it?'

'You know this love business. Cupid strikes and everything goes up like a rocket.'

'I know all about this love business, but you're carrying it too far. I mean, a banner on the church, and the children coming for a service. Whatever they must have thought I don't know. And Bel. What about her?'

'She's mad as heck, but I can't stop it. I'm on a roller-coaster and where it leads I have to go.'

'But Dicky, think of Georgie . . .'

'Can't stop. She's gorgeous Georgie as far as I'm concerned.'

'She is very attractive I know . . .'

'Isn't she?' Dicky's face lit up. 'Very, very attractive. It's the combination of that blonde hair and those petite features . . . and she's just the right size for me! I can't think why I haven't realised it before now. Seen her day in day out when I've been in for a drink and then one day I looked at her and wham! bang! there I was head over heels. It was as if I'd never seen her before that day. I felt as though I'd been pole axed. She's the yeast in my bread, the sugar in my tea, the icing on my cake, the fizz in my drinks, the cream in my coffee, the sherry in my trifle, the . . .'

'Dicky! Please think of your position. You're the Scout leader. You've an example to set.'

Dicky's face fell. 'I know. I've been a Scout since I was eight. In my blood as it were and if I had to give it up well . . . it doesn't bear thinking about. But . . . what can you do when love takes you by the throat? You know the feeling?'

'Indeed I do.'

'We're twin souls then, you and me. I've just met Willie, he told me about Dr Harris, how's things this morning with her?'

'Coming on nicely. Came through the operation OK, just got to wait to find out how successful it's been.'

Dicky put a hand on his arm and gave it a squeeze. 'Lovely lady. It must be hard for you. I'm so sorry. Give her my regards won't you? Must press on.'

'Thank you, I will. Will you pay some heed to what I've said?'

'Of course.'

'There are four lives at risk not just yours, you know.'

Dicky nodded. 'I know. I won't use the church again for a banner or anything, but I can't promise any more than that.'

'Dicky!'

Dicky grinned. 'My best wishes to Dr Harris. Very fond of her I am.' His eyes twinkled and Peter had to laugh. Dicky handed Jimbo a loaf of bread. 'That's all this morning. Thanks. Be seeing yer! Bye!' He dashed out of the door laughing.

As Jimbo totalled up Peter's shopping he said, 'I'm very very sorry about that rumour my mother spread. I told her not to say a word but there was no stopping her. I'm so grateful that Caroline didn't hear it.' He looked up anxiously. 'She didn't, did she?'

'No. Mercifully. It was an understandable mistake.'

'You're too generous. She means well, just has this domineering streak you know. She's very upset at what she's done.'

'Well, then, perhaps she'll think twice next time.'

'We should be so lucky. I'm dreading what she might get her teeth into next. I've an idea it could be opposition to the bells ringing. If I could just channel all her energy in the right direction before she . . .'

'Don't worry, Jimbo. How much?'

'Twelve pounds ninety-seven.'

'Thanks.'

Jimbo wrapped Caroline's flowers. 'Don't forget the flowers! Here you are. Our love to her. She's a great lady.'

'Thank you, you and I, both of us have been very lucky.'

Jimbo couldn't resist saying, 'Well, looking at the two of us I should say they've been lucky too!'

Peter couldn't help grinning, and as he left he said, 'It always does me good coming in here, gets life in perspective, I don't know how you do it.'

Caroline opened her eyes to see who had come in to visit her. 'Darling! I hadn't expected you tonight as well as this afternoon! How lovely! Are you sure you can spare the time?'

'Of course I can. Saturday is my day off after all. These flowers are from Jimbo and Harriet with love, I forgot to bring them this afternoon.'

'Of course. I'd forgotten it was Saturday. They're lovely, how kind of them. I'll get someone to put them in water. Were the children all right when you took them home?'

'Absolutely.' He didn't tell her how they'd cried when it was bedtime, nor the way Alex had clung to him and asked when she'd be home, nor about Beth's tantrum at bathtime when she'd laid on the floor and screamed and drummed her heels because he'd forgotten to put the bath bubbles in, when it was she who didn't like them very much. Nor that Beth had gone to sleep with Caroline's favourite scarf hidden under her pillow which for her sake he pretended not to notice, nor indeed that Alex had got his baby beaker out from the cupboard and insisted on having his bedtime drink in it.

'Really?'

'Well . . . they wanted you, naturally, but we got over that bit. How are you tonight, my darling? If you want me to go because you're tired just say so.'

'I am tired but I don't want you to go. Sometimes I just fall asleep even when I'm talking to someone.' She gazed somewhere behind his head and then said, 'I've never had an operation before, you know.'

'I know, neither have I. I think you're being awfully brave.'

'Not really. Peter . . .'

'Yes?'

'Peter, there's nothing left of me now you know. Not the me that's *me*!'

'From where I'm sitting there seems to be all the bits left that I love, so what's the problem?' He reached out and lifted her hair at the front and pretended to inspect it. 'They haven't removed your brain too have they?'

'Don't make me laugh, it hurts!'

'Sorry! Well, they haven't have they? You're still my Caroline whom I adore.'

Caroline turned her head away from him and stared at the wall. 'But everything that makes me a woman has gone. I might as well be a hundred for what's left that's feminine. Whilst ever I had everything else intact there was, foolishly really, just a tiny bit of hope that I *could* possibly have your children even though my womb was tantamount to nonexistent. It was all very silly of me I know, because I couldn't have carried a baby in fact, but now absolutely all hope is gone.'

'As Rhett Butler would say "Frankly, my dear, I don't give a damn". You and I will continue having a wonderful married life together and no surgeon, whoever he is, is going to put a stop to that.'

Caroline shuffled painfully about in the bed trying to get herself more comfortable. She was silent for a while and Peter thought she must be falling asleep again but she said, 'What I'm so afraid of is that I feel less of a person than I was before. How can you possibly want me after this?'

'Caroline, I'm not going to stop loving you just because, as Sheila Bissett would say, you've had everything taken away. It won't make one jot of difference to me and we won't let it make one jot of difference to you either.'

'Do they all know?'

'I expect so by now.'

'I wish they didn't have to.'

'Unavoidable. By the way, your mother's been on the phone, four times. She's phoned the consultant twice and threatened what she'll do to him if anything goes wrong. Apparently they've realised he was in the same year as your father at medical school. She's coming down when you come out.'

'Oh right. I can understand her wanting to come, and I'm grateful that she is, but I wish she wouldn't, I shan't feel like being stirred up.' She fell silent and lay with her eyes closed. Without opening them she continued speaking. 'I felt you pray for me yesterday. Well, not pray but kind of call out to me. I can't remember when it was. Were you here when they brought me back from theatre?'

'A while after.'

'You said my name twice and I came back into the room to see what you wanted, it was really very odd.'

'Ah, right! I see my flowers have come.'

She smiled at him. 'They're beautiful. Thank Jimbo and Harriet for theirs for me will you?'

'Of course. Shall I sit with you until you sleep?'

'Yes, please. I'll go to sleep now.'

Peter rested his elbows on the edge of the mattress and held her hand close to his cheek and then kissed it. 'God bless you.'

'And you. Give my two little ones a kiss from me. I hope they're not being too difficult.'

119

'No, not at all. Good as gold. Between us Sylvia and I are managing very nicely, though we shall all be glad when you're back.'

'I do love them. So much. And you. I love you dearly.'

'I know, and I love you.'

Faintly he heard her say, 'We're so lucky aren't we, you and I?' She squeezed his hand and smiled and then fell asleep.

In church on Sunday when Peter was saying prayers he told the congregation about Caroline's operation, that it was for cancer and would they give thanks with him for her safe recovery.

No one prayed more fervently than Grandmama. She'd lived a thousand years since she'd met Peter on the Friday morning and he'd told her the real truth of the matter. Thank heavens she hadn't met Caroline and said something. That didn't bear thinking about. If only she'd listened to Jimbo and done as he'd said. But she hadn't and she'd blundered on in her usual bossy way. But she was right about some things. After all he often took notice of her ideas for the Store. He never said he would, but next time she went in he'd have done whatever she'd suggested. Not always, but a sufficient number of times to make her feel useful. But for now she'd pray. Between her fingers she could take a peep at the twins sitting with Sylvia because they'd made a commotion in Sunday School and had to be brought out. Dear, dear little things. Wriggling about a lot, but then who wouldn't at their age?

When the service was concluded Grandmama made her way to the twins and gave them each a pound coin. 'Now this is for you to spend in the Store when Sylvia gets a chance to take you after school. It's closed today but you can go in tomorrow, can't you? Something nice, remember?'

Through tight lips Sylvia forced herself to say 'What do you say children?'

'Thank you, Mrs Charter-Plackett.' The two of them studied the shiny coins for a moment and then stored them away in their pockets.

Having made sure the children had behaved politely Sylvia turned her attention to Grandmama. 'I can't disappoint the children when they're so upset about their mother, but if it was my decision I'd throw that money back at you. You can't buy favour with us, not with none of us.'

'How dare you!'

'I dare all right. I've found out it was you who started that rumour about Dr Harris being . . . you know. How could you? How could you?' Sylvia stamped her foot and a small crowd, beginning to gather in the aisle because they couldn't get past, were paying delighted attention to Grandmama getting told off.

'It wasn't done maliciously, I just put the facts together.'

'But they weren't facts were they?'

'They seemed like it.'

'Well, they weren't. Can you imagine how she would have felt if you'd met her and said that and her knowing what she was having to face? If we still had a ducking stool that's exactly where you'd be, in the pond and drowned for your wicked ways. It happened more than once in that pond in years gone by to nasty old gossips like you.'

Someone in the crowd contributed to the discussion with 'And for what she did to Sheila Bissett. That was cruel that was.'

'It was. Downright cruel.'

Grandmama began to feel in need of help, things

were getting very ugly. To her relief Jimbo came to her rescue.

He declared rather more loudly than there was any need, 'Mother! There are you. Coming home for lunch?' He elbowed his way to the middle of the crowd and took her arm.

Sylvia found she had a lot of support. 'Sylvia's right. You tell her, Mr Charter-Plackett, you tell her to keep her meddling ways to herself. Nasty she's been, real nasty.'

'We all make mistakes. It wasn't done to be nasty,' Jimbo retorted sharply.

'Go on, get off home with your Jimbo, it's only because we all like him so much that we can excuse yer, but don't you try us too far. Else Sylvia'ull be right, they'll find yer floating in the pond.'

There was a bit of elbowing and nudging and Jimbo knew he had to get her out of the way before things got uglier still. 'Come along, Mother, right now.' She looked tempted to stay a moment and give them a piece of her mind from the security of Jimbo's arm, but he led her off and as they went down the aisle they could hear some of the congregation saying, 'Spreading such tales.'

'Disgusting.'

'Poor Dr Harris.'

In his usual forgiving way Peter shook hands with Grandmama and asked after her health but she couldn't face him and lowering her eyes, thanked him and went quietly away with Jimbo.

Sunday lunch at Jimbo and Harriet's was a boisterous meal but it gave Grandmama the opportunity for reflection. The children didn't appear to notice how quiet she was but Harriet did and when they'd reached the coffee stage and the two girls had left the table she enquired from

Grandmama how she was feeling. 'Are you not well, you're very quiet.'

'I'm quite well, thank you.'

'Not like you, that's all.'

Fergus passed her the sugar and said 'It's all right, Grandmama, we all know what's up. I saw Sylvia giving you a drubbing. Didn't know she had such a temper.'

'Fergus!' Jimbo couldn't face another smoothing of Mother's ruffled feathers.

'Be quiet, Jimbo, he's quite right.'

Harriet raised her eyebrows and Finlay grinned. 'Your face was red!' Fergus began to laugh uproariously.

Under the table Jimbo kicked Fergus' ankle, but Grandmama gave a tight little smile and answered, 'It was very embarrassing. But she was quite right. I should never have said it. I should have waited to see.'

'Never mind, Mother, we have to be thankful Caroline's come through the operation OK.'

'Indeed. Now boys it will soon be half-term. Have you any plans? I've money going spare if you're fancying a day out somewhere or a visit to the cinema or something.'

They began discussing how best to spend their Grandmama's money and no one mentioned the matter of her rumour-mongering again, except Harriet and Jimbo in the kitchen after his mother had left.

'My word! That's a turn-up for the book! Your mother feeling apologetic! Don't forget the dishwasher powder. Here.'

'Well, perhaps this time she will have learned her lesson. I understand she also has had a tiff with Muriel, so she's got that to sort yet.'

'Do you think we might be sailing into calmer waters with your mother now?'

'Since when has she *ever* sailed in calm waters? That's just wishful thinking.'

Harriet sighed. 'You're right, but I do believe it's brought her up short. She's never been so apologetic.'

'Right that's it, everything's done. I don't know how seven people can use so many dishes and pans. I didn't even know we had so many.'

'So many children or so many pans?'

'Both. Do you ever fancy having another one? Make it five, eh? How about it?' He had pinned her against the dishwasher and, with both hands resting on the cupboard above, he kissed her soundly. When they'd finished she answered him. 'Definitely not.'

'Go on. Let's.'

'At your age? Or mine come to that. No, Jimbo, I've just got back into the swing of things and I'm not being tied to the house yet again. Four children is enough for anyone.' She pushed him away and went to see if anyone fancied going for a walk.

While they were out at Bickerby Rocks only Harriet saw Dicky and Georgie hand in hand disappearing out of sight down the hill towards the car park.

Chapter 11

When Bel went over to the school at eight o'clock on Monday morning to open up and check the heating had come on she was unprepared for what she saw chalked in letters two feet high out in Jacks Lane. The words were strung in a line along the tarmac. 'I LOVE GEORGIE'. The letters were written in a kind of dancing, prancing, sprightly style which added to the potency of their message.

Her lovely open friendly country woman's face became flushed from her hairline right down to her throat. She'd kill him she would. There was a limit. She'd wondered why he hadn't been in the house when she got up, they usually left together, him for his newspaper and then work and her for the school. She'd scrub it off with the playground broom. But she'd have to do her own jobs first. No, she wouldn't. She'd scrub it off first and then see to the school.

Bel did check the heating before she collected the broom and bucket from her broom cupboard in the school kitchen and went out, the water in the bucket sending up swirls of steam into the early winter cold. She began with I and then progressed to LOVE . . .

'What's this then?'

Bel looked up to see who was speaking to her. It was the postman, Ted.

'You can read I'm sure, at least I hope you can.'

'Oh, I can. Don't need to see it all anyways. I've already read it.'

'You're early this morning then.'

'No, not really, it's outside the pub as well, saw it there first. Bryn done it has he?'

Bel seethed. 'Outside the pub as well?'

'Just seen it.'

She snapped, 'No, it isn't Bryn.'

'Who is it then? Who's daft enough?'

Bel pondered for a moment and then answered by denying all knowledge of who it could be.

Ted laughed. 'Whoever it is they're stupid to do it right outside the pub. Bryn's like a bear with a sore head just lately, tore me off a strip just for delivering a letter of his to one of the weekender's cottages by mistake. Course they didn't come back for two weeks did they, so his letter was really late. Weren't my fault. Didn't do it on purpose. He can have a nasty temper and not half.'

Bel finished scrubbing off GEORGIE, picked up the bucket and left Ted to ruminate on his own. He delivered the school post, and two letters to Miss Pascoe and then went to the Store. There was quite a pile of post for Jimbo, he heaved it onto the counter and shouted into the back.

'Mr Charter-Plackett! I've left the post on the counter.'

Jimbo came through from the storeroom carrying a box of apples.

'Morning Ted. Thanks.' Ted reached into the box and chose an apple. He raised his eyebrows at Jimbo who nodded and Ted sunk his teeth into the reddest part of it. When he'd swallowed his first mouthful he said 'Someone's written "I love Georgie" on the road outside the school. In chalk. In big letters.'

Jimbo swung round to face him. 'Has Bel seen it yet?'

'Just scrubbing it off. Was her face red!'

'I'm not surprised.'

'Know who did it then, do yer?'

'I can give a good guess.'

Ted took another large bite of his apple. By the time he'd emptied his mouth sufficiently to be able to speak Jimbo had disappeared into the storeroom again. Ted saw the lovely Comice pears. He tested one for ripeness checked Jimbo wasn't about to come back in and popped it in his mail bag, but only just in time.

Ted asked, 'Who is it then?'

'I expect you'll know soon enough. It'll be Dicky Tutt.'

Ted's jaw fell open. 'Dicky Tutt! Dicky Tutt! Never.'

'On your bike, Ted, I'm busy.'

'In yer van, yer mean. I'm mechanised now. Well, I never. Poor Bel.'

'Bye to you, Ted, and I'd have given you that pear if you'd asked.'

Ted blushed. 'Sorry.' He went to take it out of his bag.

'Don't bother, but don't do it again.'

Jimbo wasn't quite sure how to greet Bel when she came to work after finishing at the school. But she came in with her usual cheerful greeting and made it difficult to broach the subject.

'Morning all. Isn't it bright and sunny today? We'd better make the best of it while we can. What would you like me to start on this morning Mr Charter-P?'

Linda behind her post office grille felt full of pity for Bel. Such a nice person she was, blasted shame she was having to put up with all this from Dicky. She'd seen the message in the lane, couldn't help it, plain as day from their bedroom window it had been. She'd watched poor Bel start scrubbing away but then the baby had wanted attention and she'd had to press on. And here she was cheerful as ninepence, as if nothing had happened. She'd kill her Alan if he ever did anything so blatantly obvious. Come to think about it she'd kill him if he even so much as looked at another woman never mind advertised it. Linda called across, 'Good morning, Bel. My stationery shelves could do with filling up, there's quite a few gaps.'

Jimbo rounded on her. 'Those shelves are your responsibility, Linda, not Bel's, she has quite enough on her plate at the moment. You've no customers so kindly attend to them now if you please. Bel, start shelf filling in the groceries will you, I've an appointment in half an hour and I'll need you to be on the till while I'm out. OK?' Jimbo looked at Bel and studied her face for a moment but her guard never slipped, and he had to let the moment pass.

At a quarter to ten, only fifteen minutes after Bel had come to start work the door banged open and in came Bryn. His appearance in the Store was very unusual in itself for it was always Georgie who shopped, never Bryn. Linda was glad Jimbo hadn't left yet for she rather suspected that by the look of him Bryn might possibly be quite furious; his face was purple and there were beads of sweat on his forehead, and his fists were clenched, and he was positively *grinding* his teeth.

Straightening up from filling the gaps on the bottom shelf with packets of envelopes, she said the first thing that came into her head. 'Good morning, Mr Fields. Has something upset you, you don't look well.' He was towering over her and as a precaution Linda stepped back a little. 'Is there something I can get you?'

Through clenched teeth and in a tightly controlled voice he said, 'Bel Tutt in?'

'Could be.'

'Either she is or she isn't. Well?' As though on cue Bel came through from the back with a clip board in her hand. The moment she saw Bryn she began to retreat. 'I want a word with you! Come back here!'

Bel hovered in the doorway seemingly unable to make up her mind as to what she should do. In the background she could hear Jimbo on the telephone and Mrs Jones in the mail-order office furiously stapling things together as though there was no tomorrow. She could see Linda beside Bryn looking frightened and beginning to back off towards the outside door.

Bel took a deep breath. 'There's a little word you've forgotten.'

There was a moment's silence and then Bryn said 'Please.'

Slowly Bel moved forward and went to stand beside the till. She rested a hand on the counter as though for support and waited.

'Have you seen what's been chalked on the road outside my pub?'

'No.'

'I love Georgie. That's what. I . . . love . . . Georgie.'

'I didn't do it.'

'I don't suppose for one minute you did. But your Dicky did.'

'Did he?'

'You know damn well he did. I'm up to here.' Bryn stepped towards Bel and tapped the edge of his hand on his forehead 'up to here, with your Dicky. I've banned him from the pub but still he's getting at me. Tell him from me' – Bryn stabbed at his chest with his finger – 'if this tomfoolery doesn't stop I shall have him. God help me I will. I'll have him and I'll squeeze him till there's not a drop of breath left in his stunted little body. Right!' He wrung his hands together as though they were around Dicky's throat.

'I'll give him your message.'

'If you don't, I shall. He's to leave my Georgie alone. Alone! Right? Or else as God is my judge, I'll see there's an end to him.'

'Right.'

'You can also tell your Tom Thumb from me that's he's a pipsqueak, he's a stunted, undersized, blasted little squirt. A dwarf.' Bryn paused for breath searching for the most damaging thing he could say without committing a total breach of etiquette. 'A bloody evil little dwarf.'

By the time Bryn had finished this speech he had an audience of Mrs Jones, Jimbo, two assistants from the kitchens, Harriet, Linda and Grandmama. She'd come in halfway through the tirade and been standing listening open-mouthed to what he was saying. As he moved to leave she stepped forward and blocked his way out. In her most superior voice she upbraided him for his outburst.

'My man, have you given one moment's thought as to how Bel must be feeling? She too is an injured party, you know, just as much as you. Your behaviour is most reprehensible, you should be ashamed of yourself. Have you ever given a thought as to why Georgie appears to find Dicky so fascinating? Or indeed as to why Dicky finds Georgie so engaging? Have you given it your earnest consideration? Oh no! I don't expect you have. Foolish man. Go home and think about it. And don't march in here laying down the law ever again. These are business premises not a fairground boxing ring. Such language! Venting your spleen on Bel in this way. It's absolutely disgraceful! Now, get out!'

She opened the door and waited for him to leave.

Which he did, but not without throwing a fevered glance at Bel as he left and saying to Grandmama, 'And you, Duchess, are an interfering old *hen*,' before he slammed the door behind him. There was a stunned silence as the Store reverberated with the sound of the door slamming.

The first to recover was Grandmama. She brushed her gloved hands together as though ridding herself of something thoroughly unpleasant and looking round at everyone she smiled. 'Well, now, is anyone serving in here this morning or not? I want notepaper and envelopes and a tub of single cream, for I've someone coming for coffee. Chop, chop! Bel go in the back and get Jimbo to give you a brandy out of his first aid box. You look as though you need it. Good morning, Harriet.'

'Good morning to you.'

Slowly everyone resumed their places, Mrs Jones went back to her mail-order office full of admiration for the dignified manner in which Grandmama had dealt with the situation, it took class it did to give a dressing down like that, class, nothing less. Linda to the bottom stationery shelf for notepaper and envelopes, careful to choose the most expensive she could find. Bel, white and trembling, disappeared with Jimbo in her wake. Harriet went to the chilled shelves for the cream.

'My word, Mother-in-law, you certainly gave him what for. I have never in all the time he's been here known him explode like that. Things must be serious for him to behave like that.'

'They are, Harriet, they are.'

'You know?'

'I do. That's fine, Linda. Thank you. In very good taste, I must say. Tot it up for me, Harriet, I'm in a hurry. I've Muriel coming for coffee.'

'Indeed. I thought you two weren't exactly . . . you know . . . friends.'

Grandmama looked uncomfortable. 'There's been a slight hiccough which I intend to paper over today. That doesn't sound quite right but you know what I mean. Thank you, my dear. See you soon.'

Grandmama left feeling well satisfied with her morning's work. Now all she had to do was butter up Muriel and then all would be right with her world. There was nothing quite like a demonstration of power to make one feel . . . what was the phrase she was after? Cock of the dung heap? Oh dear no, that wasn't it. Ten years younger? On top of the world? She'd think it over while she got the coffee things out. Pity she'd no family silver to bring out, but there you couldn't have everything.

After taking coffee Muriel went home to lunch very amused by Grandmama's attempts to apologise for her loss of temper and for spreading the rumour about Caroline. She, Grandmama, was a very proud woman and it must have cost her a lot to apologise so profusely. Muriel's kind heart could do no other than accept graciously and they had parted the best of friends. At least on the surface, for Muriel was tempted to wait to see what other escapades Grandmama might get up to.

'Ralph, my dear, have you heard?'

'No, I don't expect so.'

'Oh there you are!' Muriel stood in the doorway of his study and admired Ralph, his snow white, well barbered hair, his fresh complexion, his alert brown eyes and, to her, his wonderful aristocratic nose. 'You grow more handsome each time I see you!'

'Thank you, my dear. Is that the news? That Ralph Templeton grows more handsome every day?'

She laughed. 'Of course not! That was an aside. No, Grandmama tells me that Bryn has been in the Store and told Bel off quite cruelly about Dicky, and I've just seen her crossing the road to school and said how sorry I was and that she was to ignore him and she said she was, but I said it must be very difficult and she said it was, so I said she'd have to put her foot down and she said you know Dicky so I said I do and he's a very naughty boy so she said that's just right that's what he is so I said would she like you to have a talk with him and she said . . .'

'Muriel!' Ralph raised a hand in protest. 'Muriel! I am not getting involved in someone else's marital affairs. Please.'

Muriel looked quite crestfallen. 'But, Ralph, he needs someone like you to . . .'

'No, he does not.'

She went to stand beside him and putting an arm around his shoulders she bent to kiss the top of his head. 'Please, my dear, someone has to do something and we can't expect Peter to with Caroline so ill.'

'I am not. Sorry. And kissing me won't make one jot of difference.'

'Oh Ralph! Please.'

'No.'

'Then I shall.'

'I expressly forbid you to say anything at all, Muriel. Let them sort themselves out.'

'Forbid me?'

'I beg your pardon. Of course I don't forbid, but please take my advice and keep out of it.'

'How can we, the whole village is agog.'

'Then agog they will have to be. It's becoming quite sordid and I don't want to have anything to do with it.'

'You must admit though, Ralph, if they weren't all

married it would be a rather wonderful romance. Telling all the world about how your heart feels. So romantic, so . . . compelling. It's like a film. A nineteen fifties film like *Spring in Park Lane* with Anna Neagle, or *Brief Encounter* with Trevor Howard, when there was romance and not simply sex.' She sighed longingly.

'Muriel?' He put down his pen and resting his elbows on the desk studied her face. 'I do believe you like the idea of having messages left all over the village. Maybe I'm letting the romance in our marriage seep away through neglect. I shall have to think up something for you, maybe Dicky could give me some suggestions.'

Muriel blushed. 'Oh no! not something like that. That would be too embarrassing.'

'Then beware, my dear, if I discover you've been handing out advice to them all, I shall find a way of embarrassing you good and proper!' Ralph chuckled at the consternation in Muriel's face.

'That's blackmail!'

'Indeed it is. But I shall, you may take my word for it.'

'Ralph!' She sped away into the kitchen quite over-come by Ralph's teasing.

But the opportunity to speak to Dicky came the following evening and Muriel couldn't resist the chance. She'd been busy all day and it was dark before she got an opportunity to call at the rectory with a cake which she hoped in some small way might help Sylvia. It was she who came to the door when Muriel rang the bell.

'Good evening, Sylvia. I've brought a coconut cake, thought it might help.'

'Thank you very much indeed. I really appreciate that. Coconut, lovely!'

'What's the news today?'

134

'A big improvement. We're all feeling much happier. She's out of bed and she's beginning to be more like herself.'

'I'm so glad. He's with her tonight?'

'No, he's presenting the prizes at the Guides' annual whatever.' Sylvia turned as she heard the study door close. It was Dicky with an envelope in his hand. 'Got what you wanted?'

'Yes, thanks. He'd left it out for me, like he said. Tell the Rector I'll get it back to him before the end of the week. Oh, good evening, Lady Templeton.'

'Good evening, Dicky. I'll say good night then.'

'Thanks for the cake, save me baking tomorrow.'

'Good, I'm glad.'

Dicky and Muriel stepped out of the rectory together and the opportunity couldn't be missed. Before they left the pool of light cast by the lamp over the rectory door, Muriel cleared her throat and took the plunge.

'Could I have a word, Dicky?'

'Of course. Can't be long though, I've got Venture Scouts in ten minutes.'

'Oh, it won't take long. I had a word with Bel yesterday, I feel very upset for her.' Dicky, the same height as herself, looked straight into her eyes without answering. Muriel grew uncomfortable, and she wished she'd never begun the conversation at all, she really should have listened to Ralph's advice. But she had to say it. Just had to. 'I can quite understand about you being captivated by Georgie, totally understand it, she's a very attractive person and I know it can be difficult when they're the light of your life and your feelings overwhelm you and you feel quite helpless and . . . I . . . I don't mean to interfere, but it's not right what you're doing.'

'Not right? Not right to be in love?'

'Well, no, I can't say it's not right to be in love, we shouldn't turn our faces against love at any time, but you shouldn't be should you? In love, well, not with Georgie.'

'Does love ask for your credentials before it strikes?'

'Oh no, of course not. No, it doesn't, but . . .'

' "But", exactly. I can't help it.'

'All the world doesn't need to know, though, does it? You don't have to advertise the fact do you?'

'What else can I do when it's bubbling out of me? I've been well and truly clobbered by her and I can't think of anything else.'

'But your reputation. Think of that.'

Dicky gazed up the road, thought for a moment and then said very quietly, 'I don't care one jot for my reputation, not one jot. I love her and that's all there is to it.'

'Then at the very least you could think of Bel, think how it must be for her. I felt truly sorry when I heard what Bryn said to her in the Store yesterday, she must be feeling it very deeply. Often, you see, the cheerful, happy people are the very ones who hurt the most. So it's Bel I feel the most concerned for, after all, she is *your legal wife*. You should think of her, first and foremost.'

Dicky didn't answer immediately, he first looked deep into her eyes. He appeared to be weighing up if whether what he was about to say would be a good idea or not. He patted her arm and said 'The word "legal" isn't in the equation at all, so there's no need for you to worry yourself about Bel. Good night to you, Lady Templeton.'

Chapter 12

Peter had kept Caroline up to date with all the village news so when she came home ten days later there wasn't a great deal she didn't know. Except, of course, no one knew what had passed between Muriel and Dicky the previous Tuesday night. Sylvia went to collect the children from school and the first words they said to her were 'Is Mummy home?'

'She is.'

The two of them raced across the playground towards the gate.

'No! No! Mind the road!' Fortunately Miss Booth was by the gate and she stopped the two of them from leaving.

'Oh, thank you, Miss Booth. They're so excited, the Doctor came home this afternoon, you see, and they can't wait.'

'I know! They've talked of nothing else all day. I am pleased.' Miss Booth patted their heads. 'She will be happy to see you both.'

Beth nodded her head in agreement. 'We've been to see her in hospital but I didn't like that. I don't like hospitals. Come on, Sylvie, be quick!'

'We've got to cross the road properly, Beth, no matter what. Hold my hands. You as well Alex.'

Alex urged her to hurry.

They burst in through the rectory door shouting 'Mummy! Mummy!'

'In the sitting-room.' Alex rushed in and flung himself upon her and hugged her but Beth stood outside the door peeping round it watching Alex greet Caroline. 'Where's my Beth? I'm in here, darling.'

Very slowly Beth walked into the room and stood looking at her mother. Caroline spread her arms wide and said 'Come here, my darling.'

Beth unable to cope with the emotion she felt on seeing Caroline at home at last, fled to the kitchen to find Sylvia. But it was Peter who was making a drink for them all.

'Why, Beth darling, what is the matter?' he scooped her up into his arms and her chubby little arms squeezed his neck so tightly he could scarcely breathe. Her hot tears prickled onto his neck. He felt the cold of her cheeks and inhaled the fragrance of her hair, and hugged her close.

'Dearest child, Mummy's home now and quite safe. Come and say hello.'

'I can't, it hurts.'

'Where does it hurt?'

'I think it's in my heart, I think it's going to burst.'

'No, it isn't. What you need is Mummy to give you a hug, that will mend your heart. We'll go in there together.'

'Does your heart want to burst, Daddy?'

'Oh yes. It does.' He carried her through into the sitting-room and placed her on the sofa next to Caroline. 'There we are. You hug Mummy, that'll make it feel better.'

Caroline hugged her tightly and gradually Beth's fear

138

subsided, and the horrid broken jigsaw of her life fell slowly into order and she felt her world had been put to rights.

'Mummy, Daddy needs a hug, his heart's ready to burst too.' So Caroline sat on the sofa with one arm round Alex, the other round Beth and Peter kneeling in front of her his head resting against her chest. Their tears dried up and when Sylvia came in with tea, which she'd finished making on Peter's behalf, she stood with the tray in her hands in the doorway and smiled, a huge great beaming smile the like of which she felt she hadn't done for days. At last everything was back to normal and she gave an enormous heartfelt sigh of relief.

'Tea anyone?'

Caroline had refused to go to bed while the children were up. She talked and joked and listened and played herself to complete exhaustion. Peter took them up to bed and when they were happily tucked up, Alex with his teddy and Beth, with her thumb in her mouth, clutching old Boo Boo rabbit he went downstairs to Caroline.

'Peter, I'm so tired.'

'I can see that. You should have gone to bed sooner than this.'

'I know but the children, they need to see me looking more normal, they need reassuring. You know?'

'Let me help you upstairs. Have a sleep, eh?'

'That would be lovely.'

He helped her undress and when she was safely laid in bed he suggested that he'd come up about ten with a hot drink, what did she fancy?

'Tea I think and a piece of Sylvia's cake, whatever she has on the go at the moment.'

'Good idea. You need to get some weight back on.'

'Don't put pressure on me, please, I'll get round to things in my own good time.'

'Sorry, just anxious, you know.' He hung her skirt and cardigan in the wardrobe, put her shirt and underthings in the linen basket and left her to sleep.

Peter sat for a long while in his study in the easy chair. He alternately thought and prayed, underscoring his gratitude for her coming through the operation with prayers of thanks to God. He had no living relatives, no one to turn to in times of need. Only Caroline and the children on earth. They were his whole world. This terrible threat to their happiness had heightened his awareness of how much he needed her to sustain him in his daily life, how much he needed her common sense, her humour, her strength. Caroline gave so much to so many people; to him, his children, her patients, her friends, her own family, the parish. They none of them could manage nearly as well without her.

On his desk were the pile of get well cards Caroline had brought back with her from hospital. He read through them one after the other, they were from parishioners, from family, from friends, many of them unknown to him. The last one right at the bottom was from David Lloyd-Jones. He didn't pose any threat but the man could still waken feelings of jealousy. Peter had to laugh at himself.

She wasn't out of the wood yet though, the specialist had said to him, but the prognosis was excellent. The hurdle of therapy still had to be faced, but he was determined to remain cheerful on that subject, yes definitely cheerful.

The little carriage clock on the study mantelpiece chimed ten o'clock. He went into the kitchen to put the kettle on, prepared a tray with an Indian cloth Caroline had brought back years ago, found the best teapot and cups and saucers and a matching plate and a lace doily for the cake.

When he entered the bedroom Peter laid the tray on his bedside table and looked to see if Caroline was awake. She was fast asleep, with Alex cuddled up on one side of her and Beth on the other. Peter debated what he should do, but decided to leave them where they were. The two of them would both heal quicker that way, sleeping close to her. He carried the tray into the children's room and went to sleep in Alex's bed, altogether envious of his children.

Chapter 13

Grandmama burst through the front door calling, 'Harriet, my dear, where are you? Are you there? Hello, Fran, my darling!'

Jimbo came out of the sitting-room. 'Hello, Mother, what's the matter, is there a fire?'

'Not a fire, Jimbo, dear.' She held her face for him to kiss. 'I've got such news. You won't believe. Where's Harriet? What are you doing home at this time?'

'Half day, I do have one occasionally, I've a function tonight.'

Harriet had been washing her hair and came down the stairs rubbing it dry. 'Hello, Mother-in-law. What's the news then?'

Grandmama nodded her head in the direction of the kitchen. Jimbo and Harriet followed her in.

'Didn't want little Fran to hear, the children aren't home yet are they?'

'Another half an hour. Why?'

Grandmama seated herself at the kitchen table and digging into her handbag brought out a small plastic bag. 'In here is the piece I need for repairing my sewing machine. It's so old they've stopped stocking the spare parts for it now and I've searched all over and found a little man in Culworth who's managed to get it for me.'

'Is that it? Is that the news?' Jimbo was very disappointed, he'd expected a murder at least.

'Of course not. But you should be delighted for me, I've really missed not being able to use it. I'm going to make things for charity. I've a very good line in stuffed dolls, they are very stylish, of course, they're not some arty crafty rubbish masquerading as designer dolls. However, while he was finding out how much I owed him this chappie asked me if I lived in Culworth and I said no I lived in Turnham Malpas, so he said in that case then you'll know Dicky Tutt. He knows Dicky because it's where Dicky works in the office that the sewing machine man managed to get this piece from, so he knows Dicky very well, you see. Been dealing with Dicky's company for years and years. So we got talking about what a nice man he is and what fun, which he is, and I said his wife's lovely too, she's the village school caretaker and she works for my son.' Grandmama paused and looked at them both to make sure she had their complete attention. 'Then he said . . . You'll never believe this . . .'

Jimbo stood up. 'Now look, Mother, I'm not having you going round spreading rumours again. You'll please me if you keep this all to yourself, I really don't want to know. Your rumours have proved dangerous in the past, so you are stopping right there.'

Harriet intervened. 'Steady on, your mother's only telling us what he said, she hasn't made it up has she?'

'Thank you, Harriet, for springing to my defence. As Harriet said, I'm only repeating to you what he said to me.'

'I don't want to hear what some piffling sewing-machine repairer has to say about anything. Now please, Mother, say no more. If all you have to talk about is unreliable gossip then you can leave right now.'

'Jimbo! I think . . .'

'I don't care what you think! and if I hear that you've breathed one wrong word, and I say that again, *one wrong word* about Dicky Tutt then you'll have me to answer to. I mean that, Mother. Whatever this chappie claims, it in no way affects the brilliant job Dicky does with those boys.'

Grandmama stood up. 'I'll go before the children come home. If you don't want to hear my interesting news then so be it. But don't expect me to tell you anything at all, ever, in the future. Coming from someone who loves a tasty piece of gossip, I think you're being two-faced. Anyone else's gossip is all right but mine isn't.'

'No, it isn't, and you're not to repeat it to anyone. I had thought you'd learned your lesson. Apparently you haven't.'

Grandmama stormed from the house, Jimbo's 'I mean what I say' following her out.

Harriet went to put the towel to dry on the radiator. 'I'm afraid you came down a little too heavily there Jimbo.'

'Since when have you been on Mother's side?'

'I'm not, but even so I can be fair to her.'

'I've put the frighteners on her on purpose. Tough measures for a tough cookie. That's what.'

'She was only telling us what he said.'

'The thing is Mother's assuming this man in Culworth is right in whatever it is he's told her. He could be quite wrong.'

'I wonder what it was he said? You shut her up far too soon, I would have liked to have heard what it was.'

'Harriet! You're as bad as Mother.'

144

'OK. OK. I'm going over to see Caroline for five minutes. I won't stay long. Her mother's driving down tomorrow, so it's best if I go today. I'll just brush my hair.'

'Give her my love.'

'I will.'

The following morning Malcolm was late with the milk because the baby had been awake half the night, and Ted was early so they both arrived at the Royal Oak at the same time.

'Morning, Ted.'

'God you look awful.'

'It's the baby, yer long for 'em to come and then . . . He went to sleep just as it was time to get up and I dropped off by mistake. Eh! Look at this.'

He was examining the window boxes. There were three under the long window between the two entrances. Each one had been filled with winter pansies by Georgie and the ivy which had been burgeoning in the summer was hanging on by a thread now the cold weather had come. All the way along the front edge of each box were red roses, stuck into the soil. Each and every one had a small heart-shaped label attached with the word Georgie written on it with a red pen. They looked like very tall guardsmen on parade. There must have been three dozen Ted reckoned. 'He's at it again. There's no stopping him is there? The daft beggar.'

'Wouldn't like to be in his shoes when Bryn finds out. Blasted miserable sod he is nowadays.'

'Hardly surprising is it considering? Would you like it if your wife was being courted under your very nose?'

'I'm not daft, I ain't married.'

'Well, then. Leave yer milk and let's be off before he finds out.'

145

'He won't be up for a bit yet.' Malcolm left his regular crate of milk for the dining-room and went off. Ted put the letters through and checked he'd not forgotten any, not after the last time.

When finally they both got up, Georgie asked Bryn to bring in the milk as they hadn't sufficient for breakfast, so it was he who saw the roses first.

Bryn didn't know whether to laugh or cry. How could this man do this to him? How could he? He was being made a laughing stock. That was the part he resented the most; being made to look a fool. Georgie and he belonged to each other. When they'd married he'd lusted for her like nobody's business. So pretty, so petite, so lively, he couldn't resist her and they'd built such a good business, such a good following in the other pub and now here, the dining-room, the bar. They worked together so well. The hours were crippling agreed and he wasn't coping with them quite as easily as he used to, but there you are. Open all hours, what else could she expect.

Well, she damned well wasn't seeing these. He'd pull them out and get them in the wheelie bin before she saw them. Swiftly he raced along the boxes pulling out the roses as he went. The thorns scratched his fingers, tore at his hands, made his wrist bleed but he didn't care. When he'd got the last one out he glanced round to see if anyone was about and then raced round the outside to the wheelie bin in the car park, and back again in a trice.

'Bryn, where's that milk? I'm dying for a cup of tea.'

'Just coming.'

The morning went along as usual. Alan came to start work and Georgie disappeared to make the bed and to pretty herself up ready for opening for the lunchtime

146

trade. The chef arrived to start work on the dining-room food, and his assistant, a brash blonde with more bounce than brains came too. Bryn began to congratulate himself on a successful outcome to his secret piece of sabotage.

By a quarter to one the regulars were in and a very good sprinkling of people who'd booked tables and were having a drink before sitting down to eat. Jimmy was in, it being his day off, and Willie and Sylvia too.

Jimmy wiped the froth from his top lip and asked why Willie and Sylvia were in at lunchtime?

'My day off and the Rector said Sylvia should take a day off too with working so much when the doctor was in hospital. So we're having a drink and then having lunch and then we're off into Culworth.'

'Lunch, eh?'

Sylvia saw immediately what he was hoping for. 'Care to join us?'

'I'd like that if you don't mind.'

'Not at all, do we, Willie?'

Willie shook his head. 'You're welcome.'

Jimmy smiled his thanks. 'Dr Harris all right, is she?'

'Getting better every day. We're right pleased with her. The Rector's smiling again, thank goodness.'

'Caught sight of him in Culworth one day when she was in hospital, he looked terrible he did, something terrible. Poor chap. It's hard when yer love like they do and . . .'

They'd all heard the phone ring but took no notice, it was probably a booking for the dining-room, but from the sound of Georgie's voice it wasn't a run of the mill conversation. She put the receiver on the bar counter and, lifting the flap, crossed to the outside door and went out. Bryn, who was collecting up empty glasses from the table by the fire watched her go. His heart began beating rather fast. He slipped across to the counter, picked up the receiver and shouted 'Get stuffed!' into it and quietly replaced it on its cradle.

Everyone was aware a drama was being played out and they eagerly awaited Georgie's return. By the time she came back in Bryn was pretending to straighten his collection of brass toasting forks hanging above the fireplace. She marched across to the phone and stood gazing in surprise at the receiver.

'Did you put this receiver back?'

'Receiver? No.' Bryn stopped to have a conversation with a customer, keeping a wary eye on her while he did so. She was standing looking at the telephone, then in an instant they could see she made up her mind. Georgie was round the counter and standing in front of Bryn before you could say Jack Robinson.

The customers jointly held their breath.

'It's you isn't it? You've taken the roses out of the window boxes?'

Roses in the window boxes in October? What did she mean?

'Roses? Me?'

'Bryn Fields, you're lying to me. It was you, I can see it written all over your face. You lying cheating so and so.'

'What do you expect me to do? Stand by and let that little runt of a man court you as though you were free to be courted? Well, you aren't and I shan't. The worm has turned. I pulled them out and stuffed them in the bin, and I shall do whatever is needed to stop that nasty little beggar from stealing you from me. We're a team you and me.' He gestured with his arm to the counter and the customers. 'We've built this up, we've made it what it is, him with his

148

twopenny ha'penny office job couldn't keep you like I can, never in a million years.'

'What good does it do me having money in the bank? We never can enjoy it. We're always too busy. Too busy for fun. Always the bar, the bar, the bar, day after day. At least he is amusing and alive and he *cares* which is more than can be said for *you*! I'm sick of it, Bryn, sick of it. I'm going now to get the roses out of the bin and I shall find the loveliest vase I can and put them in it and stick it right here at the corner of the bar for all to see, and don't you ever dare put the receiver down on any call of mine ever again.'

Sylvia couldn't but admire Georgie's spirited defence of her lover. 'But she shouldn't say all that in front of everybody. Give Bryn his due he took her in the back when he wanted to protest.'

Jimmy disagreed. 'More fun though out in the open. What do they mean by the roses? He must have put some outside at the front. That Dicky! He's going to be in serious trouble he is.'

Willie said, 'He's daft he is, absolutely daft. Rector's not going to be pleased. It's no example for them boys, no example at all. He should behave right, he should. This is plain daft.'

At this point Georgie came back in carrying a huge cut glass vase filled with Dicky's red roses. Some were looking a bit worse for wear but most were still quite splendid. She placed the vase right where she said she would, where the counter curved round, no one could miss them.

Bryn who'd been swishing some glasses through the soapy water in the sink behind the counter watched her out of the corner of his eye. Dropping the pint tankard he was washing, which fell with a great sploosh back into the sink, he reached out and swept the vase clean off the counter. It smashed into a thousand pieces on the stone floor. Water and roses and shards of glass were everywhere. Georgie burst into angry tears and beat at Bryn with her fists, but he thrust her aside.

Two customers had to jump back to avoid the water and flying glass, two more walked out in disgust. Sylvia stood up and said, 'Get me a dustpan and brush, Georgie, I'll give you a hand.'

'You won't.' Bryn moved towards her as though daring her to interfere.

Sylvia held her hands, palms upwards in a conciliatory gesture. 'Very well, I won't.'

Willie moved to her side. 'Don't you dare threaten my wife.'

Belligerently Bryn replied, 'If you don't like what's going on then you can always leave.'

Willie drew himself up to his full height. 'I shall. This pub isn't what it was. I'm sick of witnessing your stupid quarrels, I swear they're turning the beer. We come in 'ere for a quiet drink with friends and what do we get? You smashing the place up, all because you aren't clever enough to hold on to your wife.'

Bryn moved towards him his face grim and his fists clenched, but Willie refused to be intimidated. 'Come on, Sylvia, we'll eat in Culworth, they tell me they do grand food at the Plaice by the River, I could just fancy a nice tasty piece of fish.' He took her arm and weaving their way between the tables they headed for the door. As he opened it for Sylvia to go through Willie turned and said, 'Before long you'll have no customers left and it'll serve you right. Coming with us, Jimmy?'

Jimmy got up from the table, 'Might as well, the drama seems to be over and my ale tastes rotten. They tell me the

Jug and Bottle in Penny Fawcett serves some good beer. If this goes on much longer I might start going there.' As he reached the door Jimmy put on his cap and shouted, 'Good day to you all.'

Chapter 14

While they were having lunch Willie had organised Jimmy to go up the tower and sweep the steps, check the light bulbs and generally give a tidy up in preparation for All Saints' Day. Since time immemorial parishioners, and anyone else who cared to pay for the privilege, could climb the church tower and spend time up there enjoying the view. When they came down there was tea and fatty cake to be had in the church hall. No one could remember when they had first begun serving cups of tea and still less could anyone remember when they'd begun serving fatty cake. Strangers furrowed their brows at the mention of fatty cake and the older inhabitants of Turnham Malpas nodded their heads knowingly but refused to divulge their secret recipes.

There were only certain people, with ancestors mentioned in the very oldest parish records, who by tradition made the fatty cakes for All Saints' Day. Lavender Gotobed who now lived in Little Derehams but whose family had resided in Turnham Malpas for centuries was one, Mrs Jones from the Store was another, Willie Biggs and Jimmy Glover, the Nightingales of Nightingale Farm,

Thelma and Valda Senior and in charge of organising the cakes was the current Lady at the Big House. So as there were no longer any Templetons at the Big House it was Muriel who had to ring around and check that the fatty cakes would be made and delivered in time on the day.

Willie always had the door at the bottom of the tower unlocked at ten o'clock on the morning of November the first. This was the sixteenth time he'd done it and as he settled himself on a chair by the door, wearing every conceivable item of clothing he could think of as protection against the cold, he wondered just how many people would come.

He'd said to Sylvia only that morning, 'These old customs is all right, but they're bound to lose their excitement. There's so many other things folk can do nowadays. Watch TV, go shopping in them shopping malls, driving here and there, going to the coast, computer games and these winter sun holidays they go on and that, stands to reason they'll start losing interest in a simple thing like climbing a tower for a good view.'

'You wait and see, it's tradition and they like tradition round here. Leave these four fatty cakes in the church hall for me will you? Two from you and two from Jimmy. See, I've used the very best raisins and butter, they should taste good. Your mother's recipe I reckon is the best.'

Willie perked up at that. 'Always loved making 'em she did. Never made 'em any other time. Every year she kept one back and we had it with our tea, but she never let on and we didn't either. Bad luck or some such I think she thought, but she couldn't resist. I'll be off then. When are you coming?'

'About eleven, got your tin for the money?'

'I have, I've always liked this picture of Queen Victoria

on the lid. Her Golden Jubilee tin it was. Been used every year since then for this very job.'

'You'll be late.'

'Give us a kiss.'

'Righteo, there you are.'

So he was sitting there waiting for customers. The first up the path was the Rector and the twins.

'Good morning, Rector.'

'Hello, Willie.'

'Mr Biggs, here's my money. Can we go up now?' Beth wearing her red wool hat which she'd had since the Christmas she was three and which she refused to be parted from, looked up at him with a lovely eager smile on her face.

'I reckon this is your first time.'

'It is. Mummy said we were too small before but now we're at school she says we can go.' Alex backed away and stared up at the top of the tower. 'It's a long way up.'

'It is. Yer'll need strong legs to get up there. Let's 'ave a feel at yer muscles.' Willie bent down and pretended to test Alex's leg muscles.

'And me, and me. I'm strong.' Beth offered her legs for testing too.

'Well, I reckon, Rector, with muscles like them they'll both make it.'

'So do I. They've been pestering to come since eight o'clock. Are we the first?'

'You are, sir. Mind how yer go.'

Willie's tin began filling up with the steady stream of twenty-pence pieces from the people eager to climb the tower. The weather was cold and there was an east wind which cut cruelly through the warmest coat. He couldn't imagine what it must be like up at the top.

Dicky Tutt came up the path. He stood talking to

Willie but his mind was obviously not on the conversation for he kept glancing down the church path as though expecting someone. Then he abandoned Willie altogether when Georgie came hurrying up. Willie watched as Dicky visibly restrained himself from greeting her with a kiss.

Dicky dropped his money in the tin. 'Here you are then, forty pence.'

Georgie greeted Willie with 'Good morning, cold job for you sitting there.'

'It is, but it's all in a good cause.'

'What's the money going to then this year?'

'Save The Children.'

'You should make it fifty pence not twenty.'

'Well, it's twenty, makes it too much when you've a family to take up. You'll need something warmer than that on when you go up. I'm told the wind blows something terrible up there on days like this.'

Dicky pulled a wool hat out of his pocket. 'Here you are, Georgie, wear this.'

They disappeared into the tower hand in hand. Willie couldn't believe the boldness of it. They don't care that's it, they don't care who sees 'em. It's not right.

In the past when it got really busy Willie had had to form a queue outside on the path and wait for some people to come down before letting any more climb up. There were several passing places up the spiral staircase so it didn't matter too much if people were going both up and down at the same time but the space at the top being so limited he had to make sure there weren't too many up there at once. Didn't want no one falling over the edge in the crush.

Flick, Finlay and Fergus came next and then to his horror, hard on their heels came Bryn Fields. Willie hadn't been in the Royal Oak since that lunch time when Bryn had shoved Dicky's roses off the bar counter. He really hadn't expected Bryn to come and, oh God, Dicky was up there. He'd have to think of something quick.

'Hello, Bryn, I'm afraid you'll have to wait a while, there's getting to be too many people up there.'

'One more won't make any difference, I'm going up.'

'I'm sorry, but I've got to be quite firm about this. There's already enough people up there, I've got to ask you to wait.'

'I'm not.' He fumbled in his trouser pocket and brought out a pound coin. 'Here, there's a pound and worth every penny.'

Bryn flung the coin in Willie's tin and sped off towards the bottom of the steps.

Willie got up off his chair and entered the tower door. 'Bryn, come back down.' But Bryn had disappeared round the turn of the spiral staircase and Willie had to climb the first few steps to make himself heard. 'Bryn, do as I say, come back down.' All he could see was the heels of Bryn's shoes disappearing rapidly round the next bend. There was no way Willie was going up there so whatever drama was about to unfold he wouldn't witness it.

At the top Georgie stood with her back against the wall getting her breath back. 'That's a climb and not half. You must be fit, Dicky!'

'I am! Come and look!' He leaned as far as he could over the edge, only one of his well polished brogues was on terra firma.

'Be careful! You'll be over.'

'I won't, nine lives, I've got.'

Georgie went to stand beside him. 'Just do me a favour and keep both your feet on the ground, you're giving me the heebie jeebies.'

He tucked her hand in the crook of his arm and they both looked over the village. Dicky was pointing places out to her and they were in a world of their own.

'Hello Mr Tutt! I've never been up here before. Isn't it good?'

'Hello there, Beth, where's your dad, you're not on your own are you?'

'No, of course not, he's round the other side with Alex, looking at the cars on the bypass with Daddy's binoculars. Hello, Mrs Fields. Where's Mr Fields?'

'Working.'

'I expect he'll come later when he's not busy. You can see a long way can't you? I wish I was tall enough to look over the top, I can only see through the holes. I can put my leg right through them, look.' She waved her foot out through a gap between the stone uprights. They're just the right size for me.'

Dicky smiled down at her. 'Well, you'll grow soon enough. I'm not lifting you up to see, that's a fact. I can only just see over the top myself.'

'If you were tall like my Daddy you'd be able to see everything. He can see everything wherever he goes.'

'I would, you're right. Here he is, look. Bit breezy up here isn't it?'

Peter agreed. 'It certainly is. For the sake of my nerves, Beth, bring your leg back in. In! Thank you. How are you Georgie? Long time no see.'

The biting wind battered Georgie and she pulled Dicky's wool hat closer about her ears. 'Busy. You know how it is. Open all day.' She turned her back to him, she really couldn't withstand Peter's all-seeing eyes today. Nor the disappointment she could recognise in them.

There was a hustle and a bustle at the top of the steps and bending low under the door lintel Bryn appeared, breathing heavily. He didn't speak because he couldn't, he'd climbed the stairs far too fast. His lack of speech only served to fuel his anger. Dicky hadn't noticed he'd arrived and was still looking out over the village. Georgie nudged him. He turned to look at her and smiled, a loving, possessive kind of smile. An unmistakable smile to some-one like Peter who knew all about loving and Peter's heart sank. He glanced at Bryn and realised he'd seen the look too. Bryn, uncontrollable fury in every line of his face, lurched forward and grabbed Dicky by his collar.

Gasping he snarled, 'I knew I'd find you up here. I just knew you two had planned to meet.'

'Bryn! Let go of him! Let go!' Georgie grabbed at Bryn's arm and tried to pull him away but he brushed her off.

Before anyone could say or do anything Bryn was heaving Dicky up by his collar and the seat of his trousers and was trying to lift him over the edge. Dicky was writhing, wriggling, struggling to escape but Bryn held him in a madman's grip.

'I warned you I'd do for you and I shall. You're not having her.' As he spoke he pursued his intention of heaving him over, but Dicky was hanging on to the stone balustrade and was proving far harder to heave over than Bryn had thought possible. Georgie, screaming and crying was trying to keep hold of Dicky, and Bryn was shouting, 'I'll do for you. So help me I will. Leave go, you bastard.' It all happened so quickly that it took Peter a moment to absorb what was really happening. He thrust the children behind him and stepped forward, stood behind Bryn and concentrated all his strength on gripping Bryn's arms and pinning him to his chest. There was a fierce struggle during which Peter could hear the children scream-ing and Willie shouting from the ground. 'What's goin' on up there?' Several people joined him in the fight

158

to prevent Bryn from finally tipping Dicky over the edge. Gradually Peter, with their help, began to win and Bryn started to release his hold on Dicky and all of a sudden Bryn's maniacal strength left him and he let go completely.

Dicky ashen and breathing fast straightened his clothes. Georgie stood watching the collapse of Bryn. Bryn who'd always been a tower of strength, hard working, tenacious, ambitious and here he was leaning against the balustrade, looking a broken man. All because of her.

Peter, flushed and breathing hard realised that the children were terrified by seeing their father fighting and that he had to reassure them when he hardly felt capable of doing so because he was so shocked at the thought of Dicky being killed.

He gasped, 'Hush, hush, Daddy's all right. We're all safe. Steady now, you're not to worry.' Peter breathed deeply for a few seconds and managed to pull himself together. All the people at the top had gathered on the side overlooking the village green aghast at the possibility of Dicky crashing to the ground. Dicky's face was putty-coloured and he was sweating, Georgie and the twins were crying, and Bryn stood by the balustrade his elbows resting on it and his hands covering his face in an attempt to disguise the fact that he was weeping.

Peter in his sternest voice said, 'Dear God man, you nearly killed him! What were you thinking of? Dicky, you and Georgie go down, get right out of the way. I'll come down with Bryn when he's composed himself.'

Mrs Jones offered to take the twins down with her. 'I'll go down the first and make sure they don't fall. We'll go for a piece of fatty cake shall we, perhaps your Daddy will join us when he's ready?'

Peter nodded his gratitude. Beth called out urgently,

'Don't fight Daddy will you, Mummy won't like you fighting. Please, don't fight Mr Fields again.'

'No, Beth, I shan't. I promise.'

Mrs Jones grabbed her hand and drew her towards the door. 'Don't you worry, I'll look after them. Come along, Alex. As for you, Dicky Tutt, you want your brains examining. This is all your fault!' She disappeared through the low door with the twins, and Peter heard Alex saying 'Isn't my Daddy brave?' They were followed by the people who'd witnessed the incident and who were quite glad to return to the ground. In any case it was a brilliant piece of news for the church hall. That'd make them sit up and stare and not half. Why they'd almost witnessed a murder! And all for twenty pence. If it hadn't been for the Rector they would have. Just think if he hadn't happened to be up there, would any of them have had the strength to stop Bryn? No, they wouldn't. He'd been like a man possessed. A maniac no less.

Grandmama was in charge of the teapot in the church hall. She'd already had her tea and fatty cake, even though she hadn't been up the tower. Climbing church towers, wasn't quite sensible for a lady of her mature years, and besides someone had to be there when the first ones came in for their tea, and putting on a martyred air she'd volunteered to make a personal sacrifice by presiding over the teapot.

The first rush of customers were the ones who'd witnessed Dicky's close encounter with death. Grandmama listened to the story feeling absolutely shocked at the incident and Mrs Jones said, 'We really ought to go tell Bel, she should know.'

Kate Pascoe from the school volunteered to go to the Store to tell Bel. A few minutes after she'd gone Dicky came in and sat on a chair, while Georgie went to ask for two cups of tea.

As Grandmama poured out the tea she whispered. 'Georgie, I'm so sorry to hear about what has happened. How is Dicky?'

'In shock. I'm hoping the tea will revive him a bit. I don't know how I got him down the stairs, his legs are so shaky. He's been terribly sick in the church yard, retching something awful.' Grandmama offered the sugar and the fatty cake. 'Yes, he'll have sugar. Two please. But no fatty cake it might set him off again.'

'My dear, whatever are you going to do?'

'I don't know. I just don't know.'

'Well, if you need a roof over your head I can always make up the spare bed.'

Georgie looked at her with gratitude. 'Thanks, I may need to take you up on that.' She carried the tea over to where Dicky was sitting and stood over him while he took a drink of the tea. He'd drunk half the tea when in walked Bel.

The chattering stopped. Everyone secretly glanced at Dicky and Georgie. She was standing beside him with her arm around his shoulders, too busy comforting him to notice Bel's arrival.

Bel, arms akimbo, went to stand in front of the two of them. 'Satisfied are you now? Done everything you can to completely upset the apple cart? Caused enough trouble have you? The pair of you need your heads cracking together. You most of all Dicky Tutt. You ought to be ashamed of yourself. All through you, Bryn could have been up for murder. Come to think of it though, it's a pity he didn't tip you over, it's only what you deserve.' She turned her attention to Georgie. 'As for you, madam, the sooner you get yourself straightened out the better for everyone. You've already got a man of your own, what do you want another one for? I would have thought one was enough to be going on with. That poor Bryn, you've driven him to the absolute edge.'

'To say nothing of Dicky . . .' someone said rather too loudly and those around them laughed.

Bel swung round on them. 'Funny is it? Find it amusing do you? Bit of gossip for the weekend is it? It's blinking serious. Too serious for you to make a joke of. We could have been sending for the undertaker for him' – she jerked her thumb in Dicky's direction – 'right this very minute.' She turned back to Dicky. 'As for you, you're coming home with me *now*, where I can keep my eye on you. On your feet.'

'Now, Bel . . .'

'Now, Bel, nothing. You're coming home and you, madam' – Bel stabbed at Georgie's shoulder with a sharp finger which made her stagger slightly – 'can get back to doing what you do best, chatting up the punters from behind the bar.' Bel was about to drag Dicky to his feet and take him out when the outside door sprang open and Peter and Bryn came in. It is frequently observed in Turnham Malpas that they might not get far but they do see life. Never was it more true than now. All four of the protagonists under one roof and them all there to witness it. A deathly hush fell.

Chapter 15

Dicky leapt to his feet, his face which had been close to recovering its natural healthy glow had gone drip white again at the sight of Bryn. He gave a slight hint of a whimper as Peter closed the door behind them and Bryn came right into the hall, and stopped within feet of where he stood.

Bryn was still very distressed. He appeared to be of two minds, he didn't know whether to have another go at eliminating Dicky or whether to weep again at the dreadful, fearful thing he'd attempted to do.

Peter spoke in a tense well-controlled voice. 'I should be glad Dicky and Bel if you would come to the rectory and we can have a try to sort this out. You too Georgie. This incident is extremely serious, and I am grievously distressed by it. Grievously distressed. It is so serious that if Dicky chose to he could press charges of attempted murder, which I should be honour bound to support. I sincerely hope we can avoid such an occurrence.'

'Why avoid it? Let's go for it. He's a mad man.' Dicky's voice held a hint of hysteria which aggravated Bryn. He clenched his fists again and moved threateningly towards

Dicky. Dicky picked up a chair and prodded the legs in the direction of Bryn.

Bel stepped towards him and wrestled the chair from him. 'Don't be stupid, there's enough trouble already. Come on, let's be off to the rectory.'

'I'm not going to the rectory, I'm having nothing to do with him. He's dangerous, he nearly killed me.'

'And whose fault is that?'

Peter went to open the door. 'Come along Bryn, and you too, Dicky, I insist.'

'I'm sorry, Rector, but no. There's no way I'm being closeted with that maniac in your house. Who's to say he won't try again.' Dicky shook his head. 'No way.'

Peter tried again. 'Bryn has given me his solemn word that he won't try anything again. Now for the last time, come with me to the rectory, I will guarantee your safety.' Raising his voice and coming close to losing his temper with them all he shouted, 'All of you, this minute. Well? I'm waiting.' He stood with the door open.

Bel said 'If you don't go of your own accord, Dicky, I shall boot you all the way there. So it's up to you, go on. *Go!*'

Dicky weighed up the consequences of refusing to go of his own accord and decided walking there was better than being kicked there by Bel. Slowly he headed for the door skirting Bryn with as much caution as he would a raving lion. Bel, Bryn and Georgie followed and Peter shut the door behind him. There was an air of anti-climax in the church hall when they'd left. To their extreme disappointment the anticipated fracas had not materialised.

Mrs Jones shook her head. 'Poor Bel, it's her I feel sorry for. Fancy having your husband running after someone else in broad daylight, it's bad enough if they keep it quiet.' Mrs Jones stood up and took hold of the twins' hands. 'I do, I feel really sorry for her, the poor thing. The embarrassment. The shame.'

'She's got no claim on Dicky. He's free to do as he likes. They're not married,' Grandmama blurted out.

'Not married! Are you sure?' Mrs Jones sat down again abruptly.

'No, they're not. I have it on good authority.'

A general hubbub broke out all over the hall at this bombshell.

'Not married! I don't believe it.'

'Neither do I. Be careful, we've been conned with one of the Duchess's tales before.'

'Who'd have thought it.'

'Well, I never.'

'Whatever next?'

'So he's a free agent then . . .'

'Where did you learn this?' Mrs Jones enquired of Grandmama.

'I have my sources. It was someone who's known him for years who told me. This tea's getting cold, I'll go make another pot.'

In bed that night Peter sighed and Caroline asked him what caused him to sigh so.

'I intended spending some time polishing my sermon for tomorrow, some chance of that. I have never met four such obstinate people.'

'But you did get them to listen to reason eventually.'

'Eventually, as you say. Bryn is so incensed and no wonder. When I finally got them to agree to give themselves a week to sit back and *think* where all this is leading I was exhausted. Georgie's wanting to leave Bryn. Bryn's wanting to leave the village and make a new start with Georgie, some idea he's got about running a bar on a cruise liner, I ask you! Dicky's determined that Georgie is the one for him and Bel is the only reasonable one and she's the least guilty of them all. So with the whole situation on hold for a week I hope, hope mark you, we shall reach a reasonable solution.'

'I'm just so glad Dicky isn't pressing charges.'

'Exactly! I told him that if he really wanted to wash his dirty linen in public and ruin the reputations of both Bel and Georgie, to say nothing of Bryn and his business and Dicky himself, then that was the right way to go about it and would be no solution to anything at all.'

'But it will mean two divorces if Dicky has his way won't it? That is just so painful.'

'Not two, only one.'

Caroline sat up and looked at Peter. He was laid with both his hands locked behind his head staring at the ceiling.

'Only one? What do you mean?'

Peter turned his head slightly and looked seriously at her. 'If I tell you, there's not to be one word outside this bedroom! OK?' Caroline nodded. 'No one but those four and you and I know, you see. Bel and Dicky aren't married.'

Caroline fell back on the pillow and laughed till she had tears rolling down her cheeks. 'Not married! Oh Peter! Oh Peter! What a mess! They told you this today?'

'Hush! Don't make so much noise you'll wake the children! Yes, they did, though somehow I got the feeling it wasn't the whole truth somehow, there was something they were all four holding back. However, please don't breathe a word because if they know they'll be queueing at the rectory door saying Dicky isn't fit to be Scout leader and I'm not having that. He's brilliant. There's no one can compare and I'm not having the Scout troop jeopardised by some narrow-minded bigots.'

Caroline wiped her eyes and, with a straight face bent over him and looked Peter straight in the eye and said 'I can remember a time when you were very upset about Willie and Sylvia living together before they got married. Oh yes, you had a lot to say about that, to me at any rate. You've certainly changed your tune.'

'It's a question of priorities. If no one knows, the village won't be any wiser and everything can carry on as before. He's started the Scout band as you know and Gilbert Johns has volunteered to help and I thought I might . . .'

'Peter! You've given them a week. A week of comparative peace, but what if at the end of it Dicky and Georgie decide not to get together? The idea of them all still living in the village is fraught with problems.'

'Well, we'll cross that bridge when, and if, we come to it.'

'Yes, you're right. The story of this particular All Saints' Day will last for years! They'll still be talking about it in a hundred years' time! Come to think of it they nearly got another saint added to their number on a very appropriate day! Oh dear! I've got to go to sleep. I've suddenly gone very tired. Good night, Peter.'

'Good night, my darling. I love you.'

'I love you.'

'God bless you.'

'And you.'

'Caroline, are you feeling better? About us?'

There was a silence which Peter waited for her to fill. She knew he would leave the question in the air if she didn't reply and she knew she wouldn't sleep if she didn't answer him. She searched about under the duvet for his hand and having found it, she took it to her lips and kissed

167

it. 'Thank you for being such a wonderfully understanding man. No, understanding *husband*. You've seemed to know instinctively how to go about making me feel whole, when I'm not and won't ever be. And I thank you for that from the bottom of my heart. Yes, I am feeling much better about us and when I've got the go ahead . . .'

'Which you sound confident of getting . . .'

'Which I am confident of getting, then I truly believe everything will be all right between us. When I first came home I'd gone off you terribly, it was quite horrifying, but I expect it was because I was feeling weak and very frightened or maybe that's how you feel when you've had my kind of an operation. I really could hardly bear you close to me which sounds a dreadful thing to say about someone one loves but it's true. But now I do believe I appreciate your maleness all over again.'

'Hallelujah!'

But 'Hallelujah!' wasn't the word Peter used on reading the letter which he found on the mat when he went downstairs on Monday morning.

'Damn and blast! Who the blazes has let the cat out of the bag?'

He read on . . . 'As a consequence of these events it has been brought to our notice . . . living with someone who is not his wife . . . even in these more relaxed times his position is untenable . . . and we the undersigned . . . are agreed that Dicky Tutt is no longer a suitable person to be in charge of the St Thomas à Becket Scouts . . .'

'Blast it!'

'Daddy! That was a very rude word.'

'Alex, you're quite right it was and I'm sorry.' He raced up the stairs. 'Caroline! Look at this.' He dropped the letter on her knee. 'Who's responsible for drafting this I wonder? They promised me they wouldn't say a word. Not a word. Now, apparently everyone knows.'

Caroline broke off from helping Beth to dress and scanned the letter. 'Oh dear! So they must. Here, Beth, put your tights on. No, the other way round, that's it. Just look at the signatures. Six! Six of them. How could they. Some haven't even got any connection with the Scouts. Look! Thelma Senior she wouldn't know a Scout if she met one in the street. Venetia, Vince Jones but not Mrs Jones. This is awful. It simply isn't fair to Dicky. How dreadful of them!'

Over breakfast Peter and Caroline discussed the matter further and Peter decided for a day or two at least he wouldn't reply. Pressure of work he called it. Caroline called it avoiding the issue. They were both laughing about her comment when Sylvia came in to start work.

Caroline poured her a cup of tea as she said 'Good morning, Sylvia.'

Alex jumped off his chair to show Sylvia his new shoes. 'Look, Sylvie. Look at my new shoes.'

'They're lovely, Alex. What a good choice! They will keep your feet warm. I like the colour. Morning everyone. You're looking better this morning, Doctor, in fact much better.'

'Thank you, I'm feeling better, much better. I expect you've heard the latest news?'

'About Dicky's close encounter? I have of course. There's no other subject of conversation.'

'Peter got a petition this morning, asking for Dicky Tutt to be removed from being Scout leader. Someone's found out that . . .'

Peter cleared his throat. 'I didn't think we . . .'

'Sylvia will know soon enough, someone's let it out that

Dicky and Bel are not . . .' – Caroline glanced at the children and continued by saying – 'are not living in wedlock.'

'Well, we all know who that was, don't we?'

Caroline raised an eyebrow. 'Do we?'

'I was in the church hall checking to see if they needed any help before I climbed the tower and I heard the Duchess tell everyone. Said someone who'd known Dicky for a long time had told her.'

'That blasted woman!'

'Peter! *Pas devant les enfants.*'

'Sorry.'

Alex said 'That's two times today, Daddy.'

'I beg your pardon. Could be four or even five before this day's out. This whole situation is developing into a major crisis when there's no need at all. If everyone had just kept still tongues in their heads it would have all blown over. However, it's Monday so it's Penny Fawcett first. Anything you want from their market Sylvia? Caroline?'

'Fresh vegetables, Rector, please, particularly potatoes.'

'Caroline?'

'Nothing thanks. I think I'll take the children to school this morning. The fresh air and a change of scene will do me good.'

'What a splendid idea. Yes, you do that. I'm off. Bye, children. Bye, darling.'

'Don't forget your cloak, it's cold.'

'OK'

After Caroline had left the children at school she didn't feel like returning home straight away so she wandered into the Store hoping for a chat with anyone who happened to come in. She'd been feeling really cut off since her mother had gone back, and felt it was time she took steps to widen her horizons.

Jimbo welcomed her with open arms. 'Come for a hug have you? It's lovely to see you out. Here, sit on this chair and I shall serve you with a coffee if I may. Just made it, so it's absolutely fresh.'

'Oh yes, please. That would be lovely. How's things?' Jimbo handed her a cup and offered her sugar. 'Thanks I will. Don't usually but Peter says I must get some weight on, so I will.'

'You need to.'

The coffee was too hot to drink so Caroline put it down on the shelf nearest to her and asked Jimbo again if he had any news.

Before he could answer her Linda came in. 'Oh, Doctor Harris, how lovely to see you out. I am pleased. Life getting back to normal is it?'

'Well, not quite but nearly.'

'My word, your two little ones must have had a nasty shock on Saturday. I'm glad I wasn't there. Are they all right?'

'Thankfully I don't think they realised what was happening. They were so worried about their father fighting, that was what impressed them the most! Alex gave me a very graphic description when he got home. He was rather proud of Peter and couldn't or wouldn't understand that he wasn't really fighting.'

'Thank God for the Rector is all I can say. What a blessing he was there. Then when the Duch— Mrs Charter-Plackett let on that they weren't married. You should have seen everyone's faces, they couldn't believe it. They were gobsmacked I can tell you . . .' Linda propped her hip against a shelf and looked set for the morning. 'Mrs Jones said . . .'

Jimbo ever mindful of his business interrupted. 'Excuse me, Linda, but you were ten minutes late to begin with and I see you've someone tapping their foot by your counter. Could you get started, please. The customer is king in our set-up.'

'Sorry, I must say.' She hastened off and then had to come back for the key to open the post office till. Jimbo took it out of his pocket and she almost snatched it from him. He raised his eyebrows at Caroline. 'Come in the back. Bring your coffee.' Jimbo called out to Linda, 'If I'm needed I'm in my office. Bel shouldn't be long.'

He settled Caroline on his chair and perched on the stool.

'Peter is not best pleased at what your mother said in the church hall on Saturday. It has proved to be true, I know, but Peter had been hoping it could be kept secret.'

'I know, I know. She told me a week or so ago that she had some news about Dicky but I wouldn't let her tell me. I said she musn't say a word to anyone at all, keep mum, et cetera. But I expect the temptation proved too much.'

'The other thing is, Jimbo, you'll soon know so it won't matter if I tell you first, Peter had a petition put through the letterbox this morning, stating that Dicky should be sacked from the Scouts. It was in your mother's hand-writing and her name was the first signature, I'm afraid.'

Jimbo groaned. 'Oh no! I don't believe this. After all I said to her. Obviously I didn't say enough. I wish to goodness she'd never come here. She's worse than a child. As soon as Bel comes I shall go pay her a visit. She really is the end. The absolute limit.'

'Who is?' Standing in the doorway was his mother. Dressed immaculately in black and white she was the epitome of the well-dressed older woman.

'Close that door.'

'I beg your pardon?'

'I said close that door.'

She did. 'Well? Who is?'

'You are, Mother. I asked you not to say a word about what the sewing–machine man told you. But what do you do? You blurt it out in front of half the village. As if that wasn't bad enough I hear you've signed a letter of protest about him. It simply will not do. What you do reflects on me. My position in this village is paramount to the success of my business. Are you determined to ruin it for me? Besides which it's most unkind of you, quite thoughtless, in fact, to be a party to that petition.'

'Don't speak to me in that tone of voice. I am your mother!'

'I do not need reminding.'

'In any case it was bound to come out in view of Saturday. Bound to. Sooner rather than later I say. And I meant what I said about him in that letter, my grandsons' moral rectitude is under threat and I won't tolerate it, even if you condone it.'

'I never said I condoned it, I said it was none of my business.'

'Fudging the issue, that's all that is. If you'd let me tell you at the time, you would know all the story. When I said Dicky was married the man in the shop said, "Dicky Tutt married! Not Dicky, he isn't the marrying kind. Likes to play the field does Dicky, he wouldn't let himself get trapped into marriage." So I said, "Well, he is married now." He said, "Well, I know for a fact he isn't." I said, "Well, he is." And he asked me her name and of course I said "Bel". His whole demeanour changed then, you could have thought I'd said a dirty word, he gave me a funny look, handed me my change and shut up like a clam. When I thanked him for saving my life with the spare part

173

for my beloved machine he turned his back on me and didn't even say goodbye. So it's not just that Dicky isn't married it seems to me there's something else as well!'

'Mother! You're at it again! I warned you you'd have me to reckon with and . . .'

Caroline could see that Jimbo was working himself up into a colossal temper, his normally pallid skin was flushed deep red and his hands were clenching and unclenching at a furious pace, so she interrupted him. 'Mrs Charter-Plackett, out of Christian charity I think it would be a good idea to let this suspicion go no further than these four walls. What on earth the significance is of the man behaving so oddly when you said his wife's name was Bel I really cannot guess, but for everyone's sakes, please don't repeat it.'

'As if I would. I must apologise for my son's bad temper, he got that from his father not from me.' Grandmama smiled at Caroline and in a completely different tone said, 'Now, my dear, I am glad to see you out and about. You are looking well.'

Linda called out, 'Mr Charter–Plackett! Can you come, they're queueing at the till and Bel's not here yet.'

'Right ho! I'll love you and leave you. Stay as long as you want, Caroline.' Jimbo pushed past his mother and left.

Caroline watched him go. 'I'm going too. It's the first time I've been out I don't want to overdo it.'

'Of course not. Any time you're fancying a little walk, call and see me, I keep my cottage very warm and cosy and we'll have a cup of tea and a chat.'

Caroline stood up. 'Thank you, I'll remember that. Take you up on it some time, perhaps.'

'You'll be most welcome.'

*

When Grandmama answered her door bell that afternoon, she hoped it might be Caroline but she found Peter standing there. The reproachful look in his eyes shamed her. Why did the man always expect the best and look so sad when he didn't find it? They were all of them only human.

'What a lovely surprise, Rector, do come in.'

She offered him the best and biggest chair and sat herself down on the sofa. Peter sat with his forearms resting on his knees and his hands locked together.

'Mrs Charter-Plackett. I've come to say how sorry I am that you told everyone about Dicky and Bel. The last time you started up a piece of gossip it was totally unfounded and would have been very damaging not to say heartbreaking to Caroline if she had heard it. This time what you said is true, but you didn't know for certain it was the truth when you said it, and how I wish you hadn't.' He looked so sadly at her that her heart began to thump. 'I really do wish you hadn't. What do you have to say to me about it?'

This was it. This was when he was going to bring the best out in her when she didn't want him to. She'd only spoken the truth. But, as he said, maybe it would have been best left unsaid. 'Well, I . . . I'm sorry to have disappointed you. I didn't think.'

'Exactly. You see there isn't a Scout troop in the whole of Great Britain with a more dedicated leader than Dicky. He's excellent with the boys, quite excellent. We have boys attending from all three of the villages and way beyond and they are very lucky to have him. And so too is the church lucky to have him. He started the troop from scratch and has built it up in no time at all and he has the most tremendous influence on those boys, a wonderful influence for good. You only have to look at Rhett

Wright to see how much good he can do. If you'd known the old Rhett you wouldn't believe the change in him and it's in part due to Dicky and his hard work. I will not, will not ask him to resign.'

'I see.'

'Do you though?'

Grandmama picked an invisible thread from her skirt to give herself a moment to think. 'You mean he stays for the greater good?'

'That's right.'

'But he's living in sin.'

Peter studied what she said. 'Indeed, yes I suppose he is. But what difference does that make to his work?'

'None. I suppose.'

'Obviously it would be better if he wasn't living with Bel and why they don't marry I don't know . . .'

'It's the deceit of it, wearing a ring when they aren't.'

'But it is *their* business not yours nor mine. So am I any nearer to persuading you to withdraw your signature? You see Mrs Charter-Plackett, you have such an influence in this village.' Grandmama smiled somewhat smugly. 'Oh they wouldn't admit it for the world, they wouldn't want you to get above yourself you see, but you have. It's partly through Jimbo, he's so well liked for he's such a generous kind-hearted man, and partly through yourself. Your style . . . and bearing and of course your intelligence. You're no fool. You could be such an influence for *good* you see if you let yourself.'

By the time Peter had finished this speech Grandmama was glowing with pleasure. The dear man. He'd got right to the heart of the matter. Right to the nub. 'I withdraw my signature. They'll all be disappointed but there you are. Common sense and the greater good has prevailed.'

'I can't thank you enough. That's wonderful, I knew you were too liberal-minded not to see my point of view. Now, can you do one more thing for me?'

'Whatever you ask.'

'Persuade the others to withdraw their signatures too?'

Alarmed, Grandmama said, 'Oh, I don't know about that. They were very adamant.'

'Could you invite them round for a strategy meeting? I'm sure it wouldn't be beyond your powers of persuasion to encourage them to agree with your point of view.'

'I could try. Yes, I could try. I'll do that. It'll be a hard nut to crack, but yes I will. I'll tell them they've got to for the boys' sakes. Don't you worry, Peter, you'll be able to tear up that letter by the end of the week. Leave it to me.'

'Thank you.'

'I'm sorry for Georgie though, you know, she is very distressed. She's so sickened by Bryn, and Dicky's brought such happiness and excitement to her life. It's all gone wrong between her and Bryn you see, and I can't think of anything more terrible than being in a marriage which has gone rotten to the core. I don't believe in divorce, you know for better or worse and all that, but I do feel very sorry for Georgie. A bad marriage must be hell. I beg your pardon, Rector, but it must be.'

Peter shook his head. 'I don't believe in divorce either, but I do begin to think that there must be times . . .'

'I can't believe the good Lord wants his children to be unhappy and if they've given it their best shot . . . Well. I've told her to grab happiness when she has the chance.' She stood up. 'Don't let me keep you, a young man like you doesn't want to listen to an old lady's ramblings. Off you go. I promise to do as you wish.'

Peter looked down at her with such a loving smile on his face and said, 'No, as *you* wish, surely?'

There was nothing else she could say but, 'Yes, that's right, as I wish.'

Chapter 16

The week's respite which Peter had got the four of them to agree to, wasn't working as far as Bryn was concerned. He hadn't had an inkling that Georgie was unhappy, not an inkling and out of the blue he had been presented with Dicky in courting mood and Georgie enjoying his attentions; to say he was stunned was an understatement.

He'd a sneaking feeling that maybe somewhere along the line he'd let her down but it was all too late to retrieve himself. She was sleeping in the other bedroom and providing his meals and working in the bar but there was no rapport between them. Barely even politeness, certainly not any conversation. Takings had slumped dramatically since Saturday, once the initial excitement was over, nobody wanted to drink in a pub where the landlord appeared to be capable of murder. Which he had been that day. Bryn could have thrown Dicky over, gone down carried him back up and thrown him over again for the sheer satisfaction of it. He'd been mad. Completely mad. He didn't know how much longer he could continue like this. What was the point of being tied to someone who wished they were with someone else and a thousand miles away from you?

He'd come to recognise his mistake in not nurturing his marriage, thereby causing it quietly, unobtrusively, to die. It was a long time since he'd given Georgie any real thought. Oh, he'd paid for her clothes, admired her hair, enjoyed her bubbly personality, appreciated her hard work and her willingness but not thought about love. That was it. Love. Somehow he'd left that out of the equation and here he was with a wife being courted by an upstart of a dandy of a man, who'd captured her heart.

Perhaps if they moved away like he'd suggested. Bought another pub, or even heavens above, got that job running a bar on a cruise liner that he'd seen advertised in the trade paper last week. It was a cruise line which worked on the basis of cheap and cheerful and pack 'em in, but it would be a start. That might excite her. Not only might, it would. He seized on the idea like a drowning man a life raft. Yes, that just might . . . Bryn heard her coming down the stairs. He didn't greet her because he didn't know what to say any more. When he heard the thud of something heavy being put down on the stone floor of the passage he turned to see.

Georgie was dressed for going out. Beside her was a large suitcase.

'It's no good, is it? I'm . . .'

'You're not leaving? What about the bar?'

Georgie's face crumpled. ' "What about the bar," he says. That just about sums it up. You'll jolly well have to find someone else won't you? There's always Alan and that girl from Penny Fawcett who keeps pestering for a job. Alan will do more hours, he needs the money.'

'That's not fair, we're in this together you know, we both took it on, you're abandoning me.'

'That's true we did take it on together, but it's your name over the door and I'm afraid you'll have to get on with it.' She pulled on her gloves and bent to pick up the case. 'I'm abandoning you only after you've abandoned me.'

'Don't, please, don't go Georgie. Nothing's changed I still feel . . .'

'You're scoring well today Bryn. That's the second bull's eye in less than five minutes. "Nothing's changed", how right you are.'

'I don't know what you're talking about, it's all riddles to me.'

'Exactly. You're so turned in on yourself you can't see beyond the end of your nose. I shall be at Mrs Charter-Plackett's for the time being if you need me, not that there's anything to say between us.'

'Mrs Charter–Plackett's? Not Dicky's?'

'No, not Dicky's. There's enough gossip without me doing that, and there is Bel to consider. I'm having a respite, to sort myself out.'

'But Mrs Charter–Plackett! That old bat. Why her?'

'She's a kindred spirit.'

'What's that mean?'

'Somehow she understands what it means to be miserable, when you're married.'

'Is that how you think of it? Miserable?'

Georgie looked sadly up at him. 'I'm afraid I do and for some time now. I'll be off then.'

Bryn watched her go. Habit made him offer to carry her case for her, but she shook her head and left by the back door. He stared at the door after she'd closed it. The sound of it shutting struck him right to the heart. That was it then. Marriage, Georgie, the pub. Ashes. All ashes. He might as well not have lived the last twenty-two years. It had all been for nothing. There was a banging at the back door. Three bangs. That was the brewery delivery. He picked up his keys and went to open up the cellar.

Georgie might have escaped, but he still had ordinary everyday life to face. Still had to keep going with the nitty-gritty of a daily grind he was beginning to loathe. Bryn felt weighed down with cares. He looked down at his feet surprised to find there was no ball and chain fastened to them. How could there not be when it was so difficult to walk?

'This bedroom's lovely, Mrs Charter-Plackett. Lovely! So warm and . . . well lovely!'

'I'm glad you like it. These turquoise shades give such warmth to a room don't they? Elegant but welcoming I always think. There's plenty of space in the wardrobe, look.' She opened the mahogany doors and displayed the empty coathangers. 'Fill it up, there's plenty of drawer space too, if you need it. Settle yourself in and I'll make a coffee shortly and we'll sit by the fire and talk.'

Georgie thanked her. 'It's most kind. I shan't stay long. Just till I get my head sorted.'

'Of course, I'm giving you a breathing space. I think it would be nice if you called me Katherine. It seems silly in this day and age to be calling me Mrs Charter-Plackett when we're living in the same house. Come down when you're ready.'

They sat by the log fire, a speciality of Grandmama's. She had trained Greenwood Stubbs, the estate gardener, to keep her well supplied. Mr Fitch had said he didn't mind and she paid him for them so it was all fair and square.

Georgie found the fire comforting. Like the two of

them had said before, you can dream dreams in front of a fire. What were her dreams?

'So what are your dreams?' Georgie jumped at the question, surely she wasn't a mind-reader? It took her a moment to find an answer.

'In the best of all possible worlds what I'd really truly like is to be in a nice house with Dicky, each with our own careers and coming home in the evenings to spend time together and . . .'

'That sounds very ordinary. Very unadventurous.'

'What would you have us do?'

'I had thought of a new life together in Australia or New Zealand or Canada or somewhere. The colonies, of course, not the USA, far too brash for permanent living.'

Georgie laughed. 'Me? In Australia?'

'Why not. You and Dicky would make a wonderful pair for managing a bar. You with your knowledge, Dicky with his jokes and his outgoing personality. Excellent!'

'I've had enough of the licensed trade to last me a lifetime. Thank you very much.'

'Ah! but is it the combination of Bryn and the licensed trade you hate, or is it just the licensed trade. You've got to distinguish between the two.'

'Ah! Right.' She gazed into the fire and said 'I hadn't thought someone like you would be so understanding. You don't appear to be an understanding person at all.'

Grandmama shuffled a little uncomfortably in her chair. 'Well, I do have my good moments. I've made a few mistakes since I came here, but I am trying hard. For instance tonight I've got a meeting of the people who put their signatures to that letter I wrote about Dicky.'

Georgie stared at her. 'You wrote that letter then?'

'I'm afraid so. The Rector made me see the error of my ways and I'm having a try at changing their minds. So I'm afraid tonight you'll have to stay in the bedroom or go out. It wouldn't do for you to be seen to be here.'

'Thank goodness for that! You will do your best? Dicky wouldn't be Dicky without his Scouts. They are his life's work. Whatever I do I mustn't part him from that.'

'No, indeed, I think you're right. Perhaps Australia wouldn't be such a good idea. How's Bryn?'

'Shattered.'

'I see.'

'Do you know what his first words were when he realised I was leaving?' Grandmama shook her head. 'He said "What about the bar." If ever I needed confirmation that was it. "What about the bar." I couldn't believe it.'

'Oh dear! What about Bel?'

'Dear Bel. She's been so nice about it all. So understanding. She's the one I feel guilty about, more than Bryn. Bel's not at all upset about Dicky being in love with me, she's very philosophical about it. What will be will be she says. I might go across there tonight and have a talk, though we've promised Peter we wouldn't see each other, so perhaps I'd better not.'

'Don't rush into decisions. You know how impulsive Dicky can be.'

Georgie grinned. 'I certainly do. He's the loveliest man, you know. He sees the world through child's eyes, yet when he's with the boys he kind of grows in stature, literally. One click of his fingers and they're all lined up, no nonsense. There's such *strength* there as well as all the joking and laughter. I do love him. He's such fun. The light of my life you could say.'

'He sounds lovely.'

'Oh, he is!'

'You're very lucky.'

'It doesn't feel like luck at the moment. Bryn's guilty of

attempted murder, and Dicky and I drove him to it. It was only the Rector's being so persuasive that prevented Dicky from pressing charges, after all, who could blame him? He'd had a terrible fright, the poor love. Perhaps I'll stay in the bedroom while you have the meeting, maybe I should leave Bel and Dicky to talk things out on their own.'

Dicky came in from work desolate. He'd promised Peter a whole week of thinking things over and only two days of it had gone by, and he longed to see Georgie and what was worse he was no nearer a solution.

'Bel! It's me.' He could smell his dinner cooking, pork, he thought and stuffing. The kitchen was its usual haphazard self just like it always was when Bel was cooking. She had the most casual approach to the subject anyone could have, but it always turned out well. She worked on a bit of this and a bit of that basis and wouldn't have been able to find the scales if she looked for them for a week. The kitchen was tiny and it was best to keep out when she was in there. He squeezed himself round the door and got them both a lager from the fridge. 'I won't pour yours just yet.'

'Right. Five minutes.'

'Right.' Dicky seated himself in an easy chair and looked round the room. Bel had made this such a comfortable home. They hadn't the money for all the frills but she'd done a marvellous job with what they'd had available. It had been a bare barren tip when she'd come and somehow out of nothing a home had materialised. Whatever happened, he wasn't abandoning the Scouts, because the Scouts was where he made a real contribution. It was where he counted. It was where no-good loser Dicky Tutt could stand tall. He couldn't count the boys he'd helped over the years, this was the second troop he'd started and it was the best.

His job? Well, he did it, he did it to the best of his ability but it was a useless, waste-of-time, cog-in-a-machine, kind of job. No future, no way. But the Scouts, he gave them and they gave him such energy, that was when he came alive. Now he'd got the band going! He had a vision of them entering competitions, not just entering but winning. He raised a clenched fist and punched the air.

Bel came in and saw him. 'Daydreaming again?'

Dicky grinned. 'I suppose so. You know me, Bel! Always moving on to the next thing, I can't stand still.'

'You're right there, you can't.' Bel put the hot plates down on the table. 'Get stuck in.'

'Can't resist. It looks wonderful, Bel, I don't know how you do it.'

'Hard graft?'

'Yes, of course. You do work hard. I've always admired you for that.' Dicky put his knife and fork back down again. 'It's no good, I've no appetite. Whatever am I going to do?'

'You're going to eat your dinner and get washed and changed and go to Scouts. It's Scout night and that's what you're doing.'

'OK! OK! Why are you always so practical? Can't we just talk for once?'

'When I've eaten my dinner, we'll talk for half an hour and then you've got to go.'

She silently carried on eating her dinner without so much as even a glance in his direction. She ate her tinned fruit and ice-cream, finished her lager and sat back. 'First and foremost I want you to be happy . . .'

Dicky shook his head. 'There's you to consider, can't leave you out of it.'

'If you being happy makes me happy then we're all right, aren't we? You won't be happy without those boys. They're your life's work, not some piddling office job in a factory, though you can't manage without the money it's still not what you really want to do. So you've got to stick at that and you've got to stick at Scouts. Question is do you want Georgie so much that you're willing to give it all up?'

'I want the lot. You, Georgie, the job and the Scouts. Greedy aren't I?'

'No, you're a man, it's to be expected.'

'Bel!'

'With my two jobs I could just about manage, so don't worry about me. You do your own thing.'

'But where would you live?'

'Haven't worked that out yet. But what about Georgie? How could she live here, with Bryn just down the road. It wouldn't be easy.'

Dicky finished his drink put down the glass and heaved a great sigh. He got up went round the table and put his arm round Bel. 'Where would I be without you?'

Bel pushed him off. 'Don't go all sentimental it doesn't suit you, Dicky. You've fallen in love with a married woman and she can't live here and you can't leave easily because we've a mortgage as long as your arm for this place, and I don't want to lose you, and you don't want to lose me and altogether you've made a damned mess of things, and all you're doing is wanting me to solve it for you. Well, I can't. Frankly I wish at the bottom of me that we'd told the truth about not being husband and wife when we first came here. Don't you?'

'With hindsight, yes I do. But we both felt so vulnerable it seemed the safest thing to say nothing at all at the time.'

187

'They'd have got used to us, we know that now but we didn't then.'

'That's right. Not at the time. So we've made the mess and I don't know how to get us out of it.'

'Neither do I!' She burst into tears, jumped up and struggled up the spiral staircase to the bedroom, leaving Dicky bewildered. He couldn't remember the last time he'd seen Bel cry. She must hurt very badly indeed. All this trying to be reasonable. It was her kind heart that was making her try to see it from his point of view. She didn't want to stand in his way because she loved him so much. But she didn't want it to happen; didn't want to lose him.

So much for a week to think things over. He was getting nowhere. Every word Bel had said was true. While he cleared the dishes into the kitchen he thought about it. The easiest thing to do would be to give up Georgie, the pain this idea caused made him almost double up with anguish. He couldn't! He couldn't! Not Georgie! Not to see her again. Ever again. No, that wasn't the way. He checked the time on the kitchen clock, the duck was almost at seven o'clock. When it reached half past it would be in the pond. He'd bought that ridiculous clock for Bel years ago and she'd never been parted from it. His mouth trembled. Dear Bel! Dear Bel! How he loved her, how he relied on her. And here she was giving up everything so he could be happy. He didn't deserve her.

Dicky went upstairs to get washed and changed. As he got to the top his spirits began to lift. In his mind he started running over all the things he had planned for tonight for the boys. When he got back he'd ring Georgie, just to say good night. Saying good night wouldn't be breaking his promise, would it? Peter had said don't see each other, well, he wouldn't be, would he? A whole week without being with her, his spirits dipped again. Nothing would be solved and he'd go circling round, pulled this way and that for the rest of his life. One thing he did know he'd regret it for ever if he didn't get Georgie. Those two days they'd spent away together had been the happiest he could remember in all his life. Being with her had added such zip and excitement; every step they took, every stair they climbed, every view they admired had that extra zest.

He examined his face in the bathroom mirror. Somehow it didn't seem the kind of face that should be able to be in love, or indeed still less inspire it in anyone else. As he shaved he remembered her fingers trailing through his hair, her lips kissing his, her hands caressing his body. The ecstasy his memories brought him caused him to shudder. He'd done it before with others, but never with such joy, such abandonment and such honest *truth*. Love! You thought about it, imagined it, had even convinced yourself in the past that you were in love, but when you were, really truly in love, then there was no mistaking it. Briefly he wished it would be Georgie in there in the bedroom when he went to get his uniform out of the wardrobe. Then the sense of disloyalty to Bel this brought about made him feel guilty.

When he got in the bedroom, Bel had gone. He listened and could hear her running the kitchen taps. Dear Bel. How could he manage without her?

That afternoon Peter had called to see Muriel and Ralph about a reading they were doing for him in church the following Sunday.

'Do come in, Peter. Tea?'

'No thanks, I've drunk enough tea today to float a battleship. Everywhere I go they all seem to think I'm in need of restoration, but I think it's much more likely they're after an eye witness report of Saturday's events!'

Ralph chuckled. 'Well, you must confess you were the hero of the hour. It was absolutely shocking and the ripples haven't stopped yet, have they?'

Muriel joined them just as Ralph finished speaking. 'It's about the reading is it, Peter?'

'That's right.'

Ralph said, 'Dicky and Bel not being married was a complete surprise to you too, was it?'

'Oh yes, it was.'

'Muriel and I were asked to sign the petition, they thought it would carry more weight, but we declined.'

'I'm glad.'

'Though they do have a point.'

Muriel said, 'I don't think it matters, we can't afford to lose him.'

Ralph, surprised by her emphatic support of Dicky, said, 'I thought you agreed with me?'

Muriel looked embarrassed. 'Well, I kind of do, but he does love her very much.'

'Does he?'

Muriel fidgeted with her beads, crossed her knees, looked anywhere but at either of them and then said, 'He told me.'

Ralph astonished at her duplicity said, 'You spoke to him after I'd said you should keep right out of it? When?'

'A while ago.'

'I see.'

'It's very hard, Ralph, when you love like he does and after all he's not entirely wrong in doing so is he, him not being married?'

'No, I suppose not, but when you talked to him you

didn't know that did you?' She didn't answer him. 'Did you?'

Muriel looked to Peter for support. 'I . . . I . . . perhaps I should have said.'

Peter asked her what it was she should have said.

'That I guessed they weren't married. Dicky told me in a kind of a roundabout way, when I spoke to him. Perhaps I should have told you.'

Ralph was appalled. 'So you've known for weeks and never said a word.'

She'd been looking at the floor during her revelation, but now Muriel brought her eyes up to look straight at Ralph. 'Yes. I have.'

'But, Muriel, what about his loyalty to Bel? He can't just throw that away without a backward glance, now can he?'

Muriel shook her head.

Peter said, 'Everyone's making a lot too much fuss about all this. It would have been better if it hadn't come out, no one would have been any the wiser and the village would have carried on without a thought of asking Dicky to resign. As it is, Mrs Charter-Plackett spilled the beans, and it's all too late. Don't worry, Muriel, at least you have the virtue of having kept it to yourself. Now about the Bible reading.' He got the paper out of his briefcase and pressed on with his explanation of how he wanted things done on Sunday.

After he left, Muriel said, 'I need to finish the ironing,' and stood up to leave.

'Muriel!'

'Yes!'

'My dear, I'm not angry, just surprised. I thought we had no secrets.'

'We haven't, not really. But you'd said we should keep

out of it and the chance came up and I feel for people who are in love. Before I met you again, I would have been shocked, truly shocked at all this, but I can understand now, and it is hard when you love and you mayn't and you want to and you can't help it and you can't keep quiet about it and you want all the world to know when you know it shouldn't.' Her voice trailed off rather lamely and she finished by saying, 'If you know what I mean.'

'I do know what you mean, and I love your dear kind heart and I'm proud you see the world in such a kindly manner, and I can understand how you understand how Dicky feels. I'm honoured that having met me and loved me, you understand the passions involved. You're a very understanding loving person and I love you all the more for it. Dear me, that's almost as confused as what you have just said but we both know what each other means don't we?'

'Oh yes! I thought you would have been annoyed if I'd told you I'd spoken to him so I . . .'

Ralph stood up and put his arms round Muriel. 'No more! have done! Now we both know we love people to be in love like we are, and have the happiness we share.'

'The trouble is I don't know how the four of them can possibly solve it. Something or someone will have to be sacrificed.'

'Only they can solve it my dear, we're lucky. Not everyone finds the path to love as easily as we did.'

'Oh yes, Ralph! What a good day it was when you came back and found me.'

He kissed her and then said, 'We came very close to drifting apart, my dear, remember, you refused me first of all.'

'Don't remind me.' Muriel sighed. 'I must have been mad. That's what I mean, about knowing about love, I didn't then, but now I do. I do sincerely hope that they find a solution to all this, though what it will be I can't really think. It alters your vision of things doesn't it? Love?'

Chapter 17

Grandmama had rung all the people who'd signed her petition and finally convinced them that they needed to attend a meeting at her cottage to discuss strategy, that very night. They'd never actually assembled all together before, because when she'd sought support for her petition she'd simply called at their houses and they'd willingly signed as a result of her persuasive tongue. Now she had to get them to make a volte-face.

She was surprised to find Sheila Bissett one of the first on her doorstep.

'Come in, Sheila, do. So lovely of you to make the effort and struggle round. How many weeks now before the plaster's off?'

'Two weeks, with any luck. Shall I be glad! Just to be able to take a bath will be a luxury.'

Mentally Grandmama wrinkled her nose at the prospect of Sheila not taking a bath.

'What is it you want us for? I thought we'd done our bit?'

'I'll tell you when they've all arrived. Now, where is it best to put you?'

'I'll sit here with this little footstool for my leg. Can you take my crutches?'

'Of course. Sit down. I'll make coffee in a moment, when the others come.'

'Georgie's not here then?'

'Georgie? Why should she be?'

'I saw her in your garden. I spend a lot of time looking out of the window you see. Nothing much else I can do at the moment.'

Grandmama swallowed hard. 'Well, yes, she is, just for a little while. She needed somewhere to hide.'

'And she *chose* to hide here with *you*?'

Overtones of their previous battle could be heard in Sheila's voice but Grandmama was saved from answering because the doorbell rang and Thelma and Valda were in the sitting-room almost before Grandmama had invited them in.

As they seated themselves, Vince Jones arrived and Venetia and so the little cottage sitting-room was filled to bursting point.

Grandmama rapped with the poker on the brass fender. 'Excuse me. Thank you! I think we'll discuss the business of the meeting first and then I'll serve coffee.'

The ensuing conversation took all of Grandmama's diplomatic skills, and then some to resolve anything at all. Her complete change of heart took them all totally by surprise. She finally had to talk to them about their Christian duty, a course of action which made her uneasy, because she wasn't sure it was or maybe it was, after all Peter wanted her to do it and he couldn't be more Christian if he tried.

At last she'd persuaded Vince Jones and the Senior sisters, leaving Sheila Bissett who was being awkward on purpose and Venetia Mayer who saw it as her mission in life to protect the young since she'd become assistant youth club leader and attended every morning service without fail after her fright over the witchcraft incident.

Venetia fluffed her thick jet black hair, crossed and recrossed her slender legs much to Vince Jones' delight and uttered the one question she, Grandmama, couldn't answer. 'But Mrs Charter-Plackett, it is only days since you gave us a very convincing argument for signing the petition, who or what has changed your mind? I haven't changed mine, so why have you? You haven't yet *really* told me why I should.'

'Charity. Christian charity. Plain, simple back-to-basics, Christian charity. We're changing our minds for the greater good. Yes, definitely the greater good. Dicky is the best Scout leader any troup could hope to have. There can't be a troup in the whole county with so many boys and such a long waiting list. You try getting a boy in at the moment. The question is if he goes can we find someone to replace him? Any volunteers?' She looked round them, challenging them to offer their services.

Sheila wouldn't surrender. 'Well, I disagree. What is the good of having a Scout leader who doesn't conduct himself as he should. Things are so lax nowadays, standards should be upheld and I'd be amazed if the Rector wants to keep him anyway. I'm sure he must have fallen on our letter with a sigh of relief.'

Too quickly Grandmama said, 'He didn't.'

Quick as a flash Sheila saw the situation. 'Oh I see, it's the Rector who's behind all this, isn't it? He's made you see the error of your ways, hasn't he?'

'I did agree with his point of view.'

Sheila sighed. 'I know just what you mean. I swear he could make me say black was white if he'd a mind.' Not to be too easily persuaded however she said, 'I wish you'd been more honest from the beginning of this meeting, wish you'd admitted it was him behind your change of heart.'

Grandmama's lips pressed into a straight line, what an aggravating woman this Sheila really was, seeing everything so clearly just at the wrong moment. 'Right. Well, it's all out in the open then. Seeing as the Rector wants us to withdraw the letter then we must. We've no alternative.'

Sheila, musing on the times when Peter had persuaded her to do things she'd never intended, decided to give in because she knew faced with Peter himself she'd have given in immediately. 'Very well then. So be it. But you must understand it's only because the Rector wants it that I'm giving in, not because of you. I withdraw my signature as from now.' Mischievously aware she was scoring a point off Grandmama, Sheila said, 'Those in agreement with me raise a hand.'

She looked round the group and they signified their capitulation so the meeting was taken clean out of Grandmama's hands.

Well satisfied, Sheila cried. 'Carried! Now for the coffee. Sorry I can't help. My leg, you know.'

So the following morning Grandmama called at the rectory to tell Peter he could tear up the letter. Caroline answered the door. 'Do come in Mrs Charter-Plackett, how nice to see you. Is it Peter you're wanting? He's not in I'm afraid.'

'Well, yes, but I'm sure you could pass the message on for me.'

Caroline smiled, 'Well, I'll try!'

'Tell the Rector that I've managed to get every one of the signatories to withdraw and he can tear up the letter. It took some doing let me tell you, but we made it in the end.'

'Come in and sit down, I'm feeling quite lonely, Sylvia's gone home to supervise the washing-machine repair man, Peter's out, the children are at school and well, I'd enjoy having someone to talk to.'

Grandmama accepted. Caroline took her into the sitting-room and invited Grandmama to sit on the sofa while she took one of the chairs.

'It was Sheila Bissett, we don't see eye to eye after what happened you see, you know about the Harvest meeting. The others were easy to persuade, except for Venetia she proved more difficult. She's changed hasn't she, such a lot.'

'Yes, she has. Peter will be glad. He's so concerned about the four of them.'

'Aren't we all. Georgie . . .'

'Someone said she was staying with you.'

'She is. I feel so sorry for her trapped in a bad marriage. I know we make these promises for better or for worse and you mean them at the time but heavens above there is a limit to suffering. You're looking a little better than you have.'

'Mostly, yes, thank you, this blessed chemotherapy is crippling me though I'm afraid. Absolutely knocking me for six. I'm having some really dreadful times, so bad I sometimes really wonder if it's worth it. Far worse than the operation. You know about it then?'

'Yes, I had breast cancer some years ago, I was terrified. It leaves you with a dreadful frightened feeling right inside, doesn't it? As if nothing can be permanent any more and you think it could all so easily slip away. But stick it out, in the end it will all be to the good.' Grandmama noticed that Caroline was looking puzzled.

She leaned over and patted her knee. 'I know people think of me as an old trout but I have got my understanding side too you know. Cancer can't be shrugged off like appendicitis or something, it stays hanging around in your mind making you anxious and cautious about everything you do, even when they've given you the all clear. The thing is to get on with life, put it behind you and be positive, it's the only way.'

'I've to go back in December, and hopefully then they'll give me something positive to be going on with. Fingers crossed . . .'

'If I'm any judge you're getting a healthier glow about you, I think you're going to be OK.'

'Thank you. It's been a terrible shock for us. So, how is Georgie?'

'Middling. She can't bear to be idle with having been so busy all these years, in fact one night she nearly went to give Bryn a hand she was so restless, feels guilty you see.'

'Naturally, it's been her life for so long. Are they any nearer a solution?'

Grandmama shook her head. 'No. Give him his due, Dicky has kept away. I wouldn't have him in the house in any case, that wouldn't be keeping his word, would it? I'm in enough trouble from Jimbo over having Georgie staying. But someone had to give her refuge and it couldn't have been you could it?'

''Fraid not. That would definitely have been taking sides.'

Grandmama got up to go. 'I won't tire you. You need your rest and you won't get any when those two little ones get home.'

'You're right about that. But I love them dearly.'

'Of course. They're absolutely delightful. You're very lucky.'

Caroline looked very directly into Grandmama's eyes. 'Yes, we are.'

It was Grandmama who lowered her eyes the first. Did Caroline know about the rumour she'd spread? She hoped not. 'Bye-bye, then my dear, take care. I'll see myself out, don't get up. Don't forget to give Peter the message will you?'

She shut the rectory door behind her and went to the Store to collect her fresh rolls for the freezer. The bakery had usually delivered by this time and if the van hadn't come she'd sit in the Store on the customer's chair and talk to Harriet or Jimbo till it came.

'Not here yet, Mother. I've rung, they say it's a new man who doesn't know the area so he's on his way but they don't know when he'll arrive. Last heard of the other side of the bypass delivering to the petrol station there, so he shouldn't be too long.'

'I'll sit here and have a coffee if I may. Oh, there you are Bel. Now how are things with you?'

Bel put down the gadget she used for pricing stock and smiled cautiously. 'Fine thanks. Just fine.'

'I'm sorry about all this business.'

'So am I.'

'Yes, of course. And Dicky?'

'Stiff upper lip, you know.'

'Of course.'

'And Georgie, how's she?'

Grandmama, feeling discomfited by Bel's directness, said, 'Like you said, stiff upper lip.'

'I'll get on then.'

'Yes, of course.' Jimbo had forgotten the sugar and Grandmama got up to get it for herself as Jimbo had disappeared into the back. Sometimes it was useful to sit in the Store watching the customers and keeping an eye on

Linda and the other staff. You learned a lot from keeping quiet and just watching and listening.

Through the window she saw the delivery van pull up. The driver leapt out, opened up the van doors at the rear and lifted out a large bright green baker's tray. A customer opened the door for him and he came in looking very apologetic.

'Bel! The bakery man's here!' Grandmama called out. Bel came from where she'd been pricing tins of soup as she filled the shelves and cleared a place for the baker's man to put the tray down.

'Sorry I'm late, better late than never though, I'll get quicker once I know the route . . .' His voice trailed away and he stared at Bel in amazement. 'Why! It's Bel Tutt isn't it? I'd know you anywhere. Well, would you believe it! Well, I never. I didn't know you'd moved here. What a lovely surprise.'

Bel looked stunned. She put down the order book and blushed bright red. She dabbed her top lip with her handkerchief and said, 'Why, it's you, Trevor. Long time no see. How are you?'

'Very well indeed, now I've got this job. Been out of work nearly six months, glad to have anything that's going. And how's that brother of yours, tricky Dicky? Eh? My we used to have some fun with Dicky in the Prince Albert, I'll tell them all I've seen you. Bye, Bel, see yer tomorrow. Bit earlier I hope. I'll get better at it. We'll have a chat when I'm not in such a rush.'

Bel watched him leave then her eyes were drawn to Grandmama's who'd rapidly risen to her feet. 'When he said "that brother of yours, tricky Dicky" you didn't correct him.'

Jimbo dashed in from the back. 'Oh great! The bread's come. And not before time. I'll put it out for you, Bel.'

Jimbo busied himself emptying the tray blissfully unaware of the tension under his very nose.

'Well. I'm waiting.'

Jimbo misinterpreted what she meant. 'Well, come on then, Mother dear, help yourself. Here's a couple of bags.'

His mother ignored him. 'Well?'

Bel's face had gone from bright red to deathly white. She dabbed her top lip again and babbled an answer Grandmama couldn't hear.

'Speak up! Jimbo, are you listening then I can't be accused of rumour-mongering again.'

Bel looked at Jimbo. 'I can't explain here, not in the Store.'

Jimbo looked up from the baker's tray and asked, 'Explain what?'

'I'm still waiting for your explanation. Why are. you masquerading as Dicky's wife when that man claims you are Dicky's sister.'

Bel burst out in desperate tones, 'It's none of your business. None of your business. It's private.'

'No, it's not, not any more. He's just shouted it out all over the whole shop. My son has a right to know.'

'Now look here, Mother . . .'

'No, I won't look here. There's something going on here we should all know about. I want the truth.'

'Well, you're not going to get it, you interfering old busybody. You've caused more harm in this village in the time you've been here than all the rest of us put together.' Bel fled into the back and returned in a moment with her coat and keys. 'School. Sorry.'

As the door slammed shut Grandmama said, 'I told you there was something very funny going on when the sewing-machine man was so odd when I mentioned her

202

name. I knew it. I should have persisted then, but you warned me off.' She paced rapidly about the Store. 'So I was right.'

'Mother, for heaven's sake, you're at it again. How many more times. The man's mistaken.'

'She didn't deny it did she? Oh no! Put my rolls on one side. I'll be back shortly.'

She stepped smartly from the Store and headed for the rectory. As she turned into Church Lane she glanced to check the road for traffic and caught sight of Glebe Cottages, and the thought hit her like a sledgehammer. Oh God! Surely not! It couldn't be true! That confirmed what she suspected. Of course! Those cottages only had one bedroom. That could definitely only mean one thing! Dicky and Bel must be lovers . . . they couldn't be . . . could they? But that was . . . yes, that was . . . incest . . . they were committing incest! Well, there was one thing for certain then, that letter was not getting torn up, for she meant every word of it now and she'd make the others change their minds again if it killed her. Someone had to preserve the reputation of this village and keep it a good place to live. If the mantle had fallen on her then so be it.

Peter's car was outside so the moment could not be more opportune. Breathlessly, she hammered on the rectory door.

Sylvia answered the door. 'Good day to you, Mrs Charter-Plackett.'

Instead of answering in her normal well enunciated manner, Grandmama stuttered and stammered. 'The Rrrector, he's in, is he in, in is he?'

'He is, but he's having an early lunch. Can it wait?'

'Wwwait. No, it can't. Tttell him, tell I'm here. Ts'urgent.'

'Step in, then. Wait there.' Sylvia went into the kitchen

where Caroline and Peter were eating lunch. Peter looked up. 'Rector, it's Mrs Charter-Plac—'

'It's me, Rector.' Grandmama stood in the doorway. Peter got up from his chair.

'It must be urgent for you to . . .'

'It is. Your study if you please.'

'Won't you join us for coffee? Get another cup, Sylvia, would you, please?'

Grandmama waved her hand impatiently. 'No, there's no time for that. Have you torn up that letter I sent?'

'The petition?'

Grandmama nodded.

'No, not yet.'

'Good, well don't. Things are far worse than we thought.'

Peter raised his eyebrows. 'Are they indeed!'

'Oh yes. I have just found out that Dicky and Bel are brother and sister and Glebe Cottages have only one bedroom. It doesn't take much intelligence to see which way the cookie crumbles. That's the answer to the wedding ring. A complete cover-up. I knew there was something fishy. I knew it.' She slapped her closed fist into the palm of the other hand and looked triumphantly at the three of them.

All of them registered first shock, then disbelief and then downright scorn. Peter was the first to find his voice. 'Come into the study will you?' He led the way and left Sylvia and Caroline staring at each other.

Sylvia gave a croaky little laugh and muttered, 'I don't believe this, she's finally gone balmy.'

'Balmy? She needs certifying. What a perfectly dreadful thing to say about anybody. How can it be true?'

'It can't.'

'Of course, it can't. Not Dicky and Bel. That's ridiculous. Quite disgusting in fact. I just hope Peter is giving her what for. Jimbo and Harriet will be distraught. She can be so perceptive and considerate and then there's this other side to her . . . She defies belief. What I can never quite comprehend is the way she always appears at the right place at the right time and picks up on all the gossip before anyone else does.' Sylvia flashed her a questioning look, afraid there might be more to what she said than first appeared, but Caroline continued by saying, 'I'll clear up. Might as well keep myself occupied while I wait to hear the full story.'

'Certainly not. You go and rest. You had a dreadful day yesterday with that chemo business so you deserve a rest.'

'Sylvia! You're spoiling me.'

'I'm not. Off you go.'

'Very well. But I won't lie down, I'll sit and watch TV.'

'OK. But feet up. That blessed woman. Where does she get her mad ideas from?'

After a quarter of an hour watching TV Caroline heard Peter opening the front door. Though he was trying to keep his voice low it was impossible for her not to overhear him say, 'Not a word until I have verified it one way or the other. Remember! Not even to Georgie. *No one at all.*'

She heard Grandmama answer in subdued tones. 'Very well.'

'Promise?'

'Promise.'

'Good afternoon, then. I'll be in touch.'

Caroline heard him shut the front door, and turned expecting him to come into the sitting-room but he didn't. Then she heard him shut the study door. In that case then it was serious. When he shut the study door like that, no one not even she unless the house was on fire, dared to interrupt. Then there must be grounds for what Grandmama had said. Heaven help Peter if it was true. Heaven help the village, too, if it was true.

'More custard, darling? There's still plenty left. I'm sure you're not eating enough, I want to see you putting on more weight.'

'No, thanks. You know full well I've gained half a stone since my op. If I keep on like this I shall be as big as Bel Tutt.'

Peter didn't take her up on that which she'd rather hoped he would. He hadn't said a word about Grandmama since the door had slammed on her. Caroline was bursting to know, and he normally told her everything but there were times when he shut up like a clam and she knew not to trespass. After all it was the same for her with her patients. Confidentiality and all that. She sighed.

'You're overtired, I can tell.'

'Peter! Stop mollycoddling me! I know whether or not I'm tired. And I'm not. I'm quite simply impatient to know what went on this afternoon.'

'I can't . . .'

'I know you can't, but I'm still bursting to know.'

'I am aware we promised ourselves an evening in on our own but I'm afraid I've got Dicky coming round tonight, it's rather important. We said eight o'clock.'

Caroline glanced at her wristwatch. 'He'll be here in five minutes, then.'

'Heavens I didn't realise how the time had flown. Can you manage the dishes?'

'Of course. Will you want tea or anything?'

'I think the parish whisky might be more appropriate.'

'OK. I'll be in the sitting-room if you . . . There's the door.'

206

'Help! Is there ever a right way to broach this kind of subject?'

'I have no doubt the Lord will provide the answer.'

When he and Dicky were settled in the study Peter said, 'I've asked you to come to see me tonight because of what happened this morning. I expect Bel has told you that the new bakery man is someone you knew before you moved here? And no doubt you know what he said, which unfortunately was heard all over the Store.'

Dicky didn't answer.

'Come, Dicky, I'm trying hard not to get impatient. I struggled last weekend with your close encounter with death, now it's allegations of a very serious nature and I need answers if I am to be expected to back you up.'

Still Dicky didn't answer.

'Please.'

'It's a long story.'

'Then shall we begin?'

Dicky rested his elbow on the arm of his chair and without looking at Peter began to speak, his voice was far from being the jolly laughing one everyone knew. It was quiet and distant and very thoughtful, and his words were chosen with such care. Peter braced himself for what might be going to be revealed.

'That chap, Trevor, is quite right. Bel is my sister. I make no bones about that. She's older than me by eleven months, so we've grown up together just like twins. She doesn't remember a time when I wasn't there. We don't remember our parents at all, because apparently so we've been told, when Bel was just two and I was just one year old someone, perhaps our mother, left us in our twin pushchair outside a doctor's surgery and walked away. We've seen neither hide nor hair of her since. Why she left us there I'll never know. Desperation I suppose, well at least Bel and me hope it was desperation and not . . . not because she didn't love us. They named Bel and me after the two doctors on duty that morning, and we got the name Tutt because the surgery was in a suburb called Tutt End. So it began, in a home first and then foster parents. All our lives we've looked after each other. There isn't a bond quite like that of children who've never known their parents. You stick like glue. You're all each other's got you see. You're mother, father, sister, brother, aunt, uncle, grandparent. There isn't anyone else to stand up for you.'

Dicky locked the fingers of both hands together very tightly and looked up at Peter. 'See what I mean? Like that. So close. They talked about separating us at one time, Bel for adoption and me to another foster home, but we ran away and spent two miserable nights hiding in a shed till they found us. Bel screamed and cried so much and did such dreadfully bad things that they decided she wasn't suitable for adoption so we went together to another foster home. It's hell, without roots. Not knowing who or what you are. Like living on shifting sands. When you're young you study the faces of the people in the street just in case you catch a glimpse of someone who looks like you and they might be the mother or the father you've been waiting for all through the years. Daft isn't it? We don't do that any more of course. Then when we were sixteen I got the job at the factory where I work now and Bel went into service, but didn't sleep in and we had a little tiny two-roomed flat and it was home. In capital letters it was home. The first real home we'd ever had. We could call it ours and we could lock the door and we were untouchable. We ruled our own lives, we ate what we wanted, we went out when we wanted and we were accountable to no one.'

'Whisky, Dicky?'

'Don't touch the hard stuff, Rector, thank you.'

'Right. Carry on, I'm listening.'

'About three years ago, Bel met this chap. To me it seemed like a gigantic earthquake, my whole world felt as though it was falling apart. There'd been just the two of us, still in the same flat, all those years, and here was an intruder disturbing our very foundations. For Bel's sake, for I could see she was smitten by him, I had to keep quiet, because I thought maybe my prejudice was rooted in the fact that I didn't want to lose my Bel. And it well could have been, for I loved her and she was my anchor in the storms of life like in the hymn. I always will love her, it's not difficult to love Bel.'

He looked up at Peter unable to continue, then he cleared his throat and carried on speaking. 'She's a gem. She knows me back to front and inside out. Every move. I've no secrets from Bel. Anyway he said he had a flat for them and he would persist that they should marry. Bel asked what I thought and well, what could I say? I couldn't stand in the way of her happiness, just like she won't stand in the way of mine now. Selfish love isn't real true love is it?'

Peter shook his head. 'No, it isn't.'

'So they had a wedding. It was a poor do, he said he'd no family and we certainly hadn't so it was just friends and a do at the Prince Albert after. I don't think they'd been married three months when I started getting suspicious things weren't right. They lived in their own flat, and I was definitely feeling the pinch trying to pay the rent for our home all by myself, so Bel used to ask me over quite often for a meal to help me out. Did my washing and that. Called one night unexpected, I was feeling lonely, fancy me Dicky Tutt feeling lonely! Ridiculous isn't it? Even before I knocked on the door I could hear the shouting. They didn't hear my knock so I walked straight in and he was thumping her, like nobody's business. She was thin then, like me and she wasn't half taking a battering. He was a big chap and there wasn't anything I could do to stop him. So a neighbour called the police and he was arrested.'

Dicky's hands were twisting together round and round, this way and that. He swallowed hard two or three times. 'Sorry, I can't forget how she looked when we got her to hospital. I kept saying "why didn't you tell me, why ever not?"'

'Long and the short of it was she came home to our flat, changed her name to Tutt again and that was that. Then she started putting on weight, couldn't stop eating you see, comfort or something I expect. I hadn't the heart to say anything. He started calling again and pestering her, wanting her back, apologising for this and that you know, usual rubbish. He wouldn't lift a finger to her ever again and all that nonsense. She thought perhaps she should go back, I said no she shouldn't, a leopard doesn't change its spots and I think it was the first time in our lives that we'd disagreed. It broke our hearts when we realised what had happened to us. We both hung on to each other crying our eyes out. We decided there and then we wouldn't allow anyone else to come between us, it wasn't worth it. Upshot of it was I persuaded her to go for a divorce and we decided to move. Buy a home of our own. Something of *ours*. We saw the advert for Muriel's, you know Lady Templeton's house being up for sale and by adjusting this and that and bargaining the price down a bit we realised that between us we could just about manage to buy it. Couldn't afford anything bigger

you see, and it was isolated and we'd feel secure. We loved
the village as soon as we saw it. We're mortgaged up to
our eyebrows, believe me, it's been a struggle. Anyway
the lady Bel was housekeeper to was taken very ill and Bel
couldn't leave her. So I came here and she stayed at the
lady's house till she died. We'd had no promises made at
all but we both rather hoped that the lady would leave Bel
something in her will, but, as I've no doubt you know
blood is thicker than water when it comes to wills, and all
she got was the lady's gold watch and bracelet, so that was
that.'

Peter nodded his head. 'I know, it happens so often, the
ones who do all the work get nothing and those who've
swanned in once or twice a year get the lot.'

'Exactly. You know Bel, she worked all hours those
last months, kindness itself she was, but there we are.
So Bel came here. This is the difficult bit now. You
know how small the house is, Rector. But it's ours or
it will be when the mortgage is paid off, our very own
home, every stick and stone, we're impregnable. So
now we come to this question of people thinking we
share a bedroom. As God is my witness and I don't say
that lightly, as you well know, Bel and me we do not
share a *bed* like everyone thinks. We share the wardrobe
simply because there's nowhere else to hang clothes, but at
night I sleep on the sofabed downstairs and Bel has the
bedroom.'

Peter thanked him for being so frank.

Dicky took a deep breath. 'We don't and I repeat that,
don't . . . that is . . . we're not . . . like man and wife. We
observe all the niceties. We share the wardrobe like I've
said, so I do go in Bel's bedroom to get my clothes but I
don't sleep in there. However, mud sticks, so if you want
me to resign from anything at all I will, but I won't have

Bel's life ruined over this. I simply will not. I'll sell up and go elsewhere rather than that.'

'I see.'

'That bloody Trevor, I could murder him. Turning up like that, just when we thought we were safe and secure like. It's not fair, it just isn't fair.'

'But letting everyone think you were married.'

'What else could we do? But we never told lies, we simply let everyone assume we were married. We never lied. Just never mentioned it. They'd have hounded us out in two ticks if we'd let on. We both talked about it the other night and we agreed we should have been more honest and open about it all, but we weren't because we were scared of what they would all think. It's our dishonesty that's brought all this about. Now there's Georgie. My darlin' Georgie. And here's Bel being so kind and thoughtful and considerate. I don't deserve her. I don't.'

Peter saw the distress in his eyes. Dicky drew out his handkerchief and blew his nose.

'There's nothing more to tell. Except I love Bel and don't want her hurt and I love Georgie and want her for a wife if it doesn't hurt Bel too much, which it will, but she won't let on. I love this place, know that? Not been here long but I love it, for all its tittle-tattle and feuding I love it, 'cos it's part of old England you see and I can respond to that. But' – Dicky sighed and shook his head – 'I'd better put the house on the market and say goodbye to dreams and happiness and my Scouts, and absolutely damn all that I love.'

Peter shook his head. 'I don't want that. No, that's no solution.'

'There isn't another one. We'll have to uproot and start all over again.' Dicky took out his handkerchief and blew his nose again.

In a voice more upbeat than he felt, Peter said, 'One

person I do feel sorry for is Bryn. In a way none of this has been brought about by him, but he's suffering too.'

Dicky looked up at him. 'I know I have to confess I've been feeling bad all the time about Bryn, really bad. All he's guilty of is neglecting Georgie, and there's plenty of husbands guilty of that. At first getting him riled made me laugh, but after a while I began to feel ashamed but by then I loved Georgie too much to give her up. If he'd listen to me I'd apologise to him, but there's small chance of that. He can't stand the sight of me.'

'There must be a solution somewhere to all this. Don't do anything for the moment. Nothing at all. But now the cat is out of the bag so to speak, and everyone knows, we are going to have to do *something* but I don't know what. Thank you for being so frank. The village will react quite violently to this situation and quite understandably, after all to those who don't know the facts, it appears to be incest you're guilty of, and neither they nor I could condone that. But it isn't, and somehow we've to demonstrate that everything is above board. I don't want to be guilty of ruining yours and Bel's lives. Are you absolutely certain in view of your close relationship with Bel that you've got room in your life for Georgie?'

Dicky studied this question for a long while, so long in fact Peter thought he wasn't going to get an answer, and then Dicky said, 'I'm sure there is. All round, in the long term, it would be better for Bel and for me. Perhaps then we could each get on with our own lives instead of being so . . .' He gestured helplessly with his hand and could find no words to describe the closeness of his and Bel's relationship.

Peter nodded. 'Well, then, Dicky, go home and give Bel some support. After all she has everyone to face, you can escape to the office, she can't.'

'And the Scouts? Shall I cry off tomorrow night? The others can cope for one night I'm sure.'

'Cry off. Keep a low profile. That's the best.'

Dicky stood up. 'I've taken up enough of your time, Rector, I'll be off. Thanks for listening and being so understanding.' A vestige of the Dicky Peter knew crept into his face, and Dicky smiled. 'If much more happens I shan't be able to leave the house. I've been banned from the pub, I'm never climbing a church tower ever again, I can't go to Scouts, there's not much left is there?'

'Not at the moment, but we'll sort something out. You'll see. There's always the Jug and Bottle in Penny Fawcett!'

Dicky grinned. 'Of course. There is.' Then his face became stark and full of pain again and he said, 'I've no solution, I hope you have.'

'I'll have a good try. Good night Dicky.'

'Good night, Peter, and thanks.'

'Come any time, you and Bel, the door's always open to you.'

Dicky, standing out in the road with the outside light shining directly on his face, looked up at Peter and said, 'God bless the day you came here, I don't think my story would have been so understandingly received by anyone else. You're one in a million. Good night, and thank you, from the bottom of my heart.'

Peter nodded his thanks and then shut the door. He found Caroline watching TV. She switched it off with the remote control as soon as he entered the room. Peter didn't speak or even glance at her, he flung himself down in a chair and rubbed his forehead with his hand, as though it would help to clear his head.

She stood up and said, 'Tea?'

Without looking at her he said, 'I have faced a lot of very difficult problems in my life as a priest but I think this one is above and beyond anything I've tackled to date.'

'Tea it is, then.'

Chapter 18

The next morning, it being Friday, the children from the school were scheduled for morning prayers in the church. Normally, by the time they'd done the register and got everyone assembled for the walk across to the church all the mothers had dispersed, but this Friday morning there was a large group still talking by the gate.

Kate Pascoe, heading the crocodile of children, called out, 'Excuse me ladies, could we squeeze by?' The mothers pushed their prams out of the way and made room for them all to pass through the gate.

One of the mothers asked quietly as Kate passed her, 'Could I have a word at lunchtime?'

Kate nodded. 'One o'clock in my room?'

'Thanks.'

Kate knew exactly what the appointment was for and she didn't know what to do. After morning prayers were over, she asked Hetty Hardaker and Margaret Booth to take the children back and she wouldn't be a moment, just needed a word with Peter.

'My advice is to say that you have absolutely no reason for asking Bel to leave. Which I take it you haven't?'

Kate shook her head. 'None at all, she does the job equally as well as Pat did, if not better, I can find no possible reason for sacking her. She's done nothing wrong at all, she's patient with the children, she keeps everything spotless, she's pleasant with the staff. She couldn't be bettered.'

'I thought not. Tell them you won't, and that she's coming to the school until you are told differently. Be quiet, but firm and don't let them sidetrack you into it being a question of her morals. As far as I am concerned she and Dicky are doing nothing wrong at all, I have that knowledge directly from Dicky and I believe him.'

'Thank you for that assurance.'

'I can't give details, obviously it's entirely confidential, but I can assure you it's all right.'

'Thanks. Lovely service. Much appreciated. Bye!'

With half an eye on the clock so she wouldn't be late for the conference with the mothers' representative, Kate went into the Store at lunchtime to buy a frozen vegetable lasagne. She needed something quick for her evening meal because she was off into Culworth after school and hadn't time for cooking for herself.

'Hello, Jimbo! How's things?'

'None too sprightly.' He looked down in the mouth and at odds with himself.

'I think you have the same problem as I have?'

Jimbo asked if Bel was her problem.

'Yes. I think my mothers are up in arms. I refuse to be intimidated by them, though. Peter's given me his assurance that everything is OK about Bel and Dicky. They're a scandal-mongering lot, my mothers, when it comes down to it. Anything for a bit of excitement.'

'I have every sympathy for Bel, but I will not allow my business to suffer. Village Stores are difficult enough to make viable at the best of times, so my business acumen may have to take precedence over my sympathy for her.'

'What are you going to do then?'

'We've agreed she's shelf-filling in the evenings when we're shut, not mornings. Even so I can't give her the hours she normally does without customer contact of some sort, so she'll have to be on the till if I get desperate.'

Kate paid for her lasagne and went back to school, the light of battle in her eyes.

Peter endeavoured to keep the light of battle from his eyes when Grandmama appeared at his request in his study. He'd been ready to call upon her in her cottage but thought that he would take the initiative by summoning her to see him. Might just blunt her sharp edges if she wasn't on her own home territory he'd said to Caroline.

'I agree. The difficulty about this situation is that she's so *right* on the surface. One can't condone incest at all, it is just so downright immoral, to say nothing of unlawful. But it isn't incest, but it looks like it.'

Peter groaned. 'You obviously haven't come up with one of your admirable commonsense solutions. I feel a large dose of it would be very useful.'

'I'm afraid not. Sorry. You'll have to play it by ear.'

Grandmama sat rigidly upright in the easy chair. Peter sat sideways at his desk, facing her. Whatever age she was she kept herself remarkably smart and youthful looking. She had such a strong life force he was in danger of being overcome by it. However, he wasn't going to be intimidated by this almighty formidable lady, and he was determined to keep the upper hand.

'Mrs Charter-Plackett, thank you for finding the time to come to see me. I promised I would get back to you and here I am doing that very thing.'

She nodded. 'Not at all, Peter, I just want the whole matter cleared up. This village won't tolerate the situation for much longer. They all know, not through me but because people were in the Store when that bakery man made his revelation. They all think it's disgusting, absolutely disgusting and they want them out. Scouts, the school, they're both being tainted by it.'

Peter leant back in his chair. 'How about coffee?'

'That would be welcome. Thank you.'

They chatted about the weather, about the plans for Christmas about everything but the matter in hand. Sylvia brought the coffee in and Peter couldn't help but notice that Grandmama's cup was slapped down a little too sharply for his liking. He caught her eye as she gave him his and she couldn't miss the reproof in his face. Sylvia tossed her head and marched out. When Peter tasted his coffee he found it was only instant and not percolated. A sure sign that Sylvia disapproved.

He let Grandmama have a few lifesaving sips of her coffee and then he began. 'I have a story to tell.' By the time he had finished telling her the reasons for the situation Bel and Dicky found themselves in, Grandmama was on the verge of tears. She fumbled in her bag for a handkerchief and surreptitiously dabbed her eyes.

'So you see, Mrs Charter-Plackett, I have Dicky's absolute affirmation that there is nothing untoward at all; he has given me his word and I believe him completely. However, the world at large doesn't know that and neither does anyone else except Caroline and you and me. I have shared this information with you because you are involved and I know, yes I know that, having given you my confidence you will not betray it.' Peter paused, took a final drink of his coffee put down his cup and looked Grandmama straight in the eye. They looked at each other for a moment and then Peter broke the silence by saying the very last thing he'd ever intended to say. 'What I want is for you to help me to arrive at a solution.'

'Me?'

'Yes, you. There's the situation between Georgie and Bryn and Dicky to solve which is bound up with the situation between Dicky and Bel. Now, do you have any ideas?'

'Well, no I don't. Not at the moment. But I shall give it my earnest consideration.'

'I admit, I'm completely at a loss.'

'So am I.'

'Has Georgie enlightened you at all about what she wants?'

'Not at all. She doesn't know herself.'

Peter allowed a silence to develop. Grandmama checked her cup and found to her disappointment she'd drunk it all. She looked at Peter and said, 'We can't do anything till they all declare what they want to do. Does Georgie want to go back to Bryn? Does Bryn want her back? Does Dicky want to marry Georgie? Does Georgie want to marry Dicky? If they marry then what does Bel want to do? It sounds like something from a musical comedy.'

'It's far from being that.'

'Exactly. When you know the story you can't help feeling sorry for Dicky and Bel. It must be quite dreadful to grow up knowing your mother, whoever she was and for whatever reason, abandoned you. No wonder they've clung together all these years. The poor things. We all need someone don't we? You can't believe a mother could be so cruel, can you?'

'You can't. Look, I won't take up any more of your

time. Think about it and if you come up with any ideas, let me know, but directly not through a third party.'

'Of course. Absolute secrecy.'

'Meanwhile I'll be thinking too.' Peter stood up and smiled down at Grandmama.

Her heart flipped. If she could solve this for him she would. Given time there was no problem unsolvable. 'Of course. It's partly my fault all this trouble, I'm sorry I've been so . . .'

Peter smiled at her again. 'To err is human.'

Thankfully Grandmama smiled and said, 'Between the two of us we should be able to sort it out, after all we're not fools are we, either of us?'

'Certainly not.' He showed her out and then went to find Caroline. She was pottering in the garden.

'Caroline, you won't dig or anything will you?'

'Of course not, don't worry.' She turned to look at him. 'Do you think I should move those peonies to this side? I think they'd look more effective here, don't you?'

Peter put an arm around her waist and pulled her close. 'Happy?'

She turned towards him and put her arms round his neck. 'I am, couldn't be happier.' Caroline kissed him. 'I love you.'

'I love you. You're always happy in your garden. How about taking a garden design course, carve out a whole new career for yourself? You're very good at it.'

'If I were I wouldn't be asking you about the peonies.'

'Follow your instincts. Move them. I'll dig them out for you.'

'Peter! Sometimes you are absolutely transparent!'

'I don't know what you mean.'

'You do. You're worried I'll have a go myself, so you

221

get in quickly with an offer to do it for me. Well, I shan't. I know what I'm permitted to do.'

'I should trust you more, shouldn't I?'

'Yes, you should. Well? How did you get on with her?'

'I've taken the most awful gamble.'

Caroline listened to what he had to say and replied, 'Rather you than me.'

'Do you think I've got it wrong? You said play it by ear.'

'It will either come off quite splendidly or the situation will be ten times worse. A gamble as you say.'

'I rather hoped you'd agree with me. She's the sort of person who could solve it, you know. Grandmama's no fool as she so rightly said.'

'They might manage to solve it all by themselves if left alone.'

'They're all too deeply involved to see the wood for the trees.'

'I just hope you're backing the right horse. Despite your support, the village may still not approve. There's one thing though, they'll all have plenty to talk about. It'll keep everyone going for weeks and weeks!'

Over the weekend the bar at the Royal Oak hummed discreetly with the gossip about the four of them. In particular the discovery that Dicky and Bel were brother and sister. Discreetly because of Bryn. They didn't want to hurt his feelings, but on the other hand the gossip was far too good to miss. What couldn't be reconciled was the fact that Dicky and Bel had deceived them for so long. Why had no one twigged what was going on? What seemed even more incredible was that the Rector appeared to be condoning it. They couldn't understand that, him being so particular about things, and him having the church's attitude to take into account.

Vera had dragged Don in for a drink seeing as Jimmy was always busy driving his taxi on Saturday nights and Pat hardly ever came in since she'd married Barry. So, not wishing to spend the evening alone, Vera had persuaded Don to accompany her. 'We won't stay long, it's just to find out what's happening, that's all. You can get back to your telly as soon as.'

To her delight Willie and Sylvia were there and they'd secured her favourite table.

'Willie! Sylvia! Don's just getting the drinks.'

'How's things, Vera?' Willie asked her.

'Fine, just fine. In fact brilliant. My wages have gone up again. Thank Gawd.'

'Why's that?'

'Can't get people to work the hours. I should worry. What with Don's money, our Rhett's and mine, everything in the Wright household is great.' Vera nodded her head in the direction of Bryn. 'He's still working then?'

'There's him and Alan and wait till you see the new help.'

'New help? Who's that then?'

'Wait and see.' Willie, out of the side of his mouth, muttered, 'Here she comes.'

Vera was totally unprepared for the vision which appeared through the door marked *Private*. The woman was as tall as Bryn, with a mass of unnaturally red hair, curling and swirling around her head and well down her back. You couldn't call her fat but she was voluptuous. More than enough of her top half was exposed, the part that wasn't, was encased in a sparkling, glittering top which, cropped at her waistline, exposed a tanned midriff each time she stretched for anything the slightest

223

bit out of reach. They'd seen short skirts on some of the teenage girls in the village, but the skirt this apparition was wearing came only just short of covering her knickers.

Vera was scandalised. 'Never in all my born days have I seen anything as disgusting as that. Georgie would never have set her on. Not in a million years. Where the Dickens is she from?'

'Penny Fawcett.'

'Penny Fawcett? That dead alive hole. Giddy godfathers. I bet she sets tongues wagging.'

Sylvia giggled. 'More than tongues believe me! She's one of old Bertie Bradshaw's daughters.'

'No! Not the one the Rector caught . . .' Vera lowered her voice and whispered the rest of the story to Sylvia, finishing with 'Was it Kenny or Terry, I can't remember.'

'The very one.'

'It's disgusting. She'll be putting Don off his orange juice.' Vera moved along the settle to make room for him. 'Don't you make any of your awkward remarks tonight, Don Wright, the last one caused enough trouble. I don't want *you* being thrown from the top of the church tower, well, not before I've checked your insurance anyhow! Thanks. Cheers.' Vera raised her glass to her mouth and drank thirstily.

'Me? As if I would!'

Vera, still appalled by the sight of the new barmaid, said, 'She'll be Elektra.'

'Right name for her too.' Don made one of his rare excursions into the world of laughter which made the others look at him in surprise.

Sylvia thought it was a ridiculous name. She asked Vera what the others were called. 'Can't remember 'em all, the youngest one's called Mercedes I do know that. Reckon their mother must have had a brainstorm each time they popped out. She died years ago before they all grew up. Mind you, with five girls like Elektra there's no wonder she died young, it was the surest way to escape the lot of 'em!'

Willie, still ogling Elektra, declared she was much older than she looked. 'See her neck, yer can't disguise that, nor her 'ands. I bet she's fifty if she's a day. Pity Jimmy's not here, do 'im good to have an eyeful of her.'

Vera tut-tutted. 'Well, I'm disgusted with Bryn. Georgie always kept the place with such style, never a word out of place, everything classy like.'

With a deadpan face Don muttered, 'She'll be in his bed before long.' He waited until Bryn was looking in his direction and he called out, 'Not taken long for yer to find someone to keep the bed warm, Bryn, in a manner of speaking like.'

Elektra answered him because Bryn, caught unawares, couldn't think of an answer. 'Jealous are yer? Expect that dried up old prune sat next to yer is your wife. Bet you've forgotten what it's like.'

Don, the wind completely taken out of his sails by this bold retort, didn't know where to look.

Vera went a kind of purply red, struggled out from the settle and confronted Elektra. Being small Vera's eyes were on a level with Elektra's cleavage which made it difficult to speak with authority.

'You're a tart. That's what you are, a tart. Don't you dare speak to my husband like that. Decent people don't want the likes of you in here, with yer cheeky remarks and yer black lace knickers.'

'You old cow. Bet your knickers aren't black lace, they'll be pink interlock with them long legs with elastic.

225

Sexy I must say. No wonder that husband of yours is jealous.' She pulled at the cropped sparkling top and exposed even more of her assets.

Vera, unable to come up with a smart response to this further evidence of Elektra's unsuitability to be barmaid in the Royal Oak, picked up her glass of lager which was still half full and emptied what was left down Elektra's chest, banged the empty glass down on the nearest table and said, 'Don, we're going 'ome.' As they crossed the bar towards the door Vera said, 'Now look what you've made me do with your uncalled-for remarks.' They left in a kind of triumphant flurry.

Elektra was yowling, plucking at her top as the lager trickled down her cleavage down her midriff and then her imitation leather skirt and thence to the floor. Bryn came from behind the bar armed with a tea towel and began dabbing at Elektra's front.

Uproar ensued. The customers were cheering him on with enthusiasm, making bold hints about their relationship and inferring what a lucky man he was, and did he need a hand?

At that moment Peter walked in. Bryn unaware what had caused the ribaldry to trail off into silence continued mopping Elektra.

'You'll have to go in the back and get changed. You're absolutely wet through. Alan! Get a cloth and a bucket and . . .' Bryn saw Peter and stopped in mid-sentence. Immediately he knew that he looked all kinds of a fool. It would contribute nothing to his case as far as Peter was concerned. But did he care? No, he didn't. Hail-fellow-well-met was the best attitude to adopt. 'Good evening, Rector! What can I get for you?'

'I'll have a mineral water thank you, Bryn. Busy tonight.'

'That's right. Just had a bit of a fracas with two of the customers. All part of life's rich pattern. Eh?'

'Indeed. I've just popped in to see about arrangements for a meeting. I didn't know how you were fixed for help in the bar but I see you've got someone. Eighty pence, that right?'

'That's right, Rector.'

'Sunday evening after service I thought, in the rectory. It's fine with the others. Is it all right with you?'

'I'll get Elektra to change shifts, her and Alan should be able to manage.'

'Good.' Peter stood at the bar one foot on the brass rail and looked at the crowd. He acknowledged Willie and Sylvia and a few more from church, and drank his mineral water. There was a lot of furtive giggling amongst the customers and an occasional burst of laughter.

Elektra returned. Sylvia gasped. Nudging Willie she whispered 'I'm certain that's one of Georgie's tops. I remember her wearing it. It's not on is it?'

'It's not blinking decent, it isn't. You wouldn't think Georgie was living only yards away, you'd think she was dead. I'm amazed at Bryn. He's lost his marbles, that's what.' Willie went to the bar to buy another drink. 'Good evening, Rector. I'm afraid things aren't what they were in these parts.'

Peter smiled wryly and said, 'I agree.'

Two of the customers called good night and went, and those left behind settled down to a quiet evening. There was a game of dominoes in progress at the table by the fire, someone got up and shouted to Bryn should they put another log on, and he agreed, not caring much either way as he was chatting to Elektra. Two chaps from Culworth decided to have a game of darts and Elektra exchanged some coarse chit-chat with them. Bryn glanced at the clock. An hour to closing. And then . . . He admired Elektra's rampant red hair and thought about burying his hands in it, grasping great handfuls of it, twining it round his fingers, luxuriating in the thickness of it and . . . would she let him though? As she'd said her father had turned her out and she'd nowhere to go, he'd delightedly agreed to her having Alan's old room. Everything somehow had fallen neatly into place. As he contemplated with relish the possibility of some extra-mural activity once the bar was closed, he heard the outside door open. He looked up to see who'd come in.

It was Georgie carrying her case. She'd come back.

Bryn went hot right from his bow tie down to his brown suede shoes. His head swirled till he felt so dizzy he had to clutch hold of the bar to steady himself. Through the mists which, to his surprise, had filled the bar he saw the look of fury on Georgie's face when she spotted Elektra.

He watched her eyes taking in the whole of the saloon, Peter at the bar, the flames hungrily crackling away at the new log, the plastic flowers Elektra had put on the counter, which now appeared to him to be in the worst possible taste, and finally her eyes reached him. If it was possible he went even hotter. Her look floored him. He felt compelled to turn his eyes away, he couldn't meet hers, those lovely blue eyes which had so captivated him all those years ago; it was the horrendous sadness he saw in them he couldn't face. Georgie didn't speak. Not even to Peter. She walked across, went behind the bar and through the door marked *Private*.

Had she come back for good then?

Sylvia asked Willie this very question and he couldn't answer it, neither could anyone else. In fact the question never did get answered for it was 'Time, ladies

228

and gentlemen, please' before they knew where they were. So they all went home, Peter included, none the wiser.

Chapter 19

Grandmama was taking her turn organising the after morning service coffee in the church hall. With the service commencing at ten o'clock she was already there by quarter past nine putting out the cups. Willie had switched on the heating and the water heater so there was nothing much else to do but put out the cups, get the big coffee jugs out, spoon some sugar into bowls, put the pretty tablecloths on which Muriel had made when the hall had been renovated, get the spoons out of the locked cupboard, where was the key? Drat it, Mrs Jones had that. Where was she?

She heard the outside door shut and Mrs Jones calling out, 'Anyone here?'

'Good morning!'

'Oh! Good morning Mrs Charter-Plackett, I thought I was the first. You've done everything. You must have been early.'

'I was. I had a bad night so I decided to get up early and make the best of the day.'

'Not sleeping well then? I have some blinking good herbal stuff I use when I'm having one of my sessions when I can't sleep. Yer sleep but yer don't feel drugged when yer wake up. I've got a new bottle in mi bag, 'ere you 'ave it.' She searched about in her cavernous bag and produced a bottle of tablets still in the herbalist's bag. 'Take it, go on, buy me a new bottle next time you're in Culworth. I've still got some left in my old bottle.'

'Oh, well thank you. I could give them a try, couldn't I? I don't usually have any problem, just an off night now and again. Have you the key for the cupboard, I need the spoons.'

'Coming to something when yer have to lock up church cupboards. Things aren't what they were, are they?'

Grandmama gave her a quizzical look but as Mrs Jones didn't respond in any way she thanked her for the spoons and went round putting one in each saucer.

Mrs Jones, between counting the spoonsful of coffee needed for each jug said 'You won't have seen the new barmaid?'

'No.'

'Our Kenny was in there Friday, he says she's a tart and he should know.'

'Is she?'

'Oh yes. Between you and me she's been around rather longer than she'd like us to know. Dresses fifteen when she's nearer fifty. But as Kenny says she has a heart of gold, so we all know what that means.' Slyly she brought the conversation round to Georgie. 'Must be awful for Georgie having that tart in her lovely pub. How's she keeping? Don't see much of her nowadays. Has she said anything about going back to him? Or is she staying with you a bit longer?'

Sorely tempted to relate the conversation she'd had with Georgie which had gone on far into the previous night Grandmama remembered Peter's admonition and said briefly, 'I'm only giving her a refuge till she sorts out what she wants to do, she doesn't confide in me.'

Oh no, thought Mrs Jones, I should cocoa. 'Well, it must be very difficult for 'em, them being business partners, not like if they were managers and the brewery owned it. Different when it's a free house. More complicated money-wise isn't it?'

'There that's that. I'll be off to church. See you afterwards. I don't expect there'll be many there today. We shouldn't be too busy.'

But she was wrong. The church was filled, not so many as for a special service but there were plenty there, and they all poured into the hall afterwards too. Grandmama and Mrs Jones were kept very busy, so busy they hadn't time for gossip, but judging by the loud hum of conversation and the hoots of laughter everyone else had plenty of time for it.

After the first surge of activity Grandmama took a moment to look around. Her eyes lighted on Peter first, because he was a head taller than most of the others. He was talking to Georgie. Poor Georgie. She'd made that brave decision to go back to Bryn and make a real effort to improve their lives together and what had she found? That disgusting woman serving in *her* bar, wearing one of *her* favourite tops, and Bryn looking like the cat who'd been at the cream. What had made matters worse was her realising, once she'd gone upstairs, that Elektra was living there, something she would never have allowed. Alan, yes, but then they'd known him since he'd first started work with them at eighteen, and been pleased to offer him a home, but Elektra . . . She was a different kettle of fish altogether.

Grandmama had been secretly appalled by Georgie's

reaction. It seemed to her that Georgie had still had a lot of feeling left for Bryn, but that it had been destroyed in an instant by what she'd found. Apparently they'd had a frightful row, with Georgie telling Bryn exactly what she thought of him, something she'd never done before. Bryn had grown defiant, and told her what else could she expect when she'd left him to cope by himself, and if she didn't like the new barmaid she knew what she could do.

'Which is?'

'Just leave and let me get on with it my way.'

'We'll have no business left, our punters won't like' – she'd given Elektra a scathing glance – 'someone like her, we've a better class of pub. She's more the Jug and Bottle type.'

Elektra had taken umbrage at that remark. 'The Jug and Bottle! I wouldn't work there.'

'No? Perhaps you're right, they wouldn't want you, you're not even good enough for *them*, and that's saying something.'

Bryn had protested. 'Now come on, Georgie, there's no call to be downright nasty.'

'Isn't there? Don't forget, Bryn, I'm a partner in this business and I shall want my profit share. If she stays there'll be no profit to have. People like Sir Ralph and Jimbo and the Duchess and the Rector won't patronise us with her in here. She'll attract all the wrong kind of people.'

Elektra tossed her hair back and hands on hips retorted, 'Stuck-up lot they are, anyway, with their mineral waters and their gins and tonics.' She mimicked someone sipping delicately from their glass and laughed. 'There's plenty that will come 'cos I'm here. Give me men like Kenny Jones and their Terry, they know how to spend money . . .'

Georgie had looked Elektra up and down and said, 'You should know . . .'

'Well, really, you horrible old . . .'

'Old? Me, old? Try looking at your birth certificate some time.' So Georgie had then turned on her heel after firing that shot, picked up her case and left. She'd heard Bryn calling 'Georgie! Georgie!' but she'd ignored him.

So now poor Georgie was in even more turmoil than before.

Peter was talking and Georgie was listening and nodding her head. Grandmama noticed that Mrs Jones had drawn close ostensibly collecting used cups, but Grandmama could recognise her subterfuge. The choirboys came for their orange squash and her attention was taken making sure they didn't take all the biscuits. St Thomas à Becket choirboys were renowned for their ability to clear the plates of biscuits if you took your eyes off them even for a moment.

By the time she looked up again Dicky had joined Peter and Georgie and Mrs Jones was coming back without a single cup on her tray, and her lips tightly nipped together.

'Didn't hear a thing. They both stopped talking when I got near enough to hear.'

Grandmama saw it was her place to be shocked. 'You don't mean you were trying to eavesdrop?'

Mrs Jones grinned. 'Oh no, of course not! You know there's more than one had a word with the Rector about this business with Bel and Dicky. They've not taken kindly to knowing they share a bedroom. It's all very well the Rector saying he has Dicky's assurance there's nothing going on, but I ask yer? Stands to reason. He's a man isn't he, and a randy one at that by all accounts, so it must come over him sometimes, like it does with 'em all. Yer know.' She nudged Grandmama and gave her a wink.

Grandmama blanched. She wasn't accustomed to gossip at this level. She protested but Mrs Jones carried on. 'Who're they kidding? Not me for one. Much as I like Bel, it's not right. Just think of it. It's disgusting! Mr Charter-Plackett'll 'ave no compunction about sacking Bel. He's a lovely chap but when it comes to business . . . But there, you don't need me to tell you that. If he finds himself with a boycott it'll be curtains for Bel quick sharp. And the mothers at the school have asked if Bel can be sacked and that Kate won't do it. Says she's no cause for sacking her and she won't, not so long as she does a good job. They had a deputation or whatever they call it one lunchtime, but they met their match with Miss Kate Pascoe. Oh, I didn't see you waiting, Dr Harris. Sorry. Coffee?'

Caroline nodded her head. 'Yes, please.'

'Milk?'

'Yes, please. Good morning, Mrs Charter-Plackett.'

'Good morning, Caroline, my dear. Beautiful morning.'

'It certainly is. I don't know why, but when the two of you make the coffee it always tastes much better than everyone else's. Do you have some secret recipe or something?'

Grandmama and Mrs Jones preened themselves.

'TLC, that's our secret ingredient, isn't it Mrs Jones?'

Rather nonplussed, Mrs Jones agreed.

Caroline looked around the hall. 'I see! Oh, there he is. I've a message for Peter. See you.'

The two of them watched Caroline squeezing her way through the throng to Peter. She stood quietly beside him waiting to deliver her message.

Georgie was speaking. 'Well, Rector, there's no two ways about it, I'm not going back. Ever. I wouldn't go back even if he crawled from there to here on his hands and knees begging me every inch of the way.'

'Tonight at the meeting . . .'

'I shan't be there.'

'Georgie!'

'I'm sorry, but I shan't. As far as I am concerned there's nothing to discuss. I'm seeing my solicitor in the morning and I'm going for a divorce and making certain of where we stand with the pub, money-wise. That's that.'

Peter in the face of her resistance could only say, 'Well, if you're determined on that then there's no more to say. I may as well cancel the meeting. So this means you and Dicky . . .' He looked at the two of them in turn.

Dicky took the initiative. 'We haven't discussed what we want to do. Not yet. Georgie only made her mind up last night, so we haven't had time to talk. And there's Bel.'

Peter nodded his sympathy. 'Of course, there's Bel. I'm encountering a lot of opposition on that score, I'm afraid.'

Dicky sighed. 'I know. It'll all come out in the wash.' He saw Caroline standing patiently waiting. 'Good morning, Dr Harris. You're looking well. Better than you did.'

'Indeed I am, thank you. Much better. If you've finished I've a message for you, darling.'

'OK. Yes. I'll tell Bryn the meeting's off. Right?' He turned away and bent his head to hear what Caroline had to say.

Georgie turned to Dicky and said, 'We need to talk.'

'We'll have our dinner with Bel like she's planned and then we'll go out somewhere, just you and me. I'm sorry it's come to this.'

'I'm not.'

'Well, I am. But on the other hand it means we've got the go ahead.'

Georgie squeezed his arm. 'Oh yes it does, and what's more, no regrets now, none whatsoever.'

When they'd finished their Sunday dinner, Bel and Georgie went into the kitchen to clear up. There was scarcely enough room for the two of them but it brought about a kind of intimacy which they hadn't experienced before.

Bel said 'I want to thank you for coming to dinner today. Dicky needed a boost. I don't expect he's told you but you ought to know, we've had some very nasty letters.'

'You never have. Oh Bel!'

'Just pushed through the door, not signed or anything. Dicky's been very upset. There were two more this morning.'

'I'm so sorry. They can be very vindictive. Right from us first coming here we realised that. Very, very nasty if something doesn't suit. All this mediaeval village bit, you know. But poison pen letters! That's dreadful. Have you told the Rector?'

'Dicky won't. Says the shame would kill him, Dicky I mean, if the Rector was to read 'em. But it's so awful. We've done nothing and I want you to know this Georgie, we've done *nothing wrong*. Truly we haven't, Nothing at all.'

'I know that Bel, I know. You're not those kind of people. Dicky told me at the very beginning when we first got attracted to one another that you were his sister, so I've always known you see, but never let on to a living soul. I couldn't love Dicky like I do if what they're saying was true. He wouldn't be like he is, would he now? What's more, neither of you would be so kind and lovely. You don't need to convince me. But I do think the

Rector ought to know about the letters, after all those who wrote them are his parishoners.'

'Well, Dicky doesn't want him to know, so that's that. Don't tell anyone will you?'

Georgie reached up and kissed Bel's cheek. 'Of course not, I think too much about you to say anything if that's what you both want. You can rely on me.'

Bel handed Georgie a clean tea towel and said, 'Thanks. We'll say no more. They'll stop eventually I expect. I'm glad about you and Dicky. Very glad. He needs someone like you. A sister's not the same at all.'

'That's very generous of you, Bel. I've been worried about that. Truly worried. I didn't want to come between you.'

'It's time he branched out. I love him dearly, always will, but he needs to move on. I wouldn't say to him but it's true. Between you and me, he clings to me you see, it's not good for him.'

'But what will you do? Where will you live. Here?'

'Let's wait and see. Leave the pans, I'll do those. You take him out and . . .'

'Look Bel, I shan't want him all to myself. We're not kids. There'll still be room for you.'

Bel gazed out of the window. 'We'll see how things work out. Let's not make promises we shan't be able to keep.'

Georgie reached up and placed another kiss on Bel's cheek. 'If it's any comfort I do love him, he's just wonderful, such fun and so thoughtful. He's kind of just right for me, he makes me so happy and I hope I make him happy too. Thanks for being so generous.'

Bel laughed. 'Generous! I shall be glad to see the back of him! You can have him lock stock and barrel! I mean it!'

When they were ready to leave Bel stood at the door to

wave them off. She watched them walk down the front path with an indulgent smile on her face, but her lovely green eyes began to fill with tears. They were so absorbed in each other they didn't turn back to wave goodbye, so they didn't see her weeping and she was glad.

That night there was no moon, so without street lighting because everyone had vigorously opposed its installation ten years ago, the village was in almost total darkness. There was a light on in Linda and Alan's bedroom because Lewis was teething and unable to sleep, and there was a light above the Store where Jimbo was still working. He had spent hours sorting and planning his Christmas displays, carrying boxes of attractive packing materials and fancy cardboard boxes down into the mail-order office ready for Mrs Jones to pack the Christmas hampers, getting out the Christmas decorations from last year, planning his windows which at Christmas were his pride and joy, and generally sorting his life out for the ensuing festive rush. He rubbed his eyes and forehead and went to stand at the window looking out over the Green. Besides the Store and the mail order doing so well, he had more catering business this Christmas than ever before. If things went on as they were he'd soon be a wealthy man. So wealthy in fact he'd be able to leave much of it to his staff and elect to be in a supervisory capacity instead of at the sharp end. But when he thought about it that idea didn't appeal. Working in the Store and meeting with these good people was the best tonic he could have. He thrived on it. So did Harriet and so did the children. Such genuine whole hearted folk they were. Half past midnight. He'd better leave.

Jimbo turned off the lights, locked the stockroom door and went downstairs. He let himself out and having reassured himself that everything was secure he stood for a moment in the shadow of the doorway looking at the village. Jimbo knew he was privileged to live here. Fancy if he lived in a high-rise block somewhere. Jimbo shuddered. It didn't bear thinking about. Walking home he passed the Bissetts' house, poor Sheila he couldn't quite forgive his mother for leaving her helpless in the church hall, he passed the Senior sisters' house, the poor old things, and then his mother-in-law's old house. The chap who'd bought it seemed nice enough. As he was about to put his key in the lock of his own home he thought he heard a noise.

Jimbo stood quite still and listened. There it was again, it seemed to be coming from the direction of Church Lane. Looking across the Green he saw a small group of shadowy figures moving stealthily along towards the church. Jimbo lost sight of them so he walked as softly as he could onto the Green so he could follow their progress. But the royal oak despite its lack of leaves blocked his view. As he walked further onto the Green he heard the smashing of glass. At first he thought they must be attacking the church but as he ran and the church and Glebe Cottages came into view he saw they were attacking Dicky and Bel's windows. Without a thought for his own safety he ran into Church Lane shouting 'Hey! Hey, there! Stop it. Do you hear! Stop it!'

The noise made by the breaking glass masked his voice. He ran down Church Lane shouting, 'Stop it! Stop it!' Lights began coming on in bedrooms, windows were opened, shouts were heard. The four men were wearing balaclava type head gear which made it impossible to recognise any of them. Jimbo knew they must be able to hear his voice but they continued throwing missiles at the windows, by now Jimbo had drawn level with the churchyard wall where it ran down the side of the cottage garden, as he stepped onto the front lawn two of the men darted down the side of the cottage and Jimbo could hear glass breaking at the back. His mobile phone. Damn it! He'd left it in the Store.

The other two men were spraying paint on the brickwork at the front. Jimbo rushed at them but the taller of the two pushed him away. 'Buzz off, Jimbo! Before you get hurt!'

Then they too darted down the side of the house and Jimbo could just see them vault the churchyard wall and disappear. He followed them to the wall in time to see the other two leap it further down and speed away across the churchyard, skimming the gravestones and disappearing helter-skelter round the back of the church hall. There was no way he could catch them fit as he was, so he went back to the cottage and called up to the broken upstairs window, 'Dicky! Bel! It's Jimbo. Are you all right?'

After a moment Dicky's head appeared. 'We're OK. Have they gone?'

'Yes, there was no way I could catch them. Come on down and we'll see what we can do.' Jimbo went round to the front door, stepping carefully because of the broken glass littering the path and the front lawn.

Dicky unlocked the door, though it seemed a pointless exercise: only jagged pieces of glass were left at the edges of the door frame.

'Careful where you step, Dicky. Where's Bel? What a shock. I just wish I could have caught them. Are you sure you're OK?'

Peter came up the path, his cloak over his pyjamas, and trainers on his feet. 'My God! What on earth is happening? Did you see who it was?'

' 'Fraid not. They were wearing masks over their faces, there were four of them, I know that.'

Bel came to the door, a vast red dressing-gown over her nightclothes, her happy face creased with fear, and white as a sheet. 'Oh dear. What are we going to *do*? I was so scared.'

Dicky put his arm round her. 'Don't you worry, love, we're not going to let a pack of hooligans frighten us away. They've done their worst, but the insurance will take care of it.'

A crowd of villagers had gathered some carrying torches and most of them appalled at what had happened.

'Who do you reckon it was, Rector?'

'What a wicked thing to do.'

'They need horsewhipping.'

As well as the sympathetic cries Peter distinctly heard someone saying none too quietly 'Serves 'em right. The mucky pair.' And another one muttering 'Just deserts, that's what, we don't want 'em 'ere.'

Peter stood facing the cottage to estimate the damage. 'At this time of night there's no way we can set about making the house safe.'

Jimbo agreed. 'Look, how about it, Dicky, if I lend you my mobile phone and you stay in the house, and someone could offer Bel a bed for the rest of the night? You can't leave the house unprotected but at least if you have my phone you can ring me or Peter for help. No good ringing the police, they'll take ages to get here from Culworth. Bel, what do you think?'

'I don't like leaving Dicky, but I'm too frightened to stay.'

'Serves yer right, yer should be frightened.'

Peter fixed the speaker with a stern look, and they shamefacedly turned their gaze away from him. 'Very good idea. Look Bel, Caroline always keeps clean sheets on our spare bed, you can stay there for the night. What do you say, Dicky, to doing as Jimbo suggests?'

'Can't do any other. I'll get the glaziers to come first thing. What a damned mess. Who on earth could it have been?'

Jimbo, startled into recollecting what had happened when he'd first arrived on the scene, said, 'They were locals. That's right, they were locals.'

Dicky looked up at him. 'How did you know, if their faces were covered up.'

'They called me Jimbo. That's right they told me to go before I got hurt, and said "Buzz off, Jimbo." So they knew me. I'll ring their necks if ever I find out who it was.'

Peter vastly disappointed that it was local men looked sadly at the faces of the villagers gathered in the garden. 'We may as well all go home, there's nothing we can do except keep our eyes and ears open in the next few days and tell Dicky if we suspect we know who's done this dreadful thing. And remember if the press come asking questions we none of us know *why* or *who*. We don't want them getting on to it. This is where we all remember "silence is golden". Please don't let me . . . nor Dicky and Bel down, will you? Mum's the word. Good night everyone and thank you for your concern. God bless you all.'

Most of the villagers said 'Good night, Rector', even those who'd been less than kind in their remarks. A few went to comfort Bel and offered to come round to help clear up in the morning. 'Least we can do. Dreadful, really dreadful.'

Jimbo went back to the Store for his mobile phone and Peter went with Bel to the rectory.

Caroline came down the stairs when she heard the door open.

'Darling?' Then she saw Bel. 'Why Bel? Whatever's happened?'

Peter explained and Caroline, full of understanding, put her arms around Bel and hugged her. 'How perfectly dreadful. We'll make a cup of tea and you can take it to bed, the sheets are on.'

Bel protested but Caroline hushed her with a finger to her lips. 'No trouble at all, that's what we're here for.'

'I shall have to be up early because of the school.'

'Don't fret on that score, we're always up early because of the children, and Peter saying prayers. That's no problem. You do your best to sleep, it won't be easy I know. Just remember those dreadful people are to be pitied. Let's be thankful Jimbo was working late, and caught them at it. It could all have been a lot worse.'

When they got to bed Peter said, 'I don't want to call the police.'

'You don't?'

'No. I hope Dicky doesn't either.'

'Why not?'

'If the police know then the press will get to know and then it will all come out. Can't you just see the headlines? Turnham Malpas will turn overnight into a den of iniquity.'

'Of course, because of Dicky and Bel you mean. The one bedroom.'

'Exactly. All he's worked for will be gone overnight.'

'Well, we've had good reason to be thankful for them keeping quiet before, let's hope they can do it again. Good thing we've lost our own police station, the Sergeant would have been here in a flash.'

Peter nodded. 'I was sorry we lost him, but tonight I'm

244

quite glad. He'd have been honour bound to report it. Good night, darling.'

'Good night. There's someone crying. It doesn't sound like the children, it must be Bel. I'll go see.'

Chapter 20

The following morning Jimbo was feeling considerably below par. He ploughed on day after day carrying the burden of the business and most often he loved it, but today, somehow, a week away with Harriet, on their own, sounded like paradise. Last night had been the final straw. The papers were late, he'd had a load of vegetables to throw out because they hadn't kept over the weekend, the baker's van hadn't arrived, his accounts were getting behind hand, and to top it all he'd had a letter from a company in Culworth complaining about the food he'd provided for their company promotion meeting, when he knew all the time it was because they hadn't really been able to afford such a big splash. It wasn't the food at all. The fact that the promotion hadn't been well attended wasn't his fault, he'd only done the food and done it superbly well.

To add to his troubles it looked as though Linda would be late again. Jimbo decided that if she was that would be that. He could put up with so much, but she really was getting to be a trial. From experience he knew babies could be difficult, but he rather felt that Linda made more fuss than poor subdued little Lewis truly warranted.

He looked at his watch at ten minutes past nine and she still hadn't arrived. Running between till and post office counter he wished Harriet hadn't decided to do the farm run straight from taking Fran to playgroup. They were always busy first thing with the mothers when they'd left their children at school. He needed her right here this very minute.

The doorbell jingled and in rushed a breathless Linda. She called across, 'Sorry Mr Charter-P. Isn't it dreadful about Dicky and Bel? We hardly got any sleep and just to put the lid on it the girl who looks after Lewis on Mondays hasn't turned up, so Alan's having to look after him, and I'm all behind.'

'In that case then go back home and catch up.'

Linda stopped in her tracks. 'What do you mean?'

'Watch my lips, I shall say this only once! If you've a lot to do, go home and do it and don't bother coming back. It's obvious that you've no time for work. So you can be free of it, free to devote your time to Lewis and Alan. I've got a note of how many times you've been late, and how many times you've taken more than an hour for lunch and then left early into the bargain and I'm sorry I can no longer employ you. It's happening far too often and I'm not willing to put up with it. I'm running a business here not a charity. I shall send the money due to you as soon as I get a chance to calculate what I owe. Sorry, Linda, but that's that.'

Jimbo carried on taking the money at the till ignoring Linda's horrified expression. When she finally found her voice she said 'Oh! What a joke, for one awful moment I thought you meant it. Now, Lady Templeton, what can I get for you?'

As Muriel opened her mouth to ask for ten first-class stamps and could Linda send this letter recorded delivery,

Jimbo said, 'Stop! I meant it! Don't bother to undo your coat, just leave.' He stabbed a forefinger in the direction of the door. 'That's the way out.'

'Well. After all these years. I don't believe it. You can't sack someone who's worked for you for years. You can't do it. It's not allowed.'

'I have done it, and damn the consequences I say. That's ten pounds and ninety-five pence, please. Thank you. Five pence change. Good morning and thank you for shopping with us.' Jimbo looked at Linda with a surprised expression on his face. 'You're still here, Linda. I've shown you where the door is.'

Linda burst into tears and headed for the door, just as she was about to reach out to grasp the handle Alan burst in.

'Oh, Alan! How did you know?' She flung herself into his arms but he pushed her off.

'The keys. Where are the keys? I can't get in the pub. It's all locked up! I've hammered on the door, back and front, and there's no reply. I can't understand it, it's never happened before! I think Bryn must have been taken ill. Where've you put the spare keys? Eh?'

Because he was ignoring her predicament Linda cried louder still. She burbled out between her sobs, 'In your sock drawer, right underneath.' As he was turning to leave and go home to procure the keys a thought struck her, and gazing frantically about she screamed, 'Where's the baby?'

'The baby? The baby? Oh my God, I've left him outside the pub by the bins.' The two of them raced out leaving the door wide open.

Muriel, who hated confrontation and was standing by the post office section in a state of shock, began to tremble, it was all too much. In a faint voice she said, 'I'll help myself to a coffee if I may, Jimbo.'

'Of course, you do that.'

Muriel stepped round to the shelf where the coffee machine stood, but it was empty. 'Oh dear.'

At that moment Mrs Jones strode in. 'What's the matter with Linda and Alan? I've just seen them streaking across the Green as if the devil himself was after them.'

Jimbo sighed. 'It's a long story. I'll tell you later. Be on the till five minutes while I do the post office will you?'

'Well, all right but if I make a mistake . . .'

'I'll accept full responsibility.'

'OK, but on your own head be it.'

Jimbo strode across. 'Now Muriel . . . You didn't get your coffee.'

'No, there isn't any.'

Jimbo took off his boater and smoothed his bald head. 'I wonder if I could put back the clock and start Monday all over again? Perhaps it wouldn't be any better if I did. Shall I . . . ?' He nodded his head in the direction of the coffee percolator.

Muriel shook her head. 'Not for me, you've enough to do. Shall I come back later for my stamps?'

'I'll do it now. Who'd be an employer? I ask you? Now, let's see.'

They found the baby safe and sound though somewhat surprised, and Alan took a tearful Linda back home grateful in some ways that she'd been sacked, then he wasn't saddled with the baby to look after when he obviously had a crisis on his hands. Socks flew in all directions as he searched for the keys, grabbing them he rushed back to the pub. Opening the main door he strode into the bar and listened to the silence. It was profound. Either Bryn was laid dead somewhere or he wasn't here at all.

He searched the bar, the public lavatories, the dining-

249

room and the kitchens, the storerooms at the back, and then climbed the stairs. Knowing that Elektra had been making a bid for the lonely Bryn he was cautious which bedroom doors he opened. The door to his old room was ajar. He peeped round the door and saw the bed hadn't been slept in. Or if it had she'd made the bed first thing. Drawing a blank he went to the main bedroom. That door was shut, so taking hold of the knob firmly he gently turned it and opened it just enough to put his head round. The bed had been slept in. Both sides. He tried the third bedroom which had always been more of a boxroom than anything, that too was empty. It occurred to him to look out onto the car park. He went to the window and realised Bryn's Triumph sports car had gone.

There was no one in the lounge nor the kitchen. Obviously Bryn had packed up and left. Alan panicked. He couldn't run it on his own. He'd have to get Georgie. Would she come back though? She'd have to.

When he got to Grandmama's the two of them were just finishing a leisurely breakfast, in a lovely marigold yellow cosy country kitchen Linda would have died for. Grandmama was wearing a splendid housecoat and Georgie was in trousers and that purpley sweater Linda liked, with the pearl decoration on the front.

Georgie stood up in alarm when she saw Alan. 'What's the matter?'

'Bryn's gone.'

'Gone? Gone where?'

'Don't know. But he's not there.'

'He isn't?'

'No. Not in the pub.'

'He's slept in.'

Alan shook his head. 'No, he hasn't. I've had to get my spare keys to get in. I've been to have a look.'

'Been to look in the bedrooms you mean?' Georgie's heart began to thud.

Alan nodded. 'That's right. Elektra's not there either.'

'She's not?'

'No.'

Grandmama took a hand. 'Best get over there. Have a good search yourself.'

Alan protested. 'I've looked, I know that place like the back of my hand, I lived there. He isn't there, I tell you.'

Georgie's mind was whirling with questions. 'His car?'

'Gone.'

Georgie abruptly sat down again, dropping onto the chair with a thud. Inspired, she asked, 'His clothes. Has he taken his clothes?'

'I don't know, I didn't look in the wardrobes.'

'No, of course not. It's not like Bryn just to disappear. He'll have gone into Culworth for something urgent. Or, I know, the cash and carry, we've run out of something. Yes, that'll be it.'

Grandmama and Alan exchanged sceptical looks.

Georgie sprang to life. 'He'll be back soon. But I'd better come over. He hasn't left a note?'

Alan shook his head. 'It looks like more than just going shopping to me.'

'In that case then we'll have to get ready to open up. Has the chef arrived yet?'

'No, but it's still early for him.'

'Damn it, and I was going to the bank this morning and the solicitors, well that'll have to wait. Blast him. Blast him. And her. I'll get my coat.'

Georgie turned up her nose when she saw the state of the kitchen. Whatever Elektra was good at, it wasn't housekeeping. The sink and draining board were cluttered with dirty dishes, the waste bin was overflowing, and she noted lipstick smothered cigarette ends in a saucer on the kitchen table. Bryn was accustomed to a scrupulously clean kitchen, it surprised her what men were prepared to put up with. In exchange for what?

She saw the bedroom and realised.

Stiffening her resolve Georgie marched downstairs. 'Alan! Now look here, there's no way we can manage without some help. If we've to cover for Bryn then we need someone to clean, temporary, as of today to fill the gap. You'll have to work extra hours which I know you'll quite like. We'll manage till we find out what's going on.'

'Don't you worry we'll cope, remember that time Bryn went into hospital for his hernia, we managed then didn't we?'

'You're quite right we did. Who is there in the village could clean? Today, right now?'

'Linda could. Jimbo sacked her from the post office this morning. She could, temporary, we'll need the money. She'd have to bring the baby though, today.'

'Well, she can for now. Give her a ring. Pay's good tell her, she'll get a bonus for coming in promptly. Right, let's get cracking.'

That night the bar was crowded. The news had flashed round Turnham Malpas and the surrounding farms and villages in no time at all. All the regulars and plenty of customers who only came occasionally had found reason to be in there. Alan and Georgie were, to use an expression of Bryn's "pulled out of the place". Dicky, now that Bryn was no longer around, had called in for a drink but seeing how busy the two of them were he'd volunteered out of sympathy for their predicament and out of love for Georgie to be potman for the night.

'Eh! Dicky, you're back then, now the coast's clear?'

'So how's love's young dream tonight then?'

'We shall miss Elektra, and not half!'

'Don't suppose you wear black lace knickers?'

Dicky took it all in good part, and began to enjoy himself. He liked people and that was something he knew you had to do if you were in the licensed trade. He started telling a few jokes if a particular table was receptive, and before he knew where he was he had an audience and there was nothing Dicky liked better than an audience and he played it to the hilt.

There was a round of applause after his impromptu performance and Alan and Georgie winked at each other with approval.

'See, Alan, I knew I was right. Bryn didn't know everything.'

'Well, I agreed with you at the time. He's a bit of all right is Dicky. Everybody likes him, you see.'

A germ of an idea formed in Georgie's head, but she'd have to think hard first before she put it into words. Business decisions had to be well thought out before you took action. But it might just be the answer to a lot of problems.

Surprisingly it was Grandmama who came up with the complete solution. She called on the Thursday of the week Bryn had disappeared on the Monday, when she knew they would be quiet.

'Georgie! Georgie!' After a moment a tired-looking Georgie appeared. 'Now my dear, get us both a drink and come and sit down before you fall down. I've had an idea.'

Grandmama placed herself in the comfortable wing-chair by the fireplace. It was the middle of the afternoon and the lunchtime crowd had gone but the evening crowd had not yet arrived.

'Whisky?'

'Not at this time of day and in any case I need a clear head. I'll have a lemonade, thank you, my dear.'

Georgie plumped herself down. She was exhausted.

'My dear, you look worn out.'

'I am. Bryn did all the books and the bulk of the ordering. I never realised just how much time it took. And there's the dining-room to keep an eye on, they're short-handed in there, I've found that one of the part-timers has been taking food home so she's had to go. I feel sorry for her, but it's no good, once one does it the rest will follow.'

'I agree. Now, have you heard from Bryn?'

'No. Not a word.'

'And when you went to the bank and the solicitor's? You'll pardon me asking but I have a rescue plan and I need to know where you stand.'

'He's taken almost all the money from our private joint account. I intended getting there first and taking half which I consider is my rightful share, but being faced with the crisis on Monday, of course, I didn't get there did I? So he's hopped it with almost all of it and I'm seething about it.'

'The devil he has! You'll have to get your share back. Quite definitely yes, you will. And the business account?'

'That's safe he hasn't touched that, but then we only leave enough in there for trading, paying invoices and wages and such. Bryn always takes out whatever can be spared every month and puts it in our own account.'

Grandmama sipped her lemonade, put down the glass and cleared her throat. 'I have a plan. Do you have a plan?'

'Haven't had much time to think but I've a germ of an idea which hasn't formed yet really.'

'Well, listen to my idea first and see if it matches yours.

Until you find Bryn, financially you can't do a thing. Can't sell up, can't sell his half of the business, can't get a divorce yet, that's if you want one.'

'I want one right enough. It's insulting, downright insulting and humiliating that he's gone off with that *bitch*.' Georgie's face twisted into a grimace and her eyes glittered with tears. 'I wanted out but this . . . If she walked in now I'd murder her, believe me. It'll be her idea to take all the money, Bryn's got a bit more honour than that. But what's he doing letting her dictate to him like that?'

'Besotted?'

'I expect so. I should have thrown her out when I came back last Saturday . . . Anyway it's all too late now. You've a plan?'

'Yes. It solves all sorts of things. I understand you've been having some great times in here with Dicky helping out?' Georgie nodded. 'He's made for this kind of place you know. He could belong here.'

Georgie smiled. 'He could, you're right.'

'So, you've told me he doesn't like his job where he is, but he does do accounts, now, with a bit of tuition from my Jimbo I'm sure he could take over the accounts and ordering and things and still have enough energy left over for helping in the bar every day too, just like Bryn does, well, did. So he could give up his job, and you could employ him.'

She saw interest sparking in Georgie's eyes and pressed on with her proposal. 'Now, it wouldn't be a good idea for him to live here, there's been enough tittle-tattle, and you don't want any more of that, but that's no problem with him living just up the road. But I don't think it's right that you should live here all on your own, in a public house. Not right at all. Not safe, so how about if

Bel comes to live here with you. That then would solve the problem of everyone thinking Bel and Dicky are up to no good.' Grandmama blushed with guilt as she said this and hoped Georgie hadn't noticed. 'The whole village would then forget all about the scandalous situation which they believe exists at the moment in Glebe Cottages.'

'I do believe you might be on to something here.'

'Oh I am! I know I am. Believe me! Now should there come a time when Bryn is wanting out and wants to sell his half of this,' she waved a regal hand around her head, 'Dicky could buy him out and the two of you could marry when you've got your divorce. There!' She sat back and waited for Georgie's reaction.

'Well, it all sounds excellent, wonderful in fact, but you've forgotten one thing, even if Dicky sold his house he has such a big mortgage he wouldn't have enough money left over to buy the half share and the bank certainly wouldn't lend him it because without the house he wouldn't have any collateral. So that's a bit impossible. I couldn't lend him it either because Bryn's got what's ours.'

Grandmama shook her head. 'No, it's not impossible. I've no doubt at all that with you and Dicky here keeping up your kind of high standards the Royal Oak would go from strength to strength. It would become an excellent investment for anyone. So why not me? I have capital which I would be willing to lend him as and when the time arrives.'

'No, Katherine, I can't let you do that!'

'You can't stop me. It will be all legal and properly drawn up, believe me Jimbo has got his business brain from me not his father, I'd have it all absolutely legal and I *want* to do it. If Bryn should come back full of remorse this way nothing would be changed, Dicky and Bel would still have their house, and you could make your decisions from then on. Only Dicky would have taken a risk with giving up his job.'

'I can't believe this. I can't. That would be wonderful! The whole plan makes everything so right.'

'Exactly!'

'But what about Bel? What would she do?'

'Oh, she'd carry on with her life as it is now. No one could object to that, could they? It would leave Dicky and her whiter than white wouldn't it, her living here and doing what she usually does. She could still help Dicky with the mortgage couldn't she?'

'Oh yes. But what if Bryn comes back? He might.'

'We can't do anything legal till he makes contact anyway, so financially everything would be status quo. He can't object to Bel living here and he can't object to you employing someone besides Alan to give you a hand. The hours are crippling, you need both Dicky and Alan and a barmaid part-time too.'

Georgie stood up. 'All I can say is a big thank you. I've been puzzling my brain about the whole problem but I'm so busy I can't give it my full attention and here you are, you've come up with it all neat and tidy.' She bent forward and kissed Grandmama soundly. 'There! What more can I say, but a big thank you. I'll talk to Dicky and Bel tonight.'

'Talk to them together, Bel mustn't think we've all been plotting and planning her life behind her back.'

'Of course. Got to go, lots to do.'

'And I must be off too. We'll keep in touch.' Grandmama kissed Georgie and as she was leaving she turned back to say rather sadly, 'It'll be lonely in my cottage without you, you know, quite lonely. Bye-bye, my dear.'

Walking up Stocks Row to her cottage she saw Peter pulling up outside the rectory. She called to him the moment he got out of his car. 'Rector! Have you a moment?'

Peter nodded. 'Good afternoon, Mrs Charter–Plackett. Lovely day!'

'Can I have a word?'

'Of course, come in!'

'No, I won't do that, thank you. There's a programme I like to watch at five o'clock. You remember you asked me to solve the problem of Dicky and Bel and Georgie?'

'I did indeed.'

'Well I have, that's if they all agree.' She outlined her plan and was gratified to see the delight on Peter's face. 'I'm not telling anyone except Jimbo about the financial side of it, that's private, I'm telling you because I know I can rely on you to keep a confidence. What do you think then?'

'Brilliant. If they all agree it solves everything at one fell swoop and I know Dicky would be good for the business and he'd still be able to carry on with the Scouts. Wonderful! Thank you so much.'

'All we have to hope is that Bryn turns up some time soon.'

'Georgie hasn't heard then?'

Grandmama shook her head. 'No, not a word. Still it's early days, he might tire of Elektra quite quickly, or more likely she might tire of him! I'm glad you're pleased. Must go. See you soon, Peter!'

With his forearms resting on the roof of the car he watched her stride off to her cottage. She really was an outrageous mixture of a person. Domineering, belligerent, determined, bullying, wilful, imperious, kind, under-

258

standing, sympathetic, genteel, intelligent, the list was endless. But the debt he owed her if it all worked out! He rather hoped she wouldn't call it in one day.

Chapter 21

'So you see, Jimbo, they've agreed to my plan. Now you won't mind tutoring Dicky will you?' Jimbo opened his mouth to protest but his mother continued to speak. 'Dicky only has a month's notice to give and they say they'll have him back any time if it doesn't work out, but it will, I know it will. Now about the money . . .'

'What money?'

'My money.'

'Your money?'

'You are in danger of repeating yourself, the money I'm lending Dicky when Bryn decides he wants to sell his half.'

Jimbo went into shock. 'You haven't promised them *money*?'

Grandmama sensed opposition. 'It is *mine*.'

'I know, but you can't just go throwing it about.'

'I'm not throwing it about. Not at all. It's going to be a proper business arrangement. I'm not some foolish dod-dery old lady, I do know what I'm doing.'

'Do you though? It seems to me you've had a rush of blood to the head, or the heart, I don't know which.

One doesn't invest one's capital on a whim. Think of the risk!'

'You're a fine one to talk about risks. What about the risk you took with this place? Couldn't be called a blue chip investment could it when you bought it? A disgusting one-room shop with no stock to speak of, two dilapidated cottages, and tantamount to nil turnover. You wouldn't listen to me though would you? At least the Royal Oak is an established business with prospects, and that's what I'm investing in.'

'I invested in myself and Harriet and knew I was right. You're investing in Dicky, in truth. You'll have no shares in the business.'

Grandmama paused while she considered this fact. 'Yes, I see what you mean. I need to think about that. That won't do, will it?'

'Well, not for me it wouldn't. That is too risky by far.'

'But I want to help. After the other night Dicky and Bel need all the help they can get. They deserve it. I never heard a thing. I'd taken some dratted herbal sleeping concoction Mrs Jones gave me and I went out like a light. I wish I had, I'd have shown them what for. I don't suppose they've found out who it was?' Jimbo shook his head. 'Pity. I'm so sorry for Georgie too, there's nothing worse than a dead marriage. And I should know.'

Jimbo, who while she'd been speaking had been scribbling on a piece of paper hazarding a shrewd guess at the sums involved, looked up surprised. 'What do you mean? "You should know"?'

'That's what I had. Four years of comparative happiness and then phut! it all went up in flames.' She watched the screen-saver on Jimbo's computer while he absorbed what she'd said.

Eventually he asked quietly, 'What do you mean?'

'I never told you before, the habit of shielding you from it is deeply ingrained, but I expect you're old enough now to understand. It was because of your father that you went away to school so early, it broke my heart but it seemed better than you knowing.'

'What exactly did he do?'

Looking him fearlessly in the eye for a moment before making up her mind Grandmama said decisively, 'He had a mistress and they had three boys and he juggled himself between us. When you were home from school he spent his time with us, and then when you went back he went back to her. Had some mad idea I think, that if he kept faith with you and you never knew, it absolved him from guilt. Made everything all right he imagined, with never a thought as to how I might feel about it. I could have killed him many a time, believe me. The lying, cheating toad.'

Jimbo was appalled. Appalled that all the years of his life he'd never been aware of the misery at the heart of her. 'Mother! I'm so sorry, so very sorry. I had no idea. I just find it so hard to believe.'

'You'd better believe it! It's true! Now you're making me feel I shouldn't have told you. Maybe you're not old enough yet.'

'Mother! Not old enough? For heaven's sake. He was away working a lot, I knew that, but I didn't realise the real truth, not once. Not even when I was at Cambridge. I must have been incredibly blind, and he, and you, incredibly careful.'

'Good, I'm glad. I stuck with him you see, old-fashioned principles and all that.'

'Well, I admire you for that. I really truly do. But three half-brothers! It takes some assimilating. So that's why I'm an only one?'

262

Grandmama nodded. 'It is. I pretended it was because I didn't like childbirth, which truth to tell what woman does, but I would have liked more children. I couldn't take the risk in case he left me for good, you see. What was more, I didn't fancy him when he'd been with someone else. However, the son I've got more than makes up for not having more.' She smiled at him.

Jimbo got up from his chair and planted a kiss on his mother's cheek. 'Why have you never told me this before?'

'Pride, I'm afraid. Too proud that's me.'

'I see, I can understand that. I'm so sorry about him. So very sorry. So when he died what happened then, you've never seemed short of money?'

'She got some money and the house she lived in, but the bulk of his money and our house were mine. He did at least have the good manners to reward my tolerance of all those years, and was old-fashioned enough to acknowledge I was his legal wife. I'll give him that. Also I expect he was thinking about his son and heir.' Jimbo grimaced at that. 'A few flirtations with the stock market have increased it way beyond my wildest dreams . . . and his!'

'Where are they now? The other woman and the children? Well, they're not children now, of course.'

'I haven't any idea and I care still less. Somewhere you have three half-brothers all around your age, let's hope they never turn up by chance. I wouldn't know what the odds are on that, but I don't care.'

Jimbo went to stand at the window. There was no view, and the window was barred which limited his vision, but he wasn't looking out at anything, he was absorbed in his thoughts. 'He was always good fun my father. That's one of the things I remember best from childhood.' He turned away from the window to look at his mother. 'It must have coloured your outlook, all this going on.'

'It felt like a smack in the face with a giant, stinkingly dead cod every time he came home: smiling and laughing with his presents and his kisses. He must have felt something for me though, after all, he came home to me to die. The worst of it was I cried when he died. I wept. Grieved. I looked, and was, the genuine distraught widow at his funeral.' Jimbo nodded sadly in agreement. 'But he'd made me tough over the years and I soon got over it. I'd learned not to cry for long.'

They were both silent for a while and then Jimbo said, 'About Dicky, of course I'll teach him. It's all quite simple. And if the need to lend the money does arise then I'll help out with advice about that, too. Like you said, all legal and above board. You can't afford not to be.'

'Oh, I shall be. Now come and give your mother a kiss and I'll be off. You must get on. I see Linda's back.'

'She is indeed and not without a climb-down on my part, believe me. I have to confess I was extremely rude to her, but she caught me on a bad day. I grovelled, positively grovelled, to entice her back. However, the rustle of money finally won the day, well, my charm too, I suppose. God, did I apologise! But, we quite simply could not manage without her. She may be a poor time-keeper but she knows post office procedures through and through and she's never a penny wrong. She's got a different child-minder and she's promised to improve her time-keeping so we'll wait and see. Let's hope she learned a valuable lesson, I know I have. Harriet can't do it, she needs to be with the children.'

Grandmama stood up and collected her handbag and gloves from Jimbo's desk. 'What a lucky man you are. She's a perfectly splendid mother and a wonderful wife to you and I hope you know that and demonstrate it, daily.'

'Oh I do.'

'Good. I don't say much, Jimbo, but I am proud of you. So proud. No one but you could have made such a success of this business. Right, that's enough of sentimentality for one day. I'll be off.'

Jimbo kissed her on both cheeks and opened the door for her to leave. As she passed him she patted his cheek and said, 'At your age you won't let it affect you will you? He was just that kind of a man and in some ways you've inherited his love of the human race, except *he* didn't know when to call a halt.'

Harriet, who'd been in the kitchens supervising the staff preparing for a dinner that night, went in search of Jimbo and found him standing in his office looking lost.

'Jimbo? What's the matter? Are you all right?'

He didn't answer her immediately.

'Well?'

'Close the door, Harriet.' He paced back and forth for a moment and then looked at her. 'Do you know, I've just found out the most amazing news. Incredible really. I've got three half-brothers I never knew I had.'

Harriet was flabbergasted. 'What on earth are you talking about? Have you been at the whisky?'

'No, it's Mother, she's . . . well . . . she's . . .'

There was a split second of silence and then Harriet, eyes wide with shock, shouted *'Your mother? My God!'*

'Honestly Harriet! Of course not. For heaven's sake. No, it's she who's just *told* me. It was my father, he was playing away nearly all the time they were married, and I never knew. What am I, forty-seven, forty-eight? And she's only just felt able to let on.'

'For one dreadful minute I thought . . . that would have

265

been a laugh. Oh dear! Sorry, darling, it must hurt. I must be serious. Tell me then, if you will, or want to or can.'

So he did and Harriet was horrified. 'No wonder she's like she is. How could she have put up with that all those years? Thirty years? Right? Now at least we know the reason why she's so tough and uncompromising. Well, from now on I shall try very hard to be more understanding, she doesn't deserve to have had a husband like that.'

'No one does.' Jimbo opened wide his arms and Harriet went to him and put her arms around his neck and Jimbo hugged her tightly. 'Not even Mother!' They laughed. 'Must press on. We'll talk about it again tonight, right. The children musn't know, for her sake, and also for mine. OK? By the way, she says you're a wonderful wife to me.'

'Does she indeed? Well, well, well. It's certainly been a morning for revelations! I shall definitely have to be more understanding then.'

'We both shall. Kiss?'

Chapter 22

'Peter? Oh there you are. I'll be off then. My appointment's at eleven so I've no time to spare.' Caroline pulled on her gloves and smiled at him.

He got up from his desk and looking gravely down at her, he smoothed her cheek gently with the back of his hand. 'I'm coming.' He raised his hand to silence her as soon as he saw protest coming into her face. 'I won't brook any argument. I am coming. I will not have you face this alone. That is what being married is all about. Support. Just need to wash my hands, the print's come off all over my fingers. Won't be a minute.'

'I'm better facing things on my own.'

'This time I'm not listening. I've put an end to that, like I said.'

While he washed his hands and got his cloak Caroline stood looking out of his study window at the village. It was a bitterly cold day, with a cruel breeze blowing. She could just see Grandmama battling her way along, with her fur hat on and boots, and a huge scarf around her shoulders on top of her fur coat. Grandmama was blessed annoying with her interfering ways, but at least she'd solved the problem of Dicky and Bel. The Royal Oak was going from strength to strength with Georgie at the helm and Dicky enlivening everyone. Bel living there seemed to be working out too. She recollected hearing Bel crying in their spare bedroom the night their house had been attacked, and going to sit on the end of her bed and talking to her for what seemed hours. Poor Bel! Such a quandary for her. A variation on the eternal triangle in a way. The three of them just needed Bryn to make contact and then perhaps they could finally sort things out.

Caroline heard Peter coming racing down the stairs. 'I'm ready. Come on. We'll go in my car. Sylvia's cleaning upstairs, I've told her we're both going.'

'I expect she's pleased.'

Peter looked at her as he fastened the clasp on his cloak. 'Is she?'

'She will be. Don't pretend you don't know what I mean. It's a conspiracy between the two of you.'

Peter had the grace to look embarrassed. 'Well, yes, you're right. She does approve of me putting my foot down.'

'We'll go in the Volvo shall we? Mine's too small for comfort for you.'

'That's what I thought. In any case you haven't got the all-clear for driving yet. Right.'

Just as they were taking the sharp left turn at the signpost for Culworth Caroline put her hand on Peter's thigh and said quietly, 'Thank you for coming with me. I appreciate it. Suddenly I've gone dreadfully afraid.'

'That's understandable, but whatever the outcome, whatever the specialist says, you've always got me. I'm right up there with you, I just hope it helps.'

'It does, more than you know. I can't bear being told there's only a small chance that I shall see the children growing up. I do want to be able to live long enough to see how they turn out.' The hand resting on his thigh clenched and thumped him lightly. 'There's still so much left to do, and I want to see you when you're sixty, and seventy and eighty. What a lovely dignified old gentleman you will be.'

'That was one of the questions I tested myself with when I first met you. I realised you were the first woman I had ever known whom I wanted to know in old age.' He paused for a moment and followed on with 'And we shall, grow old together.' Taking a hand off the steering wheel he took hold of hers and squeezed it tightly. 'That's a promise.'

'I wish I had your confidence. All mine has ebbed away this morning. Every last drop has gone.'

They were silent for the next few miles and then Peter said. 'Faith that's what you have to have, faith that you'll get the all-clear and having got the all-clear, you and I will go away on our own for a few days.'

'How on earth could we manage that?'

Peter braked at the lights. Looking straight ahead he said, 'I've organised it.'

'How?'

'I've arranged for your mother and father to come down. Your mother can't wait to have the twins to herself.'

'Peter! She's never said a word! I should have been consulted. I knew nothing about it. You never asked me.'

'I know I didn't. It's a decision I made for your sake, and for mine. We both need to recuperate. It's been a long haul these last three months.'

'You can't possibly go away at this time of year so close to Christmas. What about all the work there is to do with the Midnight Service, and the old people's Christmas

Lunch and the Scouts' Christmas Party and Christmas morning and things and there's . . .'

'Yes?'

'You've so much to do.'

'I haven't, it's all done. Anne Parkin has got all the typing done, the order of service, the special carols, everything, I've checked it all and it's ready for printing out, Sheila Bissett has organised all the decorations, with I might add Grandmama's invaluable assistance, although I understand from Gilbert that Sheila's file is firmly in her hands and Grandmama is not allowed even a peep . . .'

Caroline laughed. 'Really?'

'Yes, there's a kind of armed truce, how long it will last I don't know. Gilbert has arranged the choir anthems with my enthusiastic approval, Mrs Peel and I have had a long consultation about the organ music, Willie has got his lists ready and all I have to do is go away and enjoy myself.'

'How on earth have you managed to do all that so early?'

'Determination, my darling. Determination that you and I were having a week in Crete together, all on our own, re-establishing ourselves.'

'Crete? How wonderful! I've always wanted to go there.'

'I though it might be fairly warm still and not too far away. We shall be able to leave all our cares behind us and just wander about, just the two of us. Together. On our own.'

With an amused grin on her face Caroline replied, 'If I didn't know you better I'd think you were talking in terms of a second honeymoon.'

'I am. I can't wait. It's been so long. I'll park in my place and then we'll walk through.

★

270

He stood up when he saw her come back into the corridor. Her eyes searched for him amongst the waiting patients and having found him they looked at one another long and hard. He'd spent the hour and a half she'd been away praying like he'd never prayed before. The confidence she'd lost he had also lost, but he had feared to admit to her he was as much at sea as she. He daren't smile before she did, in case the news was grim. Then as she walked towards him he realised her eyes were shining with joy, and relief ran through every vein in his body and filled him with profound rejoicing.

Caroline came close to him and looking up she said, 'I can't quite believe it but . . . it does appear things are looking quite good.' Her face shone with love. 'You were right to be confident after all. I'm so grateful to be . . .' The rest of what she had to say was smothered by Peter's cloak as he hugged her tight.

'Thank God. Thank God. Let's leave this place. Quick. I've had enough to last a lifetime.' He grasped her hand and hastened her out. As they crossed the car park he released his hold on her hand and with clenched fists raised above his head punched the air shouting, 'Hallelujah!'

'Peter, don't, everyone will hear you.'

'And why not. What news. What a relief.'

'Another check-up in three months and then six months after that. I'm just so grateful. It really was touch and go.'

'More than you realise.'

'Of course I realised, I am a doctor after all. I knew more than most.'

'But they never told you that your heart stopped did they?'

'Did it?'

'Yes, about an hour after you came out of theatre.'

'Oh God, I didn't know. Oh heavens. I'd no idea. My legs have gone all weak.'

He opened the car door. 'Here let me help you in. You frightened the life out of me.'

'You were there?'

'I was. Mind your coat. That's it.'

'I had no idea. No wonder they were so very particular about me. I thought it was because I was a medic, you know, one of their own as you might say. Peter, we need that holiday don't we? Is it booked?'

'I've an option on it, which I shall confirm this very day. So it's bells on Sunday and we leave Tuesday.

After lunch Peter called in at the Store to cancel his papers whilst he was away.

Jimbo wrote it down in his order book and as he snapped the book shut he said, 'Seems to me things have taken a turn for the better if you're going away.'

'They have. They're very pleased at the hospital, the operation appears to have been a success and she doesn't have to go again for three months. In consequence of which we're taking a holiday. Her parents are coming down to stay with the children while we go, but they don't take a morning paper.'

'I'm delighted, absolutely delighted. Harriet will be beside herself, she's been so worried.'

'So have we. I shan't want to go through all that again. Never again.'

'I should say not. Big day on Sunday. I'm feeling very nervous, this bell-ringing lark has really got to me. We've a rehearsal tonight and tomorrow night and then the real thing Sunday. We intend making enough noise to wake the dead.'

'You've no idea how I'm longing to hear the bells. This

business of having recordings and pretending it's real, well . . .'

'Exactly. We've got quite a team together you know. There's ten of us fighting for a chance to ring.'

'Brilliant. Wonderful. That's excellent news.'

'Don't suppose, Peter, you've had any news about who attacked Dicky and Bel's have you?'

'None at all. Except, between you and I, I bumped into Mrs Jones . . . is she here?' – Jimbo shook his head – 'into Mrs Jones and I gave her a long look when I asked her if she'd heard any rumours about who'd done it and she avoided my eye. She was obviously very uncomfortable and dashed away as soon as she could. What do you think?'

'She's been very cagey with me about it too. Could be Kenny and Terry know something, they're those kind of people. But if we get the police involved then the press will get to know and then the balloon will go up, oh yes. Excuse me. Bel, the bakery van's here. See to it will you. One day he'll arrive on time.'

Bel called across as she went to open the door, 'They're a man short; he's having to do two rounds.'

'That's not our fault.'

Peter took his leave. 'I must be away. Lots to do before Sunday. I'll give Caroline your good wishes.'

'Thanks.' Jimbo touched his boater and then turned his attention to the delivery man. 'Now, Trevor, this won't do. It's three times this week alone that you've not got here till the afternoon. Most of my bread trade is in the mornings you know. It's too late now and I hate selling yesterday's bread. If it's late again, I shall refuse to accept the order.'

'Sorry, Mr Charter-P. We've a new roundsman starting tomorrow, so everything will be back to normal. I don't like delivering late any more than you. I'll be here in good time tomorrow. Ta-ta for now.' Jimbo caught him winking at Bel. So . . . that was the way the wind was blowing.

'He's left the delivery note in the tray, Bel, I'll check it off for you.' Jimbo picked up the note and unfolded it. '*Dear Bel*,' it read. He quickly refolded it. 'Here, this is yours I think. Nice chap, you could do worse!'

He laughed and Bel blushed bright red as she recognised the writing. 'He's an old friend. That's all. A friend of Dicky's. There's nothing going on.'

'Come on, Bel, why not? You've as much right to a life as anyone else. Go for it, I say.'

'It's only about him coming to hear the Scout band on Sunday. Dicky's organised a performance after the service.'

'I know. Our boys have been practising for years, well not years, but certainly weeks. I swear I could play the trumpet myself I've listened to the tunes so many times. It's going to be great, what with the bells and the band. What a day.'

Though Turnham Malpas got its fair share of rain it was almost accepted as a matter of course that if they had anything special happening the weather would be fine. This Sunday was no exception. A fact which people in Penny Fawcett and Little Derehams accepted with bad grace. The element of rivalry between the three villages had been rumbling on for generations and good weather on a special day always brought out the animosity all over again. As bedroom curtains in the two villages were drawn back that morning and they all saw the clear cloudless skies and the pale winter sun, they said, 'Might have known. It's a lovely day, not a drop of rain in sight. How do they do it?'

Turnham Malpas smug in its own self-righteousness put on its Sunday best and went to the ten o'clock service, but this time for the first time for more years than they could remember the bells rang out across the fields beckoning them to church. Pure and sweet and triumphant.

Perhaps it was the novelty of the bells, or their gratitude for Caroline's good news, or a simple need to praise their Maker, but whatever had motivated them they stretched Willie's extra seating to the maximum. Just as he was beginning to think the last ones had found seats the Nightingales arrived, all seven of them. He remembered the old bench which usually stood in the churchyard, wiped the bird dirt off it with an old cloth from the boiler house storeroom, and he and Ralph carried it in and placed it right at the back near the font. Even so two of the children had to sit on the step below the font. The bells rang their final peal, and the ringers wiped their sweating faces and smiled their satisfaction at each other, and Peter and the choir entered and the service began. Peter stood on the altar steps to announce the first hymn. Behind him beside the altar was a beautiful display of flowers arranged by Sheila Bissett, and the old church silver was on display too, gleaming and twinkling in the light from the candle in the wonderful silver candlestick.

In pride of place at the front in the rectory pew alongside Caroline sat Mr Fitch. The role of benefactor sat well on his shoulders, and he couldn't resist a gracious smile in Ralph and Muriel's direction when Peter spoke of his generosity in paying for the restoration of the bells.

Peter also thanked everyone who had contributed to the Scout Band Fund. 'We are all so proud. Scout bands are quite rare nowadays, and we are very privileged to have one of our own. I understand that in the future they are planning to compete in brass band competitions. We wish them all success. Dicky?'

Dicky's face lit up with pride. He stood up and went to the altar steps to speak. 'Unaccustomed as I am to public speaking . . .' – he was interrupted here with a huge laugh – 'I should just like to say how very, very grateful all the Scouts are for the generosity of the people of Turnham Malpas, and Little Derehams and Penny Fawcett and lots of other people in the surrounding area. Without their money and without their gifts of instruments they no longer had a need for, this band would never have got off the ground. In particular a big thank you to Sir Ralph for buying us such an absolutely spanking big drum, the Royal Marines would be proud to own it. If I was a bit taller I'd have a go myself!'

There came another burst of kindly laughter.

'After the service the band will be giving a short concert, very short actually because we're still beginners, to which you are all invited. We were going to perform in the churchyard but there's so many of you here that we've moved the venue to the Green. There are lots of people I should thank, too numerous to mention, but I wish specially to thank Gilbert Johns, for all his wonderful help. Thank you, one and all.'

The congregation gathered in the road by the gate to the church hall and the band stood in formation on the Green facing them. Gilbert climbed onto an old upturned wooden crate from the Royal Oak, and with his baton raised he gathered the boys' eyes and brought them in on a clashing of cymbals and a roll on the drum. Sheila Bissett who happened to be standing beside Grandmama felt very emotional. Dear Gilbert, he was such a lovely son-in-law and here he was conducting for all the world as if he was in the Albert Hall. He'd make a lovely father in the summer when the baby came and she'd be a grandmother and wouldn't it be fun. She felt Grandmama give her a nudge. 'Isn't this wonderful? They're really quite good considering.'

Thinking there was about to be a slur cast on Gilbert's name Sheila asked sharply, 'Considering what?'

'How new to it they all are. Your Gilbert's done wonders.'

Sheila preened herself, and smiled fondly at Gilbert's energetic back. 'He has hasn't he?'

'But the bells, that'll have to stop.'

'The bells?'

'Yes, I know you'll support me. I'm going to object.'

'What is there to object about?'

'The noise. We don't need bells to remind us what time it is, we have all got clocks.'

'Shhhh! I'm listening.' Sheila thought well here's one who won't be objecting. She wouldn't allow herself to be persuaded, not by the Duchess, never again. Sheila took considerable pleasure in saying, 'Don't count on me for support, I love 'em.'

Grandmama was disappointed. When the concert concluded she joined in the applause and general admiration of the boys and as the crowd dispersed to their Sunday dinners or a pint in the Royal Oak she caught up with Dicky. 'Splendid, quite splendid. We're lucky to have you Dicky. Everything working out all right now you're full-time?'

'Wonderful, quite wonderful, we're so happy, Georgie and I.'

'Heard from Bryn yet?'

''Fraid not. Got to go, see to the boys yer know. Thanks for everything.'

'My pleasure.' She spotted Jimbo and Harriet talking to Peter.

As she drew close she could hear Peter saying, 'Who would have thought five years ago that we would have such a wonderful service as we've had this morning. The bells rehung, the church filled with young people, the band! Wonderful. I'm so thrilled. Everyone's made such an effort.'

Jimbo clapped him on the back. 'Not far to go to see why. It's you, you know. All of it's happening because of you.'

'It's the village itself that's doing it in truth.'

Grandmama interrupted. 'No, no, no, we owe it all to you, Peter. All to you. We're putty in your hands, one look from those eyes of yours and our souls are laid bare and we do exactly what you want of us.' She tapped his arm and looking up into his face she said, '*But* I'm calling in a favour.'

Peter's heart sank. He'd known from the first there'd be a day of reckoning for her sorting out Dicky and Georgie and Bel. 'Yes?'

'The bells. They're far too noisy and I expect you intend them ringing for the eight o'clock service too after today, well, I'm sorry, but it won't do. They'll have to be muffled or something or the peal shortened. They're enough to wake the dead.'

Peter was appalled. 'But . . .'

Jimbo, remembering all his hours of practice, was outraged. He grasped her arm and said through clenched teeth, 'Lunch, Mother? Now!'

'Let go my arm, dear.' She pushed at him to make him release her, but he wouldn't. 'Jimbo!'

Jimbo still gripping her arm said, 'Sorry about this, Peter, just ignore her. Come along, Mother. Lunch, right now. *Please.*'

Grandmama, furious at Jimbo's manhandling of her, tried again to thrust off his hand. Reluctantly he let go.

Peter feeling genuinely upset said quietly in his saddest voice, 'Mrs Charter-Plackett, I've longed for those bells to ring, and to have found someone willing to provide the money for their restoration, seemed heaven-sent, and I want them to ring for many many years to come. They proclaim the message of the church in a supremely special way. I wouldn't be surprised if they can hear them as far away as the bypass. There can't be anyone alive who fails to be touched in one way or another by the sound of church bells.' He smiled down at her. 'So you do see the wider implications of our bells don't you? They're for the world to hear, not just for us, are they not?'

Jimbo, his lips pressed together, his face white with temper, waited for her reply. He swore if she still objected after Peter's impassioned plea, he would personally throttle her out here on the Green in front of everyone, because despite her revelations to him, he really couldn't take any more of her aggravating ways.

Harriet, trying hard to be kinder like she'd promised she would, laid her hand on Jimbo's arm to comfort him and waited in hope.

Grandmama looked up at the splendid young man that was Peter: six feet five, with his halo of red-blond hair, and his all-seeing bright blue eyes, and that special charisma that was his and his alone, and decided she wouldn't, indeed couldn't, call in her favour. Couldn't disappoint him.

She smiled at him and said, 'My dear Peter.' She swallowed hard. 'My dear Peter, put like that how could I object to such a wonderful witness. You're quite right, the whole world needs reminding of what you stand for.'

She patted his arm and turned to Jimbo saying with an imperious note in her voice, 'Lunch, I think you said, well come along then, the children will be home before us. Don't dilly-dally.'